Sign of the Sword
By: Timothy D. Wise

Published by:
EMPORIUM PRESS
The Publishing Division of
Professor Theophilus' Emporium of Imagination, Inc.
Magnolia, Arkansas

Published by:
EMPORIUM PRESS
The Publishing Division of Professor Theophilus'
Emporium of Imagination, Inc.
Magnolia, Arkansas

Cover Design by: Timothy D. Wise

Library of Congress Control Number: 2005907621

Second Edition
ISBN: 978-0-9725549-9-2

DEDICATION:
For Laura and Lora and the friends who miss them still.

ACKNOWLEDGEMENTS:

C.S. Lewis died two years before I was born. He had been dead for fourteen years before I encountered his work in my mom's copy of The Joyful Christian, a collection of Lewis' essays, and in the cartoon adaptation of The Lion, the Witch, and the Wardrobe. By the time I was nineteen, I had read the entire Narnia series, The Space Trilogy, and a number of Lewis' nonfiction works. I had also read the Lord of the Rings saga and The Hobbitt and sampled The Silmarillion. This book is the direct result of my journeys to Narnia, Perelandra, and Middle-Earth. I learned the language of allegory from C.S. Lewis and the imagery of high fantasy from Tolkein. Upon my return from my otherworldly travels, I encountered death. One of my classmates died after being paralyzed in a motorcycle accident, and one of my brother's young schoolmates died in a car accident on the way home from cheerleader practice. As I struggled to find comfort in my religious beliefs, I found the popular metaphors of clouds, harps, and streets of gold too otherworldly to give much comfort. Looking through the lens of fairy tale allegory and high fantasy myth, however, was like seeing the realities of heaven through the mists of Avalon. Lewis and Tolkein gave me a sense of, "It must be like that," a vision that could actually bring comfort and create a sense of longing. I have tried to reproduce some of that vision in the pages that follow. So I thank Lewis and Tolkein for the legacies they left behind.

As always, I thank the friends and family members who have encouraged my writing. I think about Mr. Tilley at the Quitman, Louisiana, post office who was there when I mailed off all of those manuscripts. I think about Dr. Joy Lowe, a professor of library science at Louisiana Tech and an expert on children's literature. She read the manuscript and gave me feedback and encouragement. Mr. Tommy Liles, who sang in the church choir with me, had enough faith in my abilities to take the manuscript home and read it when he had no reason to believe it would be any good. There are too many others to count. Thanks, everyone!

Prologue

Arthur Richards sighed and turned over in bed. He had just been dreaming he was on an adventure, exploring some far green country with ancient forests, winding rivers, and ruins left behind by some ancient and wonderful civilization. He was still smiling when he opened his eyes and saw the digital alarm clock on his nightstand.

7:45 am.

The smile vanished. Arthur leaped out of bed. Covers tangled around his left leg. He shook them off as he stumbled into the hall.

"Lance! Lance!"

He rushed into the kitchen and found his twin brother sitting at the kitchen table in his boxer shorts. Songs from an MP3 player pounded through his earbuds as he lifted a soggy spoonful of cereal from the milk-filled salad bowl in front of him. Arthur stared at him in disbelief. Lance ignored him until Arthur seized his MP3 player.

"Hey! Don't touch the music."

"We've got to be at school in ten minutes!" Arthur fumed.

"Yeah," Lance said. "So what's the problem?"

Arthur threw up his arms and headed to the bathroom for a thirty-second shower.

***

The Richards twins rolled into the parking lot of Summerstown High and walked past the metal detector just as the last bell rang. Stacy Knight was standing at the door smiling as they entered. She was wearing her cheerleader uniform for the morning's pep rally.

"Go on ahead," Lance told Arthur. "I've got something to take care of."

"Yeah. Sure."

Arthur turned the corner and started toward his locker. Goose Johnson and two of his football team thugs were standing there blocking the lockers. Arthur waited for a moment.

"You want something?" Johnson asked.

"Yeah," Arthur said. "I need to get to my locker."

"That's too bad," Johnson said. "We're standing here."

"Look," Arthur said. "I just want my books. It won't take me but a few seconds to get them, and then you can stand anywhere you want to."

"I think he's telling you to move, Goose."

"Yeah. I think he's got an attitude."

Goose seized Arthur by the front of his shirt.

"You got an attitude?"

"No. I just want my books."

"Get out of here, punk." He shoved Arthur backwards.

"All right. All right." Grumbling under his breath, Arthur walked back around to the front door where Lance was still talking to Stacy.

"Go on to class, man," Lance told him. "I'll catch up."

"Goose and his punks are blocking the lockers," Arthur said. "They won't let me get my books."

"Oh, yeah? Well, what are you going to do?"

"There are three of them," Arthur said. "They all outweigh me by more than fifty pounds. What can I do?"

"Come with me."

Arthur and Stacy followed Lance down the hall.

"Lance," Stacy said. "What are you going to do?"

"You got to know how to handle people," Lance explained. "It's an art form, you know, like oil painting."

They came to the corner. Goose and his friends were still standing in front of the lockers.

"I'll make them move," Stacy said.

"That's okay," Lance said. "I've got a better idea."

Lance walked over to the janitor's closet, opened the door, and went in.

"Lance. What are you...?"

Screaming like a lunatic, Lance emerged from the closet with a bucket in his hands, and charged the three football players. Goose and his friends watched in disbelief as a sheet of water covered them. Goose was off balance and standing in water when Lance smashed into him. His feet went out from under him, and he landed flat on his back.

The bucket went banging down the hall.

Lance rolled to his feet, smiled back at Arthur and Stacy and bolted for the stairs as doors slammed open up and down the hall. Swearing profusely and brushing water from their sodden letter jackets, Goose and his friends jumped up and started after Lance. Mr. Lucas, the literature teacher, emerged from the room beside them.

"Mr. Johnson! Have you gone mad?"

***

First hour class had already started by the time Arthur left the principal's office. He couldn't keep from smiling as he passed the damp spot by the lockers. One of the custodians had mopped up most of the water, but a glistening sheen remained.

The school's newspaper and yearbook office was Arthur's favorite place on campus. It was filled with computers and decorated with artifacts—everything from an inflatable palm tree to a movie prop of a shrunken head. Someone had just added a cardboard stand-up of the Incredible Hulk from a video store. The Science Fiction Society and the Comics and Anime' Club held their meetings there. They called it the Batcave because of its décor and its basement location.

Chris Castle was sitting at a computer working on the latest edition of the school newspaper when Arthur walked in.

"Where have you been?"

"Principal's office."

"What did you do?"

"Nothing. Lance attacked some guys with a bucket of water."

"That's interesting. Do you think it's worth a headline?"

"Nah. I do wish I'd taken some pictures though. That would have been front page stuff."

"So who did he attack?"

"Goose and his caveman friends. They wouldn't let me get my books out of my locker because they didn't want to move. Lance thought they needed a little lesson in manners."

Arthur sat down at the computer beside his friend.

"They're such jerks," Chris said. "If we ever have a school shooting, I hope they get it, and I want to watch."

"That's...kind of dark, Chris."

"They wouldn't have to kill them. Just maim and disfigure them some."

"Sometimes you worry me, Chris. Somewhere inside you is a homicidal maniac just waiting to be born."

"Better than being a wimp. At least homicidal maniacs get some respect."

"What's wrong with you this morning?"

"Stacy dumped me, man."

"Oh, I'm sorry. When did it happen?"

"Yesterday."

"Did she say why?"

"No. She just said we should see other people, but that we could still be friends."

"At least she was nice about it."

"They're always nice about it," Chris said. "Do you know how many girls have told me they just want to be friends?"

"I've heard that a few times, too. I guess it's better than them telling you, 'Get lost, geek.'"

"Not much."

"You should have seen Lance throwing water on those guys," Arthur said. "That would cheer anybody up."

"It makes me depressed that I missed it." Chris smiled a little bit as he said it.

"What about homecoming?" Arthur suddenly thought of it. Homecoming was only two weeks away, and Chris and Stacy had made big plans.

"I don't know," Chris said. "I just don't know anything anymore. When we got together, it was like something I had always dreamed about. I never thought I'd date anybody like her. I thought, 'She's out of your league.' I figured she'd only want to go out with a football jock or some rich guy. Then we started going together, and I thought maybe there was some justice in the world after all. Now it looks like I was right all along."

"Don't say that," Arthur said. "I'm still convinced the geeks will inherit the earth."

"I thought that was the meek."

"Same thing. At least you got to enjoy her for a little while."

"Hmm," Chris said. "They say it's better to have loved and lost than not to have loved at all. To tell you the truth, I'm not sure I believe that now. After you've loved, you're twice as lonely as you were when you were alone before."

"That's quite true, I'm afraid," a voice said from the front of the room. The accent was British. Mr. Lucas had overheard the conversation as he was coming in. "To love is to be hurt. An English writer called C.S. Lewis said it best. If you trust your heart to anyone, it will surely be wrung and quite possibly be broken."

"So you're better off not to love at all?" Arthur asked.

"Quite the contrary," the teacher said. "According to Lewis, the only place one can be free from the pains of love is in hell."

"So you hurt either way," Chris said. "Terrific."

"How's the latest edition coming along?" Mr. Lucas asked.

"Pulitizer Prize winning stuff." Chris smiled his crooked smile. "I just wish somebody had gotten a picture of Lance soaking those jocks."

Mr. Lucas smiled.

"The report of last week's football scores was humiliation enough."

Arthur and Chris both laughed.

***

Summerstown High won the football game that night, and the whole town celebrated—even Arthur. As much as he disliked some of the players, he couldn't bring himself to cheer for the other team. It seemed unpatriotic somehow.

Arthur and Lance, still in band uniforms, climbed into

their father's Buick to drive over to Pizza Hut. Lance took the driver's seat while Arthur strapped in beside him. He turned on the radio, turned the volume to the threshold of pain, and threw the car into reverse. Arthur turned the radio down a notch as the car shot out into the road. Lance punched the accelerator, and the car leaped forward.

"Why are you in such a hurry?" Arthur asked.

"Stacy and Angie are waiting for us."

"Who's Angie?"

"Angel Stone. That's what she's calling herself these days."

"What's wrong with Angel?"

Lance shrugged. "Tired of being Angel, I guess."

"Is Chris meeting us?" Arthur asked. "You know he broke up with Stacy."

Lance didn't answer. He just turned off onto a backroad and sped up to over eighty miles an hour. Arthur sighed but didn't say anything. Lance turned the volume up again.

Half-deaf but otherwise undamaged, the Richards brothers arrived at Pizza Hut five minutes later. Half of the school seemed to have beaten them there in spite of Lance's driving. Lance didn't wait for a server to seat them. He made his way around the buffet to a booth in the corner. Stacy Knight and Angel—or Angie—Stone were waiting there.

Stacy, still wearing her cheerleader uniform, smiled as Lance approached. She had apparently been saving a place for him. Lance slid into the booth beside her. Arthur stood beside them and felt awkward. Stacy had just broken up with Chris so they could "date other people." Arthur now knew who it was she had wanted to date.

"Have a seat, bro." Lance smiled and tried to look innocent.

"Does Chris know about this?"

"We'll tell him."

"Sit down, Arthur," Stacy said. "It's okay."

Arthur hesitated for a moment. Finally, against his better judgment, he sat down beside Angel. On more than one occasion, Arthur had shared a booth with Stacy, Angie, and Chris. Now Chris was out of the picture. Lance and Stacy talked excitedly, while Arthur and Angie mostly just sat and watched them from across the table. Angie Stone was Stacy's shadow. Inseparable as the two girls were, they were as opposite as Arthur and Lance. Stacy was tall, outgoing, and physically quite mature for her fifteen years. Angie, at fourteen, was smaller and quieter and had a slender, boyish build. Angie tried hard to play the part of the popular girl. She dressed fashionably and wore cute hats, but had twice failed to make the cheerleading squad. Arthur felt that her association with Stacy was a way she had of making up for her own lack of status. *We're both bad copies*, Arthur thought. *I'm an imperfect duplicate of Lance, and you're Stacy without the personality or the figure.* That pretty well summed it up.

After what seemed like an eternity, the server arrived to take orders. Several millennia later, the pizza arrived. Lance told stories and entertained the girls.

I shouldn't be here, Arthur thought. *This is wrong.* Then things got even worse.

"Hello, Stacy."

Lance halted in mid-sentence, his arms frozen in mid-gesture. Chris Castle stood at the end of the table. He turned to Arthur.

"I thought it was you at first," he said, "but the mouth gave him away. You could have told me, Arthur."

I didn't know. Arthur coughed as he tried to choke down a wad of pizza.

"Chris," Stacy said. "I didn't do this on purpose. I really do like you, I just..."

"Save it," Chris said. "Just save it." He dropped his head and turned away.

Arthur stood up and ran after him.

"I didn't know," he said. "I swear I didn't know until we came in here."

"Arthur," Chris said. "Just go away."

He walked past the video machines, pushed open the door, and stepped out. Arthur followed.

"Chris, I—"

"I SAID GO AWAY!" Chris exploded. He pulled out his car keys, opened the door of his Mustang, and jumped inside. Arthur stood and watched as he started the car, slammed it into gear, and went screeching out of the parking lot. Arthur didn't go back inside for a long time. When he finally went back in, Lance, Stacy, and Angie were standing together at the counter. Lance was paying for the meal.

"We thought you had gone with Chris," Stacy said.

"No," Arthur said. "He doesn't want anything to do with any of us right now."

"I didn't want it to turn out this way," Stacy said. "I just didn't know how to tell him."

"He'll get over it," Lance said. "He'll have him another girlfriend by this time next week."

"No," Arthur said. "Not Chris."

Stacy seemed to wilt as he said this, and Arthur was glad. Let her share some of the pain. Lance finished paying for the pizza.

"Listen," Lance said. "We're all going over to Stacy's house to watch a movie."

"Drop me by the house, then," Arthur said.

"Please come too, Arthur," Stacy said. "I promise I'll try to talk to Chris as soon as he's had some time to cool down."

"He's mad at me too, now," Arthur said. "He told me you'd broken up with him earlier today. He thinks I knew about you and Lance all along and didn't tell him."

"I'll talk to him."

"Whatever." Arthur sighed.

Stacy and Angie left in Stacy's car. Lance dropped by the video store and rented two movies on the way out of town. They rode in tense silence for a while.

"For what it's worth, I'm sorry about how it all happened, too," Lance said, finally breaking the silence. "I'd try to talk to Chris myself, but it wouldn't do any good. He'd probably kick my butt, and I don't really blame him. I'd do the same thing if it was me." He stopped. "What in the—?"

Blue lights were flashing in the rear view mirror. A siren wailed.

"Aw, man!" Lance pulled over onto the shoulder. "I wasn't even going that fast. I...."

The state trooper zipped on past them, lights still flashing, and vanished around the corner.

"I thought he had me for sure," Lance said. He pulled back onto the road.

They drove another mile and saw the lights again. Traffic had been stopped in one lane and someone was directing cars. The state trooper's car was there, and so were a sheriff's car, an ambulance, and a firetruck. Traffic was piled back about ten cars. Cars were gradually being directed around an ambulance. The line of cars shortened until Arthur and Lance could see something in the ditch. A car had gone off the road, flipped over and over. Glass and pieces of metal littered the shoulder of the road and ragged trenches were plowed in the ground. The car was demolished. The top had been smashed in, one of the doors had been torn off, and every piece of sheet metal was buckled. The bumper was twisted into an L-shape.

The line shortened. The cars came nearer.

"That looks like Stacy's car," Arthur said.

***

Lance pulled over, threw the car into park, and leaped out. His pulse was hammering in his chest as he rushed through the crowd.

"Stay in the vehicle." Lance ignored the protests of the paramedics and the police as he ran toward the ambulance. He didn't even seem to hear them. Arthur followed him. The whole scenario seemed like some twisted alternate reality.

"Get back into the vehicle!" the voice ordered over and over again.

"Wait!" someone suddenly cried out. "Let him through. Let him through."

Lance followed the voice to the back of the ambulance and saw a young, long-haired paramedic was standing over a stretcher. The man turned as Lance approached.

"Jeff," Lance gasped. He knew Jeff's younger brother from band. He had been to their house many times. It was good to see a familiar face.

"She asked for you," Jeff said.

Stacy was strapped to the stretcher with a blood-stained sheet covering her body. Another paramedic was getting ready to load her. "Make it quick," he said.

Stacy reached for Lance. He took her hand.

"Tell Chris I'm sorry," she said. Her voice was weak, and she still had glass in her hair.

Lance tried to speak but choked on the words at first. He nodded as tears came to his eyes. "I'll tell him," he managed to say.

"I'll see you later," Stacy said. She smiled a winning smile and squeezed Lance's hand before the paramedics loaded her into the ambulance, stepped in, and pulled the doors shut. Lance watched it drive away with the lights flashing.

***

"Did you hear anything about Angel?" Arthur asked as Lance drove to the hospital.

"Angie? No, I didn't see her."

Lance pulled into the parking lot outside the emergency room door. The tires squealed as he pulled into a parking place and slammed on the brakes. Arthur sighed but didn't say anything. There was no need for Lance to drive like a maniac, but Arthur guessed it was his way of blowing off steam. They ran across the parking lot—the way lit by streetlamps—and into the admitting area.

"Can I help you?" the woman behind the desk asked.

"Is Stacy Knight here?" Arthur asked.

The woman turned and looked at the other woman who was on duty there.

"What is it?"

"She...arrived a few minutes ago."

"Is she okay?"

Another pause.

"She didn't survive the trip over. I'm very sorry."

***

Three days later, Arthur and Lance stood together in the cemetery of a small, country church as Stacy Knight was buried. Mr. Lucas, wearing the dark suit he usually wore, stood with them. Angie Stone, still hospitalized, had not been able to attend. Chris Castle had shown up for the funeral service, but had walked out before it was over. Many other friends had stayed.

Over and over throughout the service, Arthur remembered the last things he had said to Stacy; how angry he had been at her for hurting his friend and how he had tried to make her feel guilty. His feelings had been justified. He knew that. He had had no way of knowing that the words he had said to Stacy that night would be the last he would say to her. He knew that, too, but he still felt terrible.

"I've thought a lot about what you said," Arthur told Mr. Lucas as the service ended, "about how pain comes with love, but it's still worth it."

"Yes."

"I'll miss her, Mr. Lucas."

"We all will." The teacher heaved a long, world-weary sigh. Something in his manner told Arthur he had known his share of heartache. Much of his earlier life was a mystery to his students, but they knew he had not always been a teacher.

Birds sang in the trees overhead as dirt was shoveled into the open grave and an era was brought to a close. Dark clouds on the horizon signaled the coming of an early winter.

1./Carriage Ride

For Louisiana, winter came early. The week school closed for Thanksgiving vacation, an ice storm buried Arthur's world beneath its winter fury.

It might have been fun if the electricity had stayed on, but it had not. Trees had cracked, electric cables had been torn from their poles, and the lights had gone out. Traffic slowed to a crawl, and news stations warned everyone to stay off the streets. By Friday, the electric company had repaired most of the downed cables, and the roads were beginning to thaw, but Thanksgiving vacation was almost over. This had not been a fun vacation. It had been dark, gloomy, and depressing.

The gray light of early evening filtered through the blinds. Arthur Richards was in his room doing homework. He was angry about the way the vacation had turned out and angry about having to do homework. His cabin fever was reaching the critical stage. In the light of his dad's work lamp, the pages of the English literature book glowed in the dark. The lamp smeared shadowy monsters across the walls of the dimly lit room. Stray beams of light crossed an unmade bed, a pile of CDs beside a stereo system, scattered DVDs, a trash can surrounded by wads of paper, and a closet overflowing with winter clothes, comic books, and some luggage.

Arthur pulled the first page of his half-finished English composition out of the printer and read.

" ... a legendary figure, the Pendragon of Camelot, better known as King Arthur, the Pendragon of Camelot..."

Arthur ripped the page out of his binder and shredded it. He had knocked over the desk lamp in the process, and that only fed his rage all the more. He picked up his textbook and hurled it across the room. As his rage melted into shame, Arthur stood in the near-darkness and listened. No one had heard his outburst. He set the lamp back up, relieved that he hadn't broken the bulb.

I'm sorry, he thought. *I'm sorry it had to happen. I'm sorry everything had to happen.*

Arthur walked over to his unmade bed and stretched out on it, stretched out to sleep his life away. He left his shredded manuscript and English book lying on the floor. Let them rot there.

Forget English. Forget straight A's. Forget everything.

The pallid light of an outside street lamp filtered through the blinds into Arthur's dark room. Somewhere in the distance, Arthur thought he heard hoofbeats, but he knew it had to be his imagination. *It's a little early for Santa Claus,* he thought sarcastically.

A moment later, Arthur heard the doorbell ring. He could hear the recliner squeak as his father got up to answer it. He heard voices, but couldn't make out the words.

"Yeah," Arthur heard Lance say. "Sounds like fun." Somebody else spoke. Arthur didn't catch the voice.

"I'll go see," Arthur's mother's voice said in the hall. Her footsteps came closer. Arthur heard the knock on his door.

"Come in."

The door cracked open. A wedge of light slid across the floor.

"Chris Castle's at the door," Mrs. Richards said. "He says Mr. Lucas is taking some of the neighborhood kids for a carriage ride. Lance is going. You're invited, too."

"Guess Lucas felt guilty for giving us homework over the holidays," Arthur said with a smirk. "All right. I'll go. Tell 'em to wait for me." Anything to get out of the house.

Arthur's mother walked back to the living room. Arthur got up, went to the closet, and pulled on his heaviest coat. Then he remembered he wasn't wearing any long johns, so he dug the long johns out of his drawer, pulled off his jeans, put the long johns on, and then pulled the jeans back on.

Arthur walked past his parents on the way to the front door.

"Have fun," Mrs. Richards said.

"See ya, Mom," Arthur said. He braced himself for the cold and opened the door. His icy, middle class neighborhood was out there waiting for him. Then he saw it. Parked beneath a streetlight was a vision from right out of a Dickens novel: a glossy, black, horse-drawn carriage.

Mr. Lucas smiled and lifted a gloved hand in greeting as Arthur shuffled through the snow. In the orange light of oil lamps mounted on the front roof supports, Arthur could see the carriage had three benches. Mr. Lucas sat in front. Chris sat on the middle bench. Lance sat in back, on the third bench. There was a chest beside him. A leathery canopy stretched itself above all three rows. Silently Arthur wondered how long Lance and Chris could be around each other before hostilities broke out. Though they had supposedly made amends after Stacy's death, Arthur still felt the tension every time they were together.

When Arthur was close enough to the carriage, Mr. Lucas caught him by the arm and hauled him up onto the front bench. Lucas was no longer a young man, but he was surprisingly strong, Arthur suddenly realized. In his hat, long coat, and scarf, the Englishman and his carriage looked like something from a Christmas card.

Just who are you really, Mr. Lucas? Arthur silently wondered.

"Shall we go?" Mr. Lucas asked. His breath smoked.

"Ready when you are," Arthur said.

Mr. Lucas snapped the reins on the backs of his stallions. The carriage jerked into motion. Yellow-orange flames danced in the oil lamps. They threw their glow over cold cheeks, noses, and winter clothing. The horses' hooves made their hollow clippety-clop sounds against pavement that had not quite thawed. Dirty streaks of snow lay between parallel lines of tire ruts. The carriage didn't have any shock absorbers. It bumped through a hole and shook everyone around. A gray, dismal neighborhood swam past. Some of the neighbors had already put up Christmas lights.

The carriage passed a well-lit brick home.

"Let's see if Angie wants to come," Arthur said.

"Yeah, Mr. Lucas," Lance said. "We need some women to make this thing perfect. Pull over into the edge of that driveway there."

Mr. Lucas bumped one carriage wheel over a curb and onto the sidewalk in front of Angel—Angie—Stone's parents' house. Most of the carriage was out of the street.

"Hope Ms. Stone don't mind a little manure on her sidewalk," Lance said.

"Arthur," Mr. Lucas said. "Why don't you go to the door and see if Miss Angie wants to go riding with us."

"I'll go, Mr. Lucas," Lance said.

"One look at you and her mother would ground her for life," Chris said.

"Angie's mama loves me," Lance said. "Most women do."

Chris snorted.

Arthur stepped out of the carriage onto a slush-covered lawn.

"Call me if you need any help," Lance said.

Ignoring his brother, Arthur walked through the Stones' carport. He nearly panicked when he tripped over a life-size figure of Santa Claus somebody had dragged out of storage. Finally he made it to the side door. The lights were on inside. Arthur rang the doorbell. Mrs. Stone answered the door.

"Oh, hi, Arthur. Come on in."

"Is Angie here?" Arthur asked as he stepped inside.

"She's just finishing her supper," Mrs. Stone said. "We've got plenty to eat if you'd like to join us."

"No, thanks," Arthur said. "I already ate." Mrs. Stone led him through the kitchen into the dining room where Angie and her younger brother and dad were sitting around the table and looking bored. They all looked up when Arthur came in.

"Mr. Lucas is taking some of us for a carriage ride around the neighborhood," Arthur said. "We came to see if Angie wanted to go. Ryan can come, too."

"Ryan's just getting over the flu," Mrs. Stone said.

"Aw, Mom," Ryan said.

"Angie can go if it's all right with her dad," Mrs. Stone said.

"What did you say you were doing?" Mr. Stone asked. "Going for a carriage ride?"

"Yeah," Arthur said. "Mr. Lucas has an old horse-drawn carriage like they used to have in the twenties."

"Really?" Mrs. Stone brightened. "Where is it?"

"Right out front."

She walked over to the window.

"Who's going?" Angie asked.

"Lance, Chris Castle, Mr. Lucas, and me so far," Arthur said.

"It's beautiful," Mrs. Stone said from the window. "Where did he get it?"

"I'm not sure," Arthur said. "I didn't know he had it until tonight."

The whole Stone family, even Ryan, followed Arthur outside to admire Mr. Lucas's carriage. Finally it was time for the ride.

Lance reached out a hand and pulled Angie up into the carriage.

"Thank you, Lance."

Chris sighed.

Arthur climbed up into the middle bench beside Angie.

"Have a good time," Mr. Stone said.

"You boys take care of Angie for me," Mrs. Stone said.

"Always," Lance said.

"Like a fox guarding a hen house," Chris said under his breath.

"Don't mind him," Lance said. "He has issues."

"You should talk."

Mr. Lucas snapped the reins and the horses started moving. The carriage wheels bumped over the curb and into the street.

The carriage rolled past a tall, iron gate. Inside the gate was the Simmons place. The old Victorian home had been Guinevere Lane's very own haunted house for almost twenty years. The children had once dared each other to walk past it, to knock on the door, or to look in the dark windows. Now Mr. Lucas had bought the house and was in the process of restoring it.

Lance eyed a chest on the floor beneath the rear seat. "What's in this box, Mr. Lucas?"

"A moonlight snack," Mr. Lucas said. "In case we get hungry."

Everyone stopped talking as they passed the Perry house where Stacy Knight had lived with her mother and stepfather. The house was dark, the lawn was covered with undisturbed snow, and there was a "For Sale" sign out front. The place looked sad and lonely.

"Where did you get this carriage, Mr. Lucas?" Angie asked.

"I purchased it from an older gentleman in Oak Grove," Mr. Lucas said. "He said it once belonged to a local physician who had six children. It has taken quite a bit of work to restore it."

"Why did you buy it?" Arthur asked.

"A bit of a whim, I suppose. I've always been fond of antiques."

Lance smiled. "Being one yourself helps, huh, Mr. Lucas?"

"I'm not sure what you meant by that, Lance," Mr. Lucas said, "but I think you've just flunked your next examination."

"Hey, I was just kidding, Mr. Lucas," Lance said. "You're practically a spring chicken."

"Not for some time, I'm afraid."

The houses ended. There were grassy, ice-covered fields on both sides of the road. Electricity and telephone poles were spaced at near-even intervals beside the road. Gray and black cables hung with icicles. There was a road on the left where the field rose up to become a hill. Arthur found himself following the road with his eyes. On top of the hill was a cemetery.

"Why did it have to happen?" Arthur thought. Then he realized he had said it out loud.

"Sometimes it's better not to ask," Mr. Lucas sighed heavily. Something in his tone told them he had seen his share of pain. Arthur remembered hearing that Mr. Lucas had been married once and that his wife had died.

Field gave way to forest on both sides of the road. The horses' hooves sounded increasingly hollow. Snow-flocked tops of pine trees were bent over. Leafless, skeletal oaks stood clad in the dignity of an early winter. The forest spoke in creaks and rumbles, dripping water, and sifting snow as a wind swept through. Arthur looked over at Angie. She smiled slightly when she saw him, but the sadness never left her eyes.

The group had been subdued since they passed the cemetery, Arthur noticed. They had almost stopped talking. The shadow of death tinged the icy air. It would be a long time, he thought, before anybody in this group was really happy again. And spring was a whole winter away.

Mr. Lucas turned the carriage into a small drive beside the road. The path was blocked by a wooden gate with a "No Trespassing" sign tacked to it. On the other side of the gate was a narrow trail that led off into the forest.

"Do you think your father would mind us riding about on his land?" Mr. Lucas asked.

"Nah," Lance said. "Of course not."

"I'll get the gate," Arthur said.

"I'm sure that would be appreciated," Mr. Lucas said.

Arthur jumped down off the carriage. His feet hit the cold ground, and the landing jarred him to the bones. The ground was harder when it was frozen, he realized. Arthur's body felt that way too. *I've been lazy too long,* he thought as he stepped over a frozen mud puddle. Ice-covered grass and leaves crunched beneath his shoes. Arthur walked up to the rickety gate, untied a soggy, rotting piece of rope, and pulled the gate open.

"Perfect," Mr. Lucas said.

Mr. Lucas slapped the reins against the horses' backs. Frozen mud puddles cracked and popped like so much glass as they pulled the carriage through the gate. Mr. Lucas pulled back on the reins and stopped the carriage.

Arthur pushed the gate back to where it had been. Leaving the rope untied, he ran back to the carriage and climbed into his seat.

"How far does this trail go?" Angie asked.

"'About twenty miles," Lance said.

"Twenty miles?" Arthur said. "It only goes to the other side of these woods."

"It curves around a lot," Lance said.

"Not twenty miles," Arthur said. "Maybe five."

Lance shrugged.

The trail wound out of the view of the gate. The glow of the carriage lamps revealed tire ruts in the path ahead. Men in four-wheel-drive vehicles hunted these trails often. Little pine trees brushed against the sides of the carriage at one place.

"You sure you want to drive through here, Mr. Lucas?" Lance asked. "You might scratch up your nice buggy."

"Or get it muddy," Arthur said.

"If I do, it will be for a good cause," Mr. Lucas said. "We need it's magic tonight to break the spell of melancholy. I'll have plenty of time to touch it up before the Christmas parade."

If it had not been for the glow of the carriage's lamps, the darkness of night would have swallowed the carriage. Inky shadows hung on either side of them like dark curtains. Other than a tinge of ambient light from the crescent moon overhead and a few patches of gray where snow shone, the forest was pitch dark. The night was damp and full of dripping noises, and a fog was starting to rise.

"Hoohoohoo," a strange voice called out from the gloom.

"What was that?" Angie asked.

"An owl, probably," Chris said.

"Didn't scare you, did it?" Lance asked.

"No," Angie said. "Well, maybe a little."

Arthur rubbed his nose. It was numb from the cold. The carriage rolled past the shambling remains of a towering oak tree that had been killed by lightning years ago. Twisted branches and sharp limbs gave the tree a wicked look. It looked like a giant monster guarding the trail.

The carriage shifted, and the horses struggled to pull her over a small hill. Knotty tree roots filled the tire ruts. Arthur felt as though his brain were bouncing against the walls of his skull as the carriage bounced over them. The carriage cleared the roots and came to the top of a hill. The trail sloped downward for the next fifteen yards. The carriage lamps showed a wooden bridge and a small creek winding through the forest. Fog swirled in the flickering light of the lamps as the carriage creaked over the bridge. The fog was getting thicker and whiter by the minute.

"This night makes me think of some good old horror movies," Arthur said. "You could just see Wolf-Man or Dracula coming out of that fog."

"A bloke could lose 'iz 'ead on a noight like this," Chris said in a cockney English voice he used in school dramas.

"You're gonna make Mr. Lucas homesick talkin' like that," Lance said.

Mr. Lucas just smiled.

"I used to have nightmares about these people that would appear in the fog," Chris said. "It was like they were dead. They'd walk around like zombies. And just when you got close to them...they'd just disappear into the fog." Chris was quiet for a moment. "I was always afraid they'd come back and grab me, maybe pull me into the fog and make me disappear along with them."

"Don't talk about that," Angie said.

"Stop scaring the baby," Lance said in a falsetto voice. Angie turned around and hit him on the leg.

"Hey!" Lance said. "Those bony little fists hurt."

"That's right," Angie said. "Don't forget it."

"I don't know if I like this," Lance said. "Angie's starting to get liberal."

"You mean liberated?" Arthur asked.

"That, too."

The carriage rolled past a big beech tree with names carved into the trunk. The tree was covered with golden-yellow leaves that showed up as the lamps passed near them. Tough, smooth-barked limbs hung overhead. Some of the golden leaves lay on the floor of the forest.

"It looks like an Elvish tree," Chris said. "You are now entering the magical forests of Lothlorien. Is there another bridge up here?"

"Yeah," Lance said.

The trees dropped away. Mr. Lucas pulled the carriage onto a long, wooden bridge. The bridge was gray and worn, made of rough wood, and suspended about six feet above a wide, shallow creek. Still water reflected the stars and moon. Frozen sheets of ice broke the water's dark surface. The ice collected around cypress knees, roots, and a rotting wooden boat that sat at the edge, barely touching the water. A "pea soup" fog hung over the water like a gray blanket.

"Did your dad build this bridge?" Angie asked.

"No way," Arthur said. "This bridge is older than he is. It was built back in the sawmill days of the town. You know, back in about the twenties or thirties. This trail was cut to haul wood to the sawmill."

"Great fishin' in that creek," Lance said. Bits of broken fishing line were tangled around some of the cypress knees. Apparently, more than one person had tried the "great fishing" Lance had spoken of.

The carriage rattled as the front wheels left the bridge and thumped up and down again as the rear wheels dropped off. The forest closed in around the carriage. The fog had grown so thick that the horses in front of the carriage were only dim outlines. It seemed as though the carriage's lamps were the only lights in the whole dark world. Arthur felt a chill as he thought about the fog-people Chris said he'd dreamed about. The hair on his neck seemed to prickle.

They heard a howl somewhere out in the woods.

"What was that?" Chris whispered.

The fog thinned just a little bit. Arthur looked up above the trees. A crescent moon hung directly overhead.

The fog closed in again. This time it shut out everything. The carriage creaked blindly through the darkness. The horses' hooves thumped against the ground. All anyone could see was the dim glow of the oil lamps shining somewhere in the fog.

Arthur felt his hair stand straight up. Cold gripped his stomach. The horses went wild. Arthur could hear Mr. Lucas pulling wildly at the reins, but, strangely, the carriage didn't jerk. It just seemed to float. Arthur noticed he didn't hear carriage wheels or hoofbeats. *There's nothing underneath us,* he thought.

The fog distorted the sounds around them.

"Is that wind?" Lance asked.

"No," Angie said. "More like singing."

"Singing," Chris said, "but not human."

What else could it be? Arthur started to ask, but he was not sure he wanted to hear the answer.

The air was cold, painfully cold.

"Something's wrong," Angie whispered. Arthur felt her squeeze up closer to him. He put his arm around her.

Then there were the lights. They flashed through the fog like fireflies, only brighter. Then they popped like bubbles.

The carriage jerked and rattled. The sound of hoofbeats returned as the horses galloped through the night. The fog thinned out and Arthur could see the sky overhead. He searched through the treelimbs for the crescent moon he'd seen earlier, but it was nowhere to be seen. A handful of stars stared down from a purple evening sky. Some of the ones on the horizon looked strangely large.

"It was darker than this," Arthur realized.

"Whoa, Morgan," Mr. Lucas said. "Whoa, Gawain." He pulled back on the reins. The carriage bounced up and down on rough places in the trail. The stallions slowed gradually. Mr. Lucas breathed a sigh of relief.

"What the heck was that?" Lance asked.

"What were those lights?" Angie asked.

"Fireflies, maybe?" Arthur said.

"More like ball lightning," Chris said.

"Ball lightning," Lance said. "What the heck is ball lightning?"

"It may have been swamp gas," Arthur said. "I've never

seen anything like that." Arthur noticed he still had his arm around Angie. He pulled himself free without comment.

"Where's the fog?" Chris asked.

Everyone turned around. There was no fog as far down the trail as any of them could see.

"Weird," Lance said.

Arthur looked up at the sky. Why did it look so much lighter than it had a while ago? Had his eyes adjusted to the darkness, or had some clouds cleared away? Maybe some lights from town were lighting up the sky, but why all of a sudden?

Nobody spoke for a while. Mr. Lucas's carriage bumped and rattled down a twisted trail. Grass was tall in some spots and big, flat rocks shook the buggy around. The trees beside the road were gnarled and twisted. Their limbs dripped with Spanish moss. That was not uncommon for Louisiana, but where was the snow and ice?

The trail widened out on the right and became a clearing. White rocks—tall, wide, and flat—were scattered through it. One of them passed close to the carriage. The lamps fell upon it. There was a carving in the rock—an inscription.

"This is a graveyard!" Lance said.

"It can't be," Arthur said. "That's impossible."

"Look at those stones, man. What else could it be?"

"There aren't any graveyards on our land," Arthur said. "And look at the inscription. Those aren't letters. They're more like runes."

"What the heck is a rune?" Lance asked.

"A kind of old Germanic writing," Angie said.

"That's right," Chris said. "How did you know that?"

"Not all blondes are stupid, Chris," Angie said.

"This is all wrong," Arthur said. "The sky doesn't even look right."

"What are you thinking?" Lance asked. "You think we're in the Twilight Zone or something?" He started singing the Twilight Zone theme song.

"Will you shut up?" Chris said.

"You shut up, man," Lance said. "You've done nothing but moan and give attitude since you got here."

"Will you two settle down?" Arthur said.

"An excellent suggestion," Mr. Lucas said.

Chris and Lance glared at each other for a moment, then looked away. Nobody spoke for a moment. Crickets chirped in the gray of late dusk. There was another sound further away.

"What was that?" Angie asked.

"What?"

"I thought I heard voices."

Mr. Lucas eased the carriage through the cemetery. The stallions pulled them through a gate in a broken fence and out of the clearing. The trail narrowed and led uphill. The trail was better maintained here. Most of the grass and big stones had been cleared away. The sound of voices grew louder.

When the carriage reached the top of the hill, Mr. Lucas pulled the horses to a halt. Beyond the hill, the dirt trail led into a village. Crude wood huts with thatched roofs were scattered around a big, muddy clearing. Some kind of ceremony was taking place in a field that lay to the right. People were standing around a bonfire and holding up lanterns that threw off a blue light.

"What is all this?" Chris whispered.

"Better put your lamps out, Mr. Lucas," Lance said. "This could be a bunch of devil worshippers. I heard we had some around here about five years ago. Mutilated some cows."

"That's an urban myth," Chris said.

"Urban?" Lance said. "Out here?"

"Perhaps discretion is in order," Mr. Lucas said as he put out the lamps.

"Let's get out of here," Angie said.

"Listen," Chris said. "You can hear them, but they're not speaking English."

The hilltop was about a hundred yards from where the people were gathered. In the blue glow of the lanterns and the yellow glare of the fire, Arthur, Angie, and the others could see the crowd clearly. The people were dressed strangely. The men wore tunics that were cinched at the waist by belts. Their baggy pants hung down over knee-length boots. Some of the women wore long, shapeless shifts while others, mostly younger women, wore leather corsets that laced in the front.

"Notice the man with the sword," Mr. Lucas said softly.

A tall, lean man-shape stood against the glare of the fire. He held a gleaming sword over his head as the others silently watched him. The man stabbed the sword into the ground a couple of inches and began to walk, dragging the sword along behind him. There was movement, coiling movement, around the line left by the sword. At first it looked like smoke...or snakes rising from the ground. The shapes grew tall, twisted around each other, and stiffened. Then leaves sprouted, and fruit appeared. There were melons, oranges, apples....

The people cried out in delight and clapped their hands together as an orchard sprang up from the ground behind the sword-bearer. Suddenly, they went wild and rushed in on the man with the sword. Just before they reached him, he backed toward the fire, lifted up his blade, and vanished like a ghost.

"Whoa!" Lance exclaimed. "That was great!"

"What is this?" Arthur said. "Some kind of magic act."

"Let's get out of here, Mr. Lucas," Chris said.

Mr. Lucas tugged hard at the reins, turning the carriage around. There were shouts behind them, but no intelligible words. *What language were these people speaking?* The buggy flew back down the road, past the broken fence, and into the cemetery. There was barely enough light to see by.

Mr. Lucas drove the horses down a dark, winding trail and into the forest. The carriage jarred up and down on rocks and holes in the road. It hit a mud puddle and splashed everyone with muddy water.

Finally, moments later, Mr. Lucas slowed the horses down. He pulled a match out of his pocket and relit the oil lamps on the front of the carriage. Arthur held onto the seat in front of him and leaned out of the buggy. He looked back down the path behind the carriage and listened. Everyone listened.

"What's that roar?" Chris said. "Sounds like a bulldozer."

The sound was faint. It echoed through the trees.

"It's coming from in front of us," Angie said.

Mr. Lucas edged the buggy forward until he found a small clearing full of tall grass. He drove the buggy a few meters off the trail and, once again, doused the oil lamps.

"Remind me to purchase some electric lamps once we get back," Lucas said. "These are simply too much trouble."

"Why are we pulled over like this?" Arthur asked. "What do you think is coming?"

"I don't know," Mr. Lucas said, his voice hushed, "but it sounds rather large."

"I'm still trying to figure out how that guy did those things," Chris whispered. "I've seen magicians make plants grow out of hats, but that vanishing stunt was something else."

"Shhhh," Angie said.

The roaring grew louder, and a blue light danced around tree trunks as a big, metal machine roared around the bend and into plain view. Blue lights reached out before and behind it. Armored human shapes hung all over the sides of the thing. The operator sat at the top of the machine, his face bathed in the glow of instrument lights. His skin had the shriveled look of a mummy's, and his eyes glowed silver. The machine stopped in the clearing, and helmeted heads turned. Silver eyes focused coldly on the buggy and its occupants. Arthur felt his heart beating in his chest. The armored creatures were at least seven feet tall.

A mechanical voice shouted at them in a language that was not English.

There was an uneasy pause.

The same phrase was repeated. This time the voice was louder, angrier.

"We don't know your language," Mr. Lucas called back.

"No comprende'!" Lance yelled.

"That's great," Chris mumbled. "They look Mexican."

"Maybe Angie can show them some runes," Lance said.

"Will you shut up?"

The armored men looked at each other, no emotion in their mummified faces. One of them stepped down from the machine and started for the buggy. Mr. Lucas whipped the horses into motion and aimed them for the path behind the machine.

"Ride! Ride! GO!"

The buggy flew into the trail. Mechanical shouts rang out. Then one voice seemed to ring out over the others and the shouting ended. Arthur hoped the leader of the group had called off the others, but there was no way to be sure.

Mr. Lucas was whipping the reins more furiously than before. The winding path before the horses was almost pitch dark. The buggy hit a rock and rode on two wheels for a second or two. Then it bounced to the ground, rattling the teeth of its occupants.

After what could have been two minutes or ten, Mr. Lucas slowed his stallions down to a more reasonable speed. He passed Chris his matchbook.

"Light the lamps, won't you, Chris."

"Yes, sir."

Chris went to work, lighting the lamps.

"I don't think they followed us," Lance said. "Some of them started after us, but I think the guy on top called them back."

"They may just be turning that tank-thing around," Arthur said. His mouth was dry.

"I don't hear it," Angie said.

"What were those things?" Chris had voiced the same question that was on the minds of the others.

"What is any of this?" Arthur gestured wildly. "This isn't our land. This isn't our road!"

"We must have gotten lost in the fog," Chris said.

"That's impossible!" Arthur said. "You can't get lost! There's only one road through my dad's land, and this isn't it."

"Then where are we?" Chris asked, his voice hoarse.

"Lost," Mr. Lucas said. "We're lost."

2./Wrong Turn

"I can't get cell service," Arthur said as he held his smartphone. "Does anybody have it?" The others pulled out their smartphones.

"Nothing," Lance said. None of the others had it either.

"So what?" Chris said. "It's a dead spot. We're in a rural area. What are you trying to say? That we're no longer on earth?" Nobody answered. "We've got to think this through," Chris went on. "There has to be a logical explanation for this whole thing."

"It was the fog," Arthur said, his voice soft and detached. "That was the last time anything looked normal—before we went into that fog."

The others looked at him. Mr. Lucas edged the horses slowly forward. He could not have had any idea where he was going, but it seemed better than sitting still.

"When we came out of the fog," Arthur said, "the moon was gone, and the sky looked too light."

"The air felt warmer, too," Angie said, "and the trees were different."

"And we don't have a cemetery, a village, or robot monsters on our land, either." Lance said. "Maybe...maybe we got off the trail when we were in that fog. We passed through the woods or a clearing and got on another trail we didn't know was there."

"And what about the lights in the fog?" Angie asked. "The village?"

"I always heard these woods were haunted," Arthur said.

"Maybe those guys on the metal thing were aliens from outer space," Angie said.

"Aliens," Chris snorted. "Maybe this is all some kind of army experiment. Or maybe there's a movie being filmed out here, and the people filming it didn't want a crowd."

"We didn't see any cameramen or lights," Arthur said. "They'd need lights if they were going to film at night. And why did those guys yell at us in that foreign language if they were just actors?"

"Maybe it's a reenactment," Lance said. "Like a Civil War reenactment."

"For Dungeons and Dragons fans, maybe," Chris said.

"You know," Arthur said. "That almost makes sense. Lance, you may be right."

"Yeah," Chris said. "That's got to be it."

"I don't think so," Lance said. "Forget what I said."

"Why?"

"Look."

The trail had wound around a rock and onto the levee of an enormous lake. The surface was still as glass. A big, rocky island rose out of the middle. Spiked walls of weathered stone coiled around its craggy, scorched expanse like the body of a giant dragon. Its gated entrance looked like the gaping jaws of a hungry beast. From those jaws, a weathered dock extended out into the lake. Directly across the water from the dock sat a fabulous city on a hill.

The city gleamed of polished gold. Towers like the heads of so many cobras, opalescent domes, spires, and structures with purposes unguessed appeared over walls that gleamed like carved ice. The city, as far as Arthur could see, was sitting on a flat-topped mesa. It was surrounded on all sides by sheer cliff walls that made any sort of surprise attack impossible. Strange colored smoke rose past the towers and into the dark sky. The whole thing shimmered like a heat mirage. The sky behind it was spattered with what looked, at first glance, like huge, pale yellow stars.

"This is crazy!" Lance said, clearly delighted. "You were right, man. We're not in Kansas anymore."

"Shut up," Chris groaned. There was little conviction in his voice. He was clearly floored by what he was seeing.

"That's some kind of asteroid belt in the sky," Arthur said. "It may have been a moon that broke apart."

"Will you listen to yourself?" Chris gasped. "Do you

know what you're saying?"

"We're no longer on Earth," Mr. Lucas said. "This is another world entirely."

From the lake came a loud whooshing sound, a blast of heat. All heads turned back to the island. Fire was rising from behind the walls and into the sky like a giant hand. It fell back behind the walls and sent up a blast of smoke. A terrible stench hung in the air, and there were screams. They were barely audible against the roar of the flame. The glow and the roar died down. The screaming continued. A booming, robot voice brought all eyes to the lake. A long, flat ferry glided across the lake's dark skin. It was heading toward the island, toward the dock that led into its waiting jaws. Wide-eyed and silent, Arthur and the others watched as the ferry docked. In the hellish light that issued from the island's gates, they watched as four huge, armored shapes drove seven chained humans across the bridge to the island. The humans, clearly prisoners, were bound like dogs by chains around their necks. The giant figures that drove them looked very much like the silver-eyed hulks the group had seen on the trail earlier.

Something that could have been a growl or a scream came from the island. Arthur heard a rustling noise in the bushes beside the trail. He looked but didn't see anything. A cry of robot rage echoed over the lake. A human shape, chain still encircling its neck, leaped over the side of the ferry and vanished beneath the lake's dark surface.

"There he is," Angie whispered, pointing. The prisoner's head had broken the surface. He was swimming toward the lake's shore as fast as he could. With the weight of the chain that bound him, that was not very fast. He had only gone a few yards when he screamed and choked on water. His hands clawed at the air as something dragged him out of sight.

Several seconds passed. His head split the dark waters one last time. His face was a bloody mask of terror. Thrashing shapes covered him, and the water boiled with red eyes, teeth, and scaly backs and tails.

Arthur heard Chris gag. He turned around and saw his

friend throwing up over the side of the carriage.

"Are you all right?" Mr. Lucas managed to say.

Chris nodded. Then he threw up again. Arthur put his hand over his mouth. His gut heaved, but he managed to keep everything down.

Just ahead was a road leading off the levee. It led away from the lake and back into the forest. Mr. Lucas gently snapped the reins. The buggy reached the off-road and Mr. Lucas turned the horses down it. The wind changed direction. As it blew off the lake and toward the forest, Arthur and the others could feel the heat from the island. A stench of muddy, slimy water and something burning came with it. Chris nearly threw up again.

A mechanical voice shouted something unintelligible. Whatever language the cyborgs spoke, it wasn't one Arthur recognized. Mr. Lucas was listening thoughtfully. The lake was still splashing with dark, reptilian bodies.

Once the buggy was out of the sight of the robot-voiced cyborgs on the ferry, Mr. Lucas whipped the horses into a steady gallop. He seemed to want to put as much distance between his young friends and that lake as possible, but his horses were tired so he didn't push them as hard as he had earlier.

Through gaps in twisted, mossy treetops, Arthur and the others could see the shimmering city they had seen earlier. No one was trying to come up with logical explanations anymore. In fact, no one was saying much of anything. Arthur noticed that most of the trees still had their leaves. Autumn had disappeared along with the saner part of reality.

The buggy bumped up and down miles of muddy, twisting trails through the forest. No one spoke for a long time. There were animal sounds from the darkness that made everyone jump from time to time.

"We have to stop and eat soon," Mr. Lucas said. "Then we have to find shelter for the night." His voice sounded loud in the darkness. "Lance, open up that chest beside you. I've packed some sandwiches, a few cans of pop, and a Thermos bottle of tea. The tea is mine."

Lance opened the chest. Cans and sandwich bags sloshed around on ice that was starting to melt. Lance saw a plastic, insulated canister lying between two cold drinks. He reached for it. Sandwiches floated near it in transparent Ziploc bags.

"You want your tea, Mr. Lucas?"

"Please."

Lance picked up the insulated canister. He held it over Arthur's shoulder. It dripped cold drops of melted ice down his neck.

"Hey!"

"Sorry, man. Pass this to Mr. Lucas."

Sighing, Arthur took the canister and passed it over the front seat to Mr. Lucas. The teacher took it. He stopped the buggy.

"I hate tuna," Arthur mumbled.

Sandwiches and drinks were passed. Chris said he wasn't hungry, but the others ate. Mr. Lucas shoved down the braking lever, and the carriage sat still. Morgan and Gawain, the horses, seemed happy of the break. They had been driven hard.

"Something's watching us," Lance said.

Nobody spoke up to deny it.

After a brief rest, Mr. Lucas shifted the braking lever. He slapped the reins on the stallions' backs. The buggy jerked into motion. Hoofbeats echoed around dark trees, over marshes and rotting beds of leaves. The night itself seemed to edge through the underbrush—through the briars and bushes—to follow after the carriage.

Thunder cut the heavens like a gunshot. Rain started falling in blankets of water. It spattered on the horses' backs and flooded the trail with shallow streams and mudholes.

Lightning flashed. Arthur thought he saw someone standing beside a tree in the rain. Another flash. There was nothing there.

The wind blew rain into the carriage. It soaked through everyone's clothing, plastered their hair flat and straight against their heads, and ran into their eyes. The rain felt good at first. It seemed almost like a kind of cleansing—a healing—but the soggy clothes got colder and colder.

The lightning flashed. A thunderclap followed close behind. The horses almost bolted. Mr. Lucas held tightly to the reins.

"The lightning's getting too close," he said. "We have to find shelter." In the light of oil lamps, Arthur looked around at Angie beside him, Chris and Lance behind him, and Mr. Lucas in front. There was no emotion on their faces, only rain. Beads of rain dribbled from their hair and ran down their faces. It hung on their eyelashes, on their noses and chins. The lightning flashed—turned night to day. A red after-image burned itself into Arthur's eyes like a snapshot. Arthur closed his eyes and the image glared against the black of his eyelids. It showed twisted trees, bushes, and—something, a dark figure. Was it a man, a trick of the light—maybe a funny-shaped bush or a stump?

The rainfall slacked up a little bit. Arthur and the others sat in near-darkness in their cold, damp clothing and watched the rain drip off the canopy of the carriage. In the gray-blackness beyond the world of the lamps, they could hear the rain falling on the forest, spattering the muddy trail, drumming on the roof.

This is great, Arthur thought to himself. *Lost in the woods, soaking wet in an electric storm.* The horrors they had seen earlier—the vanishing man, the cyborgs with their glowing, silver eyes, the man eaten by the things in the lake—it all seemed unreal, like the rain had washed it away. Arthur could almost convince himself now that they had imagined all of it.

"I don't know where we're going to find any shelter," Chris said, breaking the silence. "We haven't passed anything for miles."

Just then the lightning flashed. Everything glared white. The blackness returned. The world had been lit up for an instant, but that had been long enough for all to see a "Y" split in the path ahead. The road forked off into two directions.

"Maybe I spoke too soon," Chris said.

"Which way, Mr. Lucas?" Lance asked. "Anybody seen a sign with a hotel on it?"

"Motel 666," Chris said darkly.

"We don't know what lies in either direction," Mr. Lucas said. "We'll have to choose a path at random. What will it be, all? Right or left?"

"Left," Angie said. "I'm left-handed."

"Don't matter to me," Lance said.

"Left," Arthur said. "I really don't care either."

"Then left it is," Mr. Lucas said. "Any objections?"

There were none. A tree stood in the center of the path. Mr. Lucas turned the horses to the left of it and chose the left path.

Arthur thought about Frost's poem, "The Road Not Taken," but he couldn't remember all the words. The path ahead was slick with mud. The horses' hooves and the buggy wheels left deep tracks. The road seemed to slope downhill. Ferns and algae grew all around the path.

"We better turn around, Mr. Lucas," Arthur said. "Those ferns are everywhere. They only grow in low, wet places."

"You're right," Mr. Lucas said, "but I don't see anyplace we can turn my stallions."

Along with the sound of the rain, they heard running water. The oil lamps lit the path in front of the horses. Water was over the road. Mr. Lucas stopped the horses. Everyone looked at him. The teacher strained his eyes against the gloom.

"What are we gonna do, Mr. Lucas?" Angie asked softly. She hadn't been talking much.

"I can see the other side," Mr. Lucas said. "It's about four meters away. I don't think the water's more than a few inches deep here."

"We gonna try to cross?" Lance asked.

"Yes," Mr. Lucas said. "I don't see that we have much of an alternative. So pray the water doesn't get too deep."

Mr. Lucas signaled the horses forward. They waded out into brown, rushing water. The carriage followed. The horses splashed through the water. Water rushed underneath the carriage, but didn't come over the floor. It was only about twelve inches deep.

The carriage slowed down. Mr. Lucas slapped the reins on the backs of the horses. They pulled. The carriage moved a couple of inches, then stopped. Mr. Lucas snapped the reins hard. The horses neighed and pulled. The carriage jerked forward, then slid back. Mr. Lucas sighed and massaged his temples.

"We appear to be stuck," he said at last.

"What do we do now?" Arthur asked.

"I don't know," Mr. Lucas said. He stood up, whipped the reins furiously and yelled.

"Pull! Pull, can't you! PULL!"

The poor horses struggled, but the carriage wouldn't move an inch. Arthur and the others knew—and dreaded—what was coming up next.

"We have to lighten the load," Mr. Lucas said. "Some of us will have to get out and push."

Nobody moved for a few seconds. Then Arthur jerked off a shoe. The others did the same. They pulled off their shoes and peeled away their socks. They rolled up their pants legs.

"I wonder how cold that water is," Chris said. He held onto the carriage seat and stepped slowly into the brown water with one foot. It rushed around his toes. He dropped off the buggy and let both feet down all the way. Icy water numbed his feet. Mud squashed up between his toes. He growled something unintelligible.

The water was too cold, everyone agreed, and the mud was too slimy. Rain fell on them. Each drop seemed like a needle of ice.

"Why don't we get behind the buggy and push," Chris said. "Mr. Lucas, you get the horses moving."

"Nobody put you in charge," Lance said. "Don't tell Mr. Lucas what to do."

"It's all right, Lance," Mr. Lucas said. "Let me know when you're ready."

Arthur, Chris, and Lance got behind the carriage. There wasn't room for anybody else in back. Mr. Lucas and Angie stood by the horses, ready to coax them forward.

"Everybody ready?" Arthur asked.

"Yep," Lance said.

Chris nodded.

"Okay, Mr. Lucas," Arthur yelled.

Arthur, Chris, and Lance, dug in and pushed. Mr. Lucas and Angie led the horses ahead. The carriage, without all the weight, glided forward. Mud ran from the spokes of the wheels in chunks. The boys stopped pushing. Mr. Lucas led the horses to the other side of the stream. They pulled the carriage up onto the shore.

"Good job, men," Lance said. The tension between Chris and Lance seemed to subside a little bit.

Arthur and Chris started for the carriage. Arthur turned back and noticed Lance was stooped over in the water. He had a strange look on his face.

Arthur watched him for a moment. "What's wrong, Lance?"

"I'm hung up on something," Lance said. "It's wrapped around my ankle." He tried to take a step forward.

"What does it feel like?" Angie asked.

Lance tugged.

"May be a root," he said. "It's kind of hard and sharp."

He bent down to feel with his hands.

"RRRRRRRRRRRRRRRRRRRRRRRRRRRRRRR!" Something sprang up—threw water everywhere—and locked around Lance's arm. It was a head—doglike—with eyes like a human. Lance screamed.

The others jumped back, started to run.

The beast ripped into Lance's chest with its claws. Chunks of cotton lining flew from his shredded coat like dandelion spores. The beast rose up on hind legs and threw the boy down in the water. Blood dampened the front of his coat as he sank beneath the water.

The beast shot between Arthur and Chris. It didn't touch them. It leaped onto Mr. Lucas and swatted him aside. Then it sprang for the horses. It bit into Gawain's hind leg with its teeth. Both horses reared up in sheer terror and bolted down the trail, an empty carriage bouncing along behind them.

The dog-thing turned on its prey, its manlike eyes and white teeth seeming to smile. They saw it more clearly than before. It was covered with muddy fur. It stood upright, had pointed ears, a doglike muzzle, and cruelly intelligent eyes. Arthur classified the beast in a split second. *It was a werewolf.*

Mr. Lucas seized a limb out of the water. He held it menacingly at the beast. The werewolf, standing upright, sprang forward, smashed the rotten limb to splinters, and leaped onto the teacher. Lucas and the beast went down, splashing and fighting in the water.

Arthur, dazed, noticed another figure standing at the water's edge. It was the shape of a man, fully seven feet tall, with glowing red eyes. He was bald, and his face was mostly hidden in shadow, but Arthur could make out gnarled distortions in the leathered skin. As the figure moved forward, the air around him crackled and grew dark. Arthur felt the atmospheric pressure drop.

Lightning flashed—blinding—about five meters away.

Image: A man holding a sword like a lightning rod, a lightning bolt dancing at the tip. Sparks flying. Thunderclap.

The werewolf shot past Arthur and ran off into the forest. Arthur scanned the treeline for the other figure, but it had vanished completely.

Lance was coughing blood when Chris pulled Lance out of the water.

Dear God, Arthur thought. *Don't let him die.* Seeing Lance, his whole life, had been like looking into a mirror and seeing a reversed image of himself. Losing Lance would be like losing a part of himself.

Someone sloshed through the water to where Chris and Lance were. The rain and darkness made him little more than a shadow. He had a sword. It was still smoking from the lightning.

"Did anybody see what happened to the werewolf?" Chris asked suddenly.

"He ran off," Angie said, her voice shaking. "I think Mr. Lucas is dead."

The teacher was slumped against a tree at the edge of the floodwaters.

Arthur looked uneasily at the man with the sword. His heart was still racing from the attack. The figure raised the sword to the gray, raining sky. Then he gazed down at Lance, but Lance didn't seem to notice. His empty eyes stared, fixed, into the sky.

"What are you doing?" Chris asked.

The man touched Lance with the flat of his blade, and he began to cough. The stranger caught Lance by the arm and lifted him to his feet. Chris stood and watched, his mouth wide open in amazement. Arthur soon saw why. His brother's coat wasn't even torn.

The stranger squinted in the gloom. The others could see that he was a rugged, olive-skinned man with a beard. His long hair was pulled into a ponytail at the nape of his neck. He looked at Arthur, at Angie, and finally his gaze came to Mr. Lucas leaning against the tree. The man waded into the water. He bent over Mr. Lucas and touched him with his sword.

Chris, Lance, Arthur, and Angie gathered around them. Mr. Lucas stood up. He looked down at his clothes. Not a single thread was torn. The teacher looked at the stranger, tall and dark before him.

"Thank you," he said slowly. "Thank you for helping us."

The stranger didn't answer.

"He doesn't understand," Arthur said.

"Can you understand me?" Mr. Lucas asked.

The stranger raised his sword. Mr. Lucas looked uneasily at him as he touched his sword to the teacher's lips. Then he pulled it away and touched it to his own.

"The tongue you speak is strange to me," the man said. He spoke English with an accent. "I am Ambrose Pendragon, son of Arthur, king of Camelot."

"King Arthur," Chris gasped.

3./Among Friends

The lightning flashed overhead.

"In our land," Mr. Lucas was explaining, "King Arthur is only an ancient legend. You say you're his *son*?"

"He is the father of my fathers for many generations."

"Then you aren't his son in the literal sense?"

"No," the man laughed. "I am not nearly so old as that."

"What language are we speaking?" Arthur asked.

"English," Lance said. He frowned. "I think."

"Your language," the stranger said, "even your very thoughts are translated into the language of this land. It is an ability the Worldsmen used in their travels."

"Who are the Worldsmen?" Arthur asked.

Ambrose looked up into the angry heavens. "Why do we stand talking in the rain? We have to find shelter."

"Is there a place near here?" Mr. Lucas asked. "We've...lost our way, I'm afraid."

"You're not from this world," Ambrose said. "How did you get here?"

"We don't know," Mr. Lucas said.

"I suspected as much," he said. "Then come with us. You will be safe."

"Who is 'us'?" Lance asked. Just then they heard a splashing sound as two men, both on horseback, forded the flooded stream. Both of them had long, dark hair and beards. One was small and wiry. The other was tall and burly. His eyes glowed silver-white beneath his craggy brow.

"These are my friends," Ambrose gestured toward the men with his sword. "They are closer than brothers to me."

"I am Amosel," the big, silver-eyed man said. "Son of Johannan."

"We call him Amos," Ambrose said.

"Are silver eyes common in this place?" Mr. Lucas

asked.

"Only for Steel-Hearts," Amos said.

He saw their blank expressions.

"It is a long story."

"I am Marcos Allesandro de Libris," the younger, smaller man said. " You may call me Marcos." His clothes were filled with bulging pockets. A telescope hung from a cord around his neck.

"He is my brother," Amos said, "though I often wonder if the Elvish stole my true brother at birth."

"Many have said that," Marcos said. "They can scarcely imagine how a lovely creature like me could have a brother like him."

"Hmmph," Amos snorted.

"I know the feeling," Lance told Marcos.

"Hah," Arthur said.

"My name is Edmund Lucas," Mr. Lucas said.

"Lucas," Ambrose said. He grasped the teacher's wrist and gazed down at the ring on his hand. "This ring. Where did you get it?"

"In London," he said. "There was a shop there. Why do you ask?"

"That symbol," he said. "It is the mark of the Worldsmen. It is forbidden here. You must not let anyone see it, especially not the Steel-Hearts. Do you really know nothing of this ring?"

"I...," the teacher began. He frowned. "Before you asked me, I would have said no. Now, suddenly, I'm not entirely sure."

"Indeed," Ambrose said. "A discussion for another time, perhaps. Who are these others?"

The teacher gestured to the young people around him. "These are my students. I present Arthur, Lance, Christopher, and Angelina."

"Such impressive names," Ambrose said. "Welcome to New Logres."

"Logres," Mr. Lucas said. "The land where Camelot was located."

"Yes," Ambrose said. "On the World of the Fathers."

Lightning flashed. "We must get inside."

Ambrose took the reigns of his horse from the man he'd called Amos. "Climb upon my horse, Lucas."

"I...thank you," Mr. Lucas said, climbing rather stiffly into the saddle. He had felt strange taking the horse from a supposed ancestor of King Arthur, but he felt he'd better not refuse hospitality.

"And you, maiden," Amos said to Angie. "Marcos will lend you his mount."

"Gladly," Marcos said, "especially since my brother lacks the chivalry to offer his own." He helped Angie onto the horse.

"Your skinny horse can scarcely bear the weight of a girl," Amos said. "I was going to lend my mighty horse to the young men."

"Perhaps it will be better if you take Lucas and ride ahead of us," Ambrose told him. "His carriage will not be far from here."

"As you wish, my lord," Amos said. "Let us go, then." Mr. Lucas followed the silver-eyed stranger down the trail while his teenage students stayed behind with Ambrose and Marcos.

"Tell me again how you taught us to speak your language," Arthur said.

"Magic," Chris said. There was an edge of sarcasm in his tone.

"Or maybe it's a kind of science we don't understand," Angie said.

"Did we see you in a village earlier?" Arthur asked. "You were making...plants grow up out of the ground. Then you vanished."

"Yes," Ambrose said. "It was me you saw."

"I just wondered," Arthur said. Rain ran down Arthur's face. A chill ran through him as he looked at Ambrose and remembered the image of a man on a horse, a man with his sword lifted into the storm-lashed sky and lightning dancing on the tip. This man could not be human. Could he?

"Are you all right, Chris?" Angie asked.

"I'm not sure," Chris said. "I think I'm going insane."

"Meeting Samhain's hounds for the first time would unnerve anyone," Marcos said.

"Samhain?" Chris said. "As in the festival of Samhain?"

"The festival of what?" Lance asked.

"It's a Celtic holiday that marked the end of summer," Chris said. "It's where we got Halloween."

"Samhain is the name of a being who rules this place," Ambrose said. "He had no name in his own world, but appeared here during the feast of Samhain and took that name as his own."

"We saw a city on a hill by a lake," Arthur said. "It was beautiful but..."

"Evil," Angie said.

"Thanatos," Ambrose said. "The city of delights and unspeakable horrors. You have seen the stronghold of Samhain's empire. You have seen Thanatos."

"How is it that you do not know about Thanatos?" Marcos asked. "There is no one in this land who has not heard of it."

"Perhaps you had better not ask any more questions until we are inside," Ambrose said. His hand was on the hilt of his sword. "The forest hears us."

Arthur looked uneasily at the trees around them. Stories of walking tree-monsters came to his mind. He shivered inwardly. After silver-eyed cyborgs, a werewolf, and a man with a magic sword, the thought of man-eating trees could not be dismissed out of hand.

The rain kept falling. Mr. Lucas and Amos returned moments later with the carriage.

"I see you had no trouble finding your conveyance," Ambrose said.

"We had only to follow the trail of shoes and socks that had bounced out into the trail."

Ambrose examined the scratches on Gawain's leg. "This animal is wounded." The marks vanished as he passed his sword over them. Arthur started to ask how he did it but doubted the answer would make sense to him anyway.

Ambrose and his friends led Mr. Lucas and his students

down a muddy road. Ambrose rode tall in his saddle. His posture and the cut of his face made him look very much like a king, even with wet hair and ragged clothing. Arthur thought of a story he'd read where a ragged vagrant had turned out to be a dead king who had magically come back to life. The story had been a sad one. The king's people had all died, his kingdom had become a pile of moss-covered stones in some English farmer's pasture, and the authorities had thought the king was crazy and had locked him away.

Ambrose led the group through a meadow, down a short path, and into a clearing. In the starlight, all could see a roof of rough lumber leading out of the side of a round, grassy mound of earth.

Ambrose rode through the clearing ahead of the others, his horse's hooves leaving marks in the tall, rain-slick grass. Drawing closer, Arthur and the others could see that a stable full of hay and horses and wagons lay beneath the roof. The stable went deep into the hillside. Apparently it had been built around a cave. A gate, located just under the edge of the roof, guarded the front of the stable. Ambrose stopped his horse at the gate, climbed over the gate, and vanished into the darkness at the back of the stable. After a moment, a door opened in the darkness. An orange rectangle of light framed the stocky shape of a man who threw his arms around Ambrose's neck as he recognized him.

"Looks like Ambrose has a boyfriend," Chris said with a smirk.

"Shut up, man," Lance said.

"In many countries it is customary for men to embrace," Mr. Lucas said. "Therefore I suggest you refrain from making harsh and hasty judgments about our host."

Ambrose returned with a short, stocky man. His black hair was braided into long ponytails. His heavy brow ridge and sloped chin gave him an apelike appearance. He wore a leather tunic and pants and was barefoot.

"My stable is in the back," the stranger said in a soft, clear voice that belied his brutish appearance. "Take your horses there. I will tend to them later."

"That really isn't necessary," Mr. Lucas said.

"Do not deny me," the man said. "My hospitality is all I have to give."

"This is Aquila, son of Corr," Ambrose said. "He is a faithful servant of the new Camelot."

Mr. Lucas drove his horses around back and into the stable. The roof was high, giving the carriage top about five feet of clearance. The floor of the stable was damp and covered with hay, muddy hoof prints, a little spilled food, and manure.

A short, blocky woman who looked very much like a female version of Aquila came through the stable door. Her homely face broke into a warm smile when she saw the young people.

"This is my lovely wife, Prisca," Aquila said.

Prisca bowed.

Horses were unhitched and unsaddled and everyone went through the door at the back of the stable. Aquila and Prisca led Ambrose and his guests into a dark, smoky chamber full of furs and earthenware vessels. The room was lit and warmed by a circular firepit that burned at the center of the room. A brick hearth surrounded the pit, and an overhead pipe channeled smoke outside. The flickering glare of the fire threw dancing shadows everywhere.

The walls of the room were rough, unpainted wood and rammed earth. Massive upright timbers held rough-hewn ceiling timbers in place. Some parts of the chamber were partitioned off into separate chambers by walls of wood and furs. A stove stood in a corner and, nearby, a manual water pump and basin. There were other pumps in other parts of the house and in the stable.

"He's got indoor plumbing," Chris said with a tinge of sarcasm.

"Everyone sit," Aquila said. "I have blankets enough for everyone." Aquila sat with his guests while Prisca hovered about in the background.

"What was that thing that attacked us?" Arthur asked during a moment of silence. "Marcos called it a hound of

Samhain. Was it a werewolf or what?"

"Yes," Ambrose said. "A *wehr-wulf* and more."

"And just what is this Samhain?" Chris asked.

"You do not know of Samhain?" Aquila asked, incredulous.

"They are not of this land," Marcos said. "Their dress and speech are strange and, for some reason, Samhain has taken notice of them."

"We must not speak openly of these things," Ambrose said. "It might place our guests in the most dire of perils."

"My brother talks too much," Amos said. "Perhaps you should command him not to speak at all."

"And deprive himself of intelligent conversation?" Marcos said.

"Please," Ambrose said. "There are things I must discuss with our guests, and they are things we must not speak of to those outside of our circle. Is this clearly understood?"

"If I break my silence," Aquila said, "you may kill me."

"By my honor as a servant of Libris," Marcos said, "I will keep my silence about these things as long as it is necessary. Yet if they are who I believe they are, everyone in this world will one day hear of it."

"Then let us ask and know," Ambrose said. "Are you from the World of the Fathers?"

Amos, Marcos, and Aquila stared at them as if awaiting an answer.

"I...don't understand."

The fire glowed against Ambrose's face.

"Are you from a world with a single glowing moon, a yellow sun, and a twenty-four hour day?"

"Yes."

"And you, Lucas. Are you a warrior of the realm?"

"I was an officer in the English military," he said.

"A warrior of the realm," Marcos said. He looked around at Arthur, Lance, and Angie. "Twin brothers as alike and as opposite as reflections in a mirror, a maiden with the countenance of an angel and the mind of a sage, and...." His voice trailed off when he looked at Chris.

"You have been expected here," Ambrose said. "Your appearance here is in fulfillment of an ancient prophecy. If Samhain learns of your presence here, if he learns where you have come from, he will try to destroy you."

There was a loud pop from the fire as a log burned in half. Sparks leaped up, and everyone jumped, everyone but Ambrose.

"But you must not fear him," Ambrose said. "I will protect you from him. He has no power over me, nor over my blade."

"What, exactly, is this Samhain?" Chris asked again.

"Samhain rules here," Ambrose said. "He is a creature that neither eats nor sleeps. He entered this world ten generations ago through A'Vilian, the Island of Doors. He has held this country in the grip of his fear since the day of his coming. He shall continue to do so until the time when stars fall like rain. The appearance of strangers from the Land of the Fathers is said to herald the coming of that day. Your very appearance here spells doom for Samhain's kingdom."

Ambrose Pendragon's voice trailed off. He gazed into the fire. The others thought he might say more, but he didn't.

***

Prisca caught Angie by the hand and led her away to one of the booths in the back of the chamber. A big washtub full of water awaited her there.

"I have prepared a bath for you, my darling," the stocky woman said.

Angie touched it with her finger. It was warm! Prisca held a brush and a bar of soap. Angie was going to get a hot bath.

"This is wonderful," she said.

"Will you bathe with your clothes on?" Prisca asked.

"Uh, no," Angie said. She realized the old woman meant to bathe Angie herself. Angie had heard about customs like this one in geography class, but that didn't make it any less awkward for her. She started to protest but was afraid she would hurt Prisca's feelings. Angie undressed as quickly as she could and sank into the water. She sighed. Warm water. It felt so good after the cold rain and the soggy clothes.

"Your poor little body," Prisca said. "You're so thin. Is there no food in the place you come from?"

"It's okay," Angie said. She was embarrassed by her lack of curves, but knew Prisca had not meant to offend.

"Now," Prisca said. "We will scrub you clean."

Prisca took the soap and brush and scrubbed Angie mercilessly. She was relieved she had any skin left by the time the old lady had dried her off and given her a coarse robe to climb into.

"So skinny," she said, shaking her head. "Poor little angel." She led Angie back into the common room and took Lance by the hand.

"Now," she said. "I will bathe you."

Lance's eyes grew wide.

"You're gonna do what?"

"She will bathe you," Aquila said, "as she did our own children."

"We-we-we don't do that in our country," Lance stammered.

"Mothers don't bathe their children?" Prisca asked, horrified.

"Well, yeah, they do."

"He does not wish to dishonor his mother by allowing another to bathe him," Aquila said. "We must respect their customs. When he marries, his wife will bathe him."

"I did not mean to dishonor your mother," Prisca said. "Please forgive me."

"It's okay," Lance said.

Arthur and Chris were both hiding their faces and trying to keep from laughing out loud. Lance followed Prisca back to the tub.

"The same bath water?" the others heard him say. Arthur and Chris laughed out loud.

"It's not that funny," Angie said, offended.

"She's right," Chris said. "We have to bathe after Lance."

"Do you have a bathroom here?" Angie asked.

"Yes, child," Aquila said. "It's across from the stable. I just placed some leaves inside."

"Leaves?" Angie asked.

"Toilet paper," Chris said.

"Come," Aquila said. "I will show you."

"Maybe bathing isn't the only thing they help you with," Chris said. Angie shot him a horrified glance. Fortunately, things were not as bad as Angie had imagined. The leaves Aquila had spoken of resembled tobacco leaves. They were big, dry, and soft.

"I will be in the stable," Aquila told Angie. "You will not be in any danger here."

Prisca, it seemed, had more than enough extra clothing for everyone. She was known for weaving cloth and making blankets and garments to sell or give away to other people in the area.

Prisca took Angie, the only girl among her guests, to a booth where she was to spend the night. The large woman stretched out on a heap of blankets. Moments later she began to snore.

Aquila stayed with the men in the big, smoke-filled chamber that was the main room. The fire cracked and popped in the center of the room. Ambrose had spoken to Mr. Lucas earlier, saying that he wanted to talk with him after everyone else had settled in for the night. So Ambrose and Mr. Lucas went to the far end of the room and spoke in low tones as Arthur and the rest of the men wrapped themselves in thick furs and blankets and stretched out on a hard-packed clay floor.

It felt good, Arthur thought, to lie down. Arthur was not used to sleeping on the floor, but that would not keep him awake long. He and his friends had passed through a weird fog, seen a man vanish, and encountered a patrol of giant, silver-eyed zombies. Then they had seen a man eaten alive, grappled with a werewolf, and been rescued by a man with magical powers who claimed to be from the ancestral line of King Arthur. They were now beyond shock. They were numb, and they were tired. Sleep came quickly. They slept from exhaustion.

4./Lore of the Worlds

Arthur awoke from a dream that made no sense. He thought he was in his room at home until he saw the beams across the ceiling and realized he was lying on the floor wrapped in blankets and furs. He squeezed his eyes shut and opened them again. The beams, the blankets, and the furs were still there, and he was still lying on the floor.

Aquila's house, Arthur whispered to himself. He propped up on an elbow and looked around. Prisca was in the corner of the room putting wood into the stove. Aquila, Ambrose, Lance, and the big man called Amos were sitting around the fire. Aquila was poking at some glowing embers with a metal prod.

Arthur wondered if this might be a dream, too. He was in another world with seven-foot-tall, corpse-faced cyborgs, weird cities like something in a Coleridge poem, werewolves, and men with powers who were kin to King Arthur. It was all incredible, but after a good night's sleep, Arthur didn't feel anything; no shock, no anxiety....

Arthur wondered if he could wake up a second time and find himself in his room. He forced his eyes wider open than they already were. He pinched himself on the arm and felt the sting. Pain was real, anyway.

Arthur lay back down, but he did not sleep.

"We will travel when the sun is high," Arthur heard Ambrose say. "The powers of my enemies are weakest by day."

"Nice outfit," Lance said. "You look like you belong here."

"Thanks," Arthur heard Angie say. She sounded embarrassed. He looked around and saw Angie standing by the fire with her arms folded. She was wearing a sleeveless cotton tunic that reached to her knees and a leather vest that tied in the front. Her hair was pulled into a tight braid in the back.

Arthur realized his mouth tasted like moldy carpet and

knew it must smell even worse. He didn't want to talk to Angie until he had eaten something to kill the morning breath so he pretended to sleep and wondered if the people in this world had invented mouthwash. Finally, Prisca served breakfast.

"What is this?" Arthur asked as he tasted a hot, white beverage Prisca had ladled into his cup.

"We call it lakos," Prisca said. Ambrose's spell did not translate the word. Apparently there was no English equivalent.

"Tell me more about this Samhain," Chris said.

"Samhain," Ambrose said, "is the ruler of the city we saw. He inhabits a human form, but he is not himself human. Ten generations ago, he came through a doorway on the Island of A'Vilian and seized the body of his human host. He cannot die as we understand death."

"The werewolf ran away when it saw you coming," Lance said. "It's like it was afraid of you."

"My sword shields me from dark enchantments," Ambrose said. "Beings of darkness are repelled by its light."

"So, why can't you just destroy him?" Chris said.

"Our powers are too evenly matched," Ambrose said. "He cannot overcome me, and I cannot destroy him. Not yet."

"Not yet?"

"My sword is controlled by powers beyond this world," Ambrose explained. "I do not control them, but I believe there will come a time when the power of my blade will be greatly increased. In that day, Samhain will fall."

"And you say our being here is a sign that day is about to come?" Arthur asked.

"I believe it is possible," Ambrose said. "As I told you last night, he must not find out who you are. If he discovers you, he will not rest until he has driven you to your deaths. For reasons you do not yet understand, you are a danger to his power. He will try to slay you before you reach your strength."

"Reach what strength?" Chris said.

"Just tell him we ain't after his power," Lance said. "We just want to go home."

"I am afraid that is not possible," Ambrose said. "I'm sorry."

"You mean we're... trapped?" Arthur felt his chest tighten.

"The only one who can send you home now is Samhain," Ambrose said. "He controls the Island of A'Vilian, the passages between worlds."

"Then how did we get here?" Lance asked.

"One of Samhain's servants might have opened the door to your world accidentally," Ambrose said. "Or, perhaps, there is someone in your world with the ability to open the ancient doors. It is also possible that Samhain himself brought you here for reasons of his own. I can only guess."

"And there's no way back?" Lance asked.

"Not in this age," Ambrose said, "but I believe this age is soon to end. On the day Samhain's reign ends, the power to walk to and from places abroad shall be restored to the hands of men. You must help me bring about that day. Put aside thoughts of home and help me restore Camelot."

"But what about our parents and our friends?" Angie said. "Stacy just died. Now they'll think we're all dead too."

"Your love and concern are good," Ambrose said, "but your only way home is through me."

"Why don't we go back to the place we came in?" Chris said. "Maybe there's a way back out."

"You're saying go back to the road by the village?" Arthur asked.

"Yeah," Chris said. "Why not?"

"Because the doors Samhain and his servants open are momentary," Ambrose said. "The passage you came through is closed. You must believe me."

"Look," Chris said to Ambrose. "We appreciate you helping us out and all that, but this is a weird place, and we can't afford to trust anybody, not even you."

"Chris!" Angie gasped.

"If we return to that place and the gate is closed,"

Ambrose said, "Will you finally believe me?"

"Yeah," Chris said. "Okay."

Ambrose and Lance helped Mr. Lucas hook the horses up to his carriage. Prisca and Aquila brought out some food and extra clothing and loaded it into the carriage. Ambrose thanked them for their hospitality. Marcos kept jabbering excitedly about something that was written on some old, yellowed scrolls he had been carrying around in his saddlebags. Amos growled something at his brother. When Amos had turned his back, Marcos made a face at Amos's back.

Arthur glanced back as Ambrose and his party led his friends away from Aquila's sunken house and into a cool, golden green morning. Ambrose rode in the carriage beside Mr. Lucas and let Lance borrow his horse. Amos and Marcos rode beside them as before.

In the light of day, they could see how strange the vegetation around them was. There were trees with jointed trunks that looked like immense stalks of cane. Some of the trees were fat with slick, green bark and long tentacles for branches. Other trees looked like any other hardwood tree, but the leaves were different from any seen on Earth.

Arthur sat next to Angie just as he had the night before. He hoped she didn't think he was dogging her every step, following her everywhere. In all honesty, he would not have minded following her because he was really starting to like her. He had to be careful, though. She was, after all, only a freshman. If she knew he was starting to like her, she might run away.

"You call our planet the World of the Fathers," Arthur said, trying to start a conversation with Ambrose who was sitting in front of him. "You're saying your ancestors came from Earth?"

"The father of my fathers was of your world," Ambrose said. "He was the great-grandson of King Arthur, the great king of Camelot."

"How did your people get here?" Arthur asked.

"From what your teacher has told me," Ambrose said,

"they very probably arrived here by the same means you did. They passed through the *Valley of Winds.*"

"The fog," Lance said. "We heard wind in there."

"And bells," Chris said.

"And strange voices?" Ambrose asked.

"Yeah," Chris said. "But how'd you...?"

"It is so recorded in the logs of my ancestor, King Aurelius of New Camelot," Ambrose said, "though many have come to see those logs as myths."

"Where did your ancestor see the fog?" Arthur asked.

"At sea," Ambrose said. "There had been the threat of invasion. The king, Aurelius's father, feared for the lives of his young queen and their sons. He ordered his court magician to take them to a secret place, a place of refuge, until the threat of invasion had passed. With them were some of his bravest knights and his most trusted servants.

"As they were nearing the isle, they came upon a wall of fog. It appeared unexpectedly, and the ocean became as glass.

"Aurelia, the queen, feared that the fog might be witchery and ordered the men to drop anchor. This was done to prevent the ship from entering the fog. Nevertheless, the fog overtook them. It is recorded in the log of Aurelius that all of them heard voices and wind and strange music. When the fog cleared, they were in a land unlike any they had ever seen. They had found a land of Elven Folk, Seraf, and Merfolk. They had come to this place."

"That does sound like what happened to us," Lance said.

"Did they ever make it back?" Chris asked.

"A small group of them were shown the way back and allowed to return," Ambrose said. "They found their kingdom destroyed. They searched for survivors but found none. Finally they chose to return to this place and set up a new kingdom among the Elven."

"Were the Elven-Folk like elves?" Lance asked.

"They are a small and beautiful people," Marcos said. "Peaceful and full of wisdom, but proud and stubborn at times. You will meet some of them. And, very likely, you will meet some of the winged Seraf."

"Winged people?" Arthur asked.

"Yes," Ambrose said.

"That's unreal," Arthur said. "Elf people. Winged people. Are there any other kinds of people here?"

"There are others. Aquila and Prisca are Trogs. The Merfolk are water-dwellers, but it is unlikely that you will meet any of them. They are seldom seen by land people."

"Merfolk?" Lance said. "You mean like mermaids?"

"And mermen," Marcos said. "Men and women of the seas with fish-like tails rather than legs."

"Why don't land people see them?" Angie asked.

"Because there are so few of them," Ambrose said,

"Once the lake around the Isle of A'Vilian was filled with them," Marcos said. "Their songs floated on the night winds. They are gone now. In the time of Samhain's appearing, the Merfolk were hunted almost to extinction. The lake around A'Vilian flowed red with their blood. Those who survived went far away into distant parts of the ocean. They are only seen by sailors who travel far from land."

"They have little love for land people," Ambrose said. "My ancestors treated them shamefully. Some are said to have helped land people whose ships were wrecked. Others are blamed for sinking ships."

"Do they really have fish tails?" Arthur asked.

"They do not have scales," Ambrose said, "but their lower bodies are shaped much like those of fish. Their skin is pale."

"What do they call your people?" Arthur asked.

"Bre'ons," Ambrose said. "You would also be called Bre'ons."

"Are there any mixed races?" Angie asked.

"Bi'ons," Marcos said, jumping in. "Those are Bre'on/Elvish hybrids. The other races do not mix so easily. Air and water. Earth and sky. Many songs have been sung about those doomed relationships."

"Watch where you're going!" Amos shouted.

Their horses scraped against each other.

"Sorry, old creature," Marcos said.

"It's all right," Amos said.

"I was speaking to the horse."

The path was still muddy from the last night's rain, but the new world was a brighter, cheerier place by day. The trees on either side of the path were green with leaves and full of twittering birds.

"I don't know what season it is here," Chris said, "but it doesn't look like fall."

The horses and the carriage crossed a green pasture. Dew sparkled from every blade of grass. A flimsy wooden bridge led over a shallow, sandy stream that divided the pastures. A line of trees ran along the stream.

Ambrose directed Mr. Lucas across the second pasture, into the forest, and back onto the trail they had ridden on the night before. They had, in fact, ridden this whole route the night before. Everything certainly looked different in the light of the sun—whichever sun it was. The star overhead was swollen and reddish. They came to the place where water had been over the road. This was the same place they had gotten stuck. Now only shallow mud remained. There were sunken dents in the mud where feet and carriage wheels had been and little pools of dirty water.

"Move toward the left," Ambrose said. "The earth looks firmer there."

Marcos was intently reading through a leather-bound book when he nearly rode into a mudhole.

"Watch where you're going!" Amos cried.

"I was reading the prophecies of Sandro the Wise," Marcos said, "his words about the visitors from other lands."

"You nearly dropped your precious book into the mud," Amos said.

"Do they always fight like that?" Angie asked.

"No," Ambrose said. "They sleep sometimes."

They came to the split in the trail. They emerged from the left fork of the "Y" that they had chosen the night before. Then they turned the carriage around and went down the right fork.

"This road joins the road to the village," Ambrose said. "We will pass the place where you first came here without having to pass Thanatos." They rode in silence for a while. A breeze blew through the forest. Birds sang in the twisted branches of alien trees.

The road soon connected to another road.

"It was somewhere along this road that you first arrived here," Ambrose said. He pointed to a muddy spot in the road. There were carriage wheel prints, hoofprints, and the prints left by a big, tank-like machine. The rain had smeared the tracks, but they were still there. "Do you see your tracks among these here?"

Mr. Lucas pulled back on the reins of his horses. Amos and Marcos stopped. Lance rode his horse over to the edge of the muddy place and stopped.

"They look like our tracks," he said.

"And those big prints must have been left by the machine those armored things were driving," Angie said.

"Steel-Hearts," Amos said.

"Why do you call them that?" Arthur asked.

"Because Samhain reshapes their bodies into weapons of death," Amos said. "Their hearts are replaced with tireless metal pumps. Their eyes can see in the dark and read heat patterns. Implants augment their muscles." He sighed. "I used to be one of them."

"What changed you?" Arthur asked.

"Love," he said simply. It was not an answer the others had expected from this silver-eyed brute.

"We apparently passed through here after our encounter with your Steel-Hearts," Mr. Lucas said.

"There's only one set of tracks," Arthur said. "The place where we came into this world is on toward the village."

"What do you figure?" Lance asked.

"It's common sense," Arthur said. "We left tracks going toward the village and going away from it. Here there's only one set of tracks. These must be the tracks we left going away from it. When we find a second set of tracks, we'll know where we came in."

"Elementary, my dear Watson," Chris said. "But if we passed through here, how come I don't remember this other trail here?"

"We passed it in the dark after I extinguished the lamps," Mr. Lucas said.

"Okay," Lance said. "There's one set of tracks here, and we left it after we saw those uglies. No offense, Amos. You look a lot better than they did."

"Thank you."

"So, we must have popped into this world someplace between here and the village."

"You've got it," Arthur said.

They found a second set of tracks after they had gone about a quarter of a mile.

"That's it, all right," Lance said. "That's where we came in at. There ain't no tracks five feet from here. Now, all of a sudden, here they are."

"Just like we rode out of nowhere," Arthur said.

"We did ride out of nowhere," Chris said.

"So, this is the place," Lance said, "but there's nothing here. It's just an ordinary piece of road."

"Stop," Chris said. "We've got to get out and look around here."

"You will find nothing," Ambrose said. "The doorway is closed."

"Yeah," Angie said. "There's no fog or anything."

"We came all this way," Arthur said. "We can at least take the time to look around."

Mr. Lucas stopped his horses and shoved down his buggy's braking lever. Lucas, Arthur, Angie, and Chris walked around, up and down the path, looking for anything that looked suspicious, anything that might be a doorway. Lance, Marcos, and Amos rode around on horseback. Ambrose meandered around and talked to the others, but his heart wasn't in the search. He already knew there was nothing to be found. Finally the others were forced to agree.

"I hate to admit it," Arthur said, "but Lance was right.

This is just an ordinary piece of road."

"Maybe the doorway's only open at night," Chris said.

"Perhaps," Mr. Lucas said. "But look. We passed through the fog and came out here. Then we went to the village and came back through this same way, back through this very spot. If the doorway had been here even ten minutes after we came through, we'd have gone back through it last night."

"That's true," Arthur said. "He's right."

"It may be open only at certain hours," Chris said. "Let's come back tonight."

"How long will it be before you believe me when I tell you that you cannot return home the way you came?" Ambrose said. "Your only path home lies in helping me restore Camelot."

"Or with Samhain," Chris said.

The others turned to him.

"You said he had the power to open those doors," Chris said. "Didn't you?"

"He will not help you," Ambrose said. "He is no one's friend. The favors he offers carry too high a price."

"Just let us come back here tonight," Arthur said. "If we don't find a way home, we'll go wherever you say."

"Very well," Ambrose said. "It will be as you say. My friend Malua lives near here. We will spend the day with him and return here tonight so you will know that what I tell you is true."

"I'm staying here," Chris said.

"I can remain with him," Marcos said. He withdrew a metal tube from his pocket. "If we see anything, I will blow twice on this whistle and signal the rest of you."

"Very well," Ambrose said. "Thank you, Marcos."

"It is no burden," Marcos said. "It will give me time to read. There are things I must study."

"Good, then," Ambrose said. "The rest of us will visit Malua for a while. It has been too long since I have seen him."

Mr. Lucas climbed back into his carriage. Ambrose, Arthur, and Angie climbed in behind him. They rode for a short distance. Less than a hundred meters up the road was a narrow side path that led off into the forest. There was barely enough room for Mr. Lucas to drive his carriage through, and tree limbs raked the canopy in some places. In other places the path was lined with briars. There were flowers on great heaps of vines. They put off a sweet, wild scent.

The path cleared. The ground ahead was swatched by decades of rotting leaves and stretches of green, velvety moss. Trees grew high overhead and made a nice shade. In the midst of them lay a tumbledown shack made of gray, weathered wood. A wide, brown pond reflected the sky behind it.

"Perhaps I should warn you," Ambrose said. "Malua is of a different tribe than we are. You possibly have never seen anyone like him. In this world, he is the only one of his kind left."

A human figure in faded clothes stepped out of the woods with a fishing pole. He looked warily at the approaching carriage.

"Malua," Ambrose called to him. "Good morning."

"Pendragon!" Malua said, his dark brown face breaking into a wide smile.

After what Ambrose had said, Arthur had expected Malua to have green skin, two heads, or horns. In reality, though, he looked surprisingly normal—from a distance, at least. He had a wide smile, a deep voice, and dark brown skin. His hair was white and wavy, like the hair of an Australian aborigine. His eyes were his most exotic feature. They were catlike and golden in color. His canine teeth were also longer than those of ordinary Bre'ons from earth.

"Malua," Ambrose said. "I want to introduce you to some new friends. Then perhaps you would like to share some of the lunch that Prisca prepared for us."

"Prisca!" Malua said. "Good cook, that one."

Once Ambrose had introduced Malua to his new friends, the whole group of them, along with Ambrose and Amos, sat down with the old man in the shade and shared the lunch Prisca and Aquila had packed for them. They spent most of the afternoon fishing, relaxing, and wandering around the pond.

***

The sun was setting. It turned the sky and the pond orange in its final blaze of light. A fire crackled underneath the trees near the cabin. Ambrose, Mr. Lucas, Amos, Malua, and the young people from Earth were finishing up a supper of well-spiced fish stew. It sent good smells through the forest.

"Maybe we'd better go back to the road and take some food to Chris and Marcos," Arthur said.

Ambrose joined Mr. Lucas, Arthur, Angie, and Lance as they climbed into Mr. Lucas's carriage. Amos stayed with Malua. Mr. Lucas lit up the oil lamps and drove his buggy back through the narrow path that had led them to the weatherbeaten cabin in the woods. The path was turning grayer and grayer by the minute as the sun dropped over the edge of the horizon.

Arthur looked down at his watch.

"What time is it?" Angie asked. She was sitting next to him again.

"Six-thirty," he said. "On Earth. I've been adding up the time. Mr. Lucas stopped by my house at about eight o'clock last night. It was about 8:30 when we drove into the weird fog. That would mean it's been around twenty-two hours since we came here. I was wondering how long the days are here. It's hard to believe we're really on another planet, but checking the day length would pretty well prove it, I guess."

"Unless we traveled through time," Angie said. "It may be that days weren't always twenty-four hours."

"Maybe," Arthur said. "Anyway, the sun set last night at about 6:15. By waiting for the next sunset, I should be able to get some idea how long the days are here."

The carriage pulled onto the main road, the road that led to the village. Mr. Lucas drove to the place where Chris and Marcos waited. Chris was pacing. Marcos was contentedly poring over passages in a book, his face lit by a lantern filled with glowing rocks.

"We brought dinner," Angie said.

"I'm not hungry," Chris said.

"I am always hungry," Marcos said.

"That's certainly true," Amos said. "He has a bottomless cave for a stomach."

"Have you seen anything?" Arthur asked.

"No," Chris said. "But we can't give up yet. We've got to wait."

They waited. No one saw any fog, heard any strange sounds, or smelled any strange scents. This was nothing more than an ordinary stretch of dirt road leading through the woods. Ambrose waited patiently with Mr. Lucas, Arthur, Chris, Angie, Lance, and Marcos as an hour passed.

"That's about how the sky looked when we first came here," Arthur said.

"I don't think anything's going to happen," Angie said. "Ambrose was right. Let's go back."

"No," Chris said angrily. "It's just now getting to be the right time."

They waited, watched, and wandered around. The forest filled with darkness and nighttime noises. Sometimes bushes rattled and animal eyes reflected the orange glare of buggy lamps.

"It looks like Ambrose was right all along," Mr. Lucas said.

"No," Chris said. "We can't give up."

"We could wait another hour," Arthur suggested.

"We may have to wait a day," Lance said. "Or a month, or a year. The door may only open when the planets are lined up just right, or it may not ever open up again."

"He's right," Arthur admitted.

"We can't stay here forever, Chris," Mr. Lucas said.

"Look," Chris said, "I want to go home."

"Of course," Mr. Lucas said. "All of us do."

"Then how come you're all treating me like I'm crazy or something, like there's something wrong with me because I don't believe everything Ambrose says?"

"We don't think you're crazy," Angie said.

"You don't really care if we make it back or not. Fine! Go back to camp. I'm staying here."

"I guess you told us so," Lance said to Ambrose.

"I take no joy in being right," Ambrose said, "but I do not believe your arrival here was an accident."

"I hope you're right," Arthur said. "So, you still think we might make it home if this Samhain is defeated?"

"Yes," Ambrose said. "I think so."

"We're not exactly warriors," Arthur told him.

"Perhaps you are," Ambrose said. "You simply don't know it yet."

5. /Into the Wilderness

The sun was almost down. Slats of golden light filtered through tall pine trees. A gentle wind whispered through the needled leaves overhead.

Arthur was riding a mini-bike. Angie and Stacy were riding double on a four-wheeler. Lance and Chris were riding dirt bikes. They hadn't had fun like this since they were children, and they had almost forgotten what it was like.

It felt so good, Arthur thought, for them all to be together again. It seemed so sweet and so magical that it almost seemed sad, yet he was not entirely sure why.

The forest was dark and the sky was aglow with the last light of dusk. Lights on roaring four-wheelers and bikes cut glowing shafts through the gathering shadows. Big tires swished through the tall, pale yellow hay grass.

Stacy and Angie shot past Arthur. Stacy turned around and smiled saucily at him. Arthur grinned and hit the throttle. His bike shot ahead. Arthur followed Stacy and Angie over a gentle hill. The dark woods were full of friends riding machines. They rode through the trees laughing. They came out of the forest on a hill overlooking a lake full of floating yellow flowers. The red sky and a big moon reflected amid the flowers on a glasslike surface. The lake was about twenty feet below them—a sheer drop— and surrounded by tall cliffs.

The riders drove their vehicles down a narrow strip of bare dirt that led through the trees. Autumn leaves spun through the air as they passed. They rode into a clearing and looked around. They peered through the gray light of dusk at the wonders that surrounded them: a fun house with a clown's face painted on the front, a metal spider with cars that dangled from the legs, a sheet metal replica of a Victorian-style haunted house, a log flume, a mirror maze. And there were food stands: hot dogs, corn dogs, and snow cones. The place was dark. It looked shut down.

Ambrose Pendragon was there, and Arthur did not exactly remember when he had shown up. The bikes and four-wheelers had also vanished, but the amusement park remained. A dirt path ran through all of the rides. There were other people with them now. How incredible it was to find an amusement park right in the middle of Arthur's dad's woods. It was so close to home! Arthur thought that long ago—in some forgotten day of childhood—he and his friends had been to the park before. If so, why had they forgotten it? Why had they waited so long to return?

They climbed into roller coaster cars, cars that ran along a track. Ambrose Pendragon stood by, helping people into the cars.

Arthur and Stacy—closer friends than ever before—climbed into one of the cars and Ambrose pulled down the safety bar. The bar was worn, and it made your hands smell funny.

"Enjoy yourselves," Ambrose said.

The roller coaster car sprang into motion and ratcheted up a steep track into a clear, moonlit sky. The car wound around the tops of pine trees, shot down to the ground, and then back up again. Stacy and Arthur passed a village of mechanical primitives that shot make-believe arrows at them. They flew by night over a big pumpkin patch full of scarecrows dressed in strange and colorful masks and Halloween costumes.

Stacy and Arthur spoke as close friends as they rode through the sky. Everything was so warm and magical.

"But how can you be here?" Arthur finally asked. "Aren't you dead?"

Arthur remembered that night at the hospital, the memorial service in the high school gym.

Stacy looked hurt, and everything dissolved.

Stacy? Arthur tried to speak, but his vocal cords were paralyzed.

Arthur woke up and found himself outside looking up at the tops of trees. Exotic birds called in the distance. He was wrapped in a blanket and lying on a seat cushion from Mr. Lucas's carriage. The air was still and gray, pre-dawn light hung over the world—whatever world it was—like the early-morning fog that floated over the still surface of a nearby pond. Marcos lay asleep on a pile of leaves, his blanket wrapped firmly around him. The leaves and grass around him were wet with dew.

Arthur and Marcos had agreed to camp near the site of the doorway and help Chris keep watch throughout the night. At the first sign of supernatural activity, they would call the others. There had been no swirling vortexes, no fog, and no haunting voices.

Even under a blanket, Arthur still felt chilled by the dampness. He pulled the coarse cloth closer to his body and thought about his dream of Stacy and the others. As he drifted off to sleep, he found himself longing to return to the world he had seen in the dream. The second time Arthur woke up, the sun was glowing through the trees on the far side of the pond. It was a reddish-orange orb, not yet high in the sky.

The sun still rises in the east anyway, Arthur thought to himself. Then he wondered if he would have been able to tell anyway. If Ambrose's planet orbited its sun backwards from Earth, would west seem like east? It was too early to think about such things. The question gave Arthur a headache. He looked at his watch. 3:01 A.M. The sun had risen in less than nine hours from the time it had set.

Arthur sat up and looked around. Marcos was sitting by the fire reading from one of his books and cooking something.

"Good morning to you," he said. He was holding a pot by the handle with his left hand.

"Where's Chris?" Arthur asked as he drew near the fire.

"Still sitting by the road, I expect," Marcos said.

"I'd better go check on him," Arthur said.

"Wait," Marcos said. "Try some of this." He took out a clay mug and filled with the steaming liquid from the pot in front of him.

"Thanks," Arthur said. He wrapped his fingers around the fired clay mug—it was warm—and took it from Marcos.

"Taste it," Marcos said. "I used to be quite the cook, but I don't get much practice anymore."

Arthur wasn't at all sure he wanted to taste his new friend's concoction. Then he took a sip. The drink was hot, thick, and sweet with a vanilla/almost-almond flavor. It was like what Prisca had served for breakfast, only sweeter. Arthur swallowed quickly.

"It's good, Marcos."

Marcos nodded. He stuffed his book into one of the saddlebags.

"I'm going to check on Chris," Arthur said. He started toward the path, the mug still in his hand.

"Wait," Marcos said. "I'll go with you."

They walked on the mossy carpet that ran beneath the trees and came to the path that would lead them to the main road.

They walked unhurriedly, sipping Marcos' brew from warm cups. The air was damp and cool and clean. The sun was still hiding out in the forest, and the world still slept. Spiderwebs stretched from the trunks of trees. They were ghostly silver, covered with spangles of morning dewfall.

Arthur was still in his dream. This was like the places all the neighborhood kids would go to have picnics, ride bikes and four-wheelers, build tree-forts....

The first day of summer vacation. That's what it felt like. Summer vacation coming alive: a feeling long untasted yet never really forgotten. And it all made him think of Stacy. In the two months since her disappearance, she had become so enshrined and idealized that she hardly seemed like the flesh and blood girl they had known. Now her memory was back with jolting, real-life clarity. Arthur almost always dreamed in color—Technicolor, he told his friends—but last night's dream.... Arthur remembered the golden light through green pine needles, the red sky reflected in a lake of yellow flowers, all of it. It was clearer than clear, realer than real.

Arthur saw Chris standing in the main road and started toward him. Marcos followed. Arthur knew Chris must have seen them coming, but he didn't give any sign of having seen.

"Time for breakfast," Arthur said.

Chris didn't answer at first. Arthur was about to say something else when Chris finally answered. "I'm not going back."

"Back where?"

Chris ignored the question.

"Did you know my parents split up while I was gone to summer camp?" Chris said. "No hint that they were going to do it. They were together when I left. When I came back, my family was finished. It was all over with, and my stuff had been thrown into an apartment. My whole life changed forever, and nobody bothered to tell me anything."

"But what does that have to do with...?"

"Who knows how much time has passed on earth while we've been here? Our friends and families may be dead and buried by now."

They heard a mechanical growling coming up the road.

"Steel-Hearts!" Marcos said. "Get off the road!"

Chris didn't move.

"COME ON!" Arthur yelled.

Chris still didn't move. Arthur grabbed him by the arm and jerked him off his feet.

"You can go to...!"

"Listen to me," Arthur said. "If those things capture you, you'll *never* make it home."

Chris finally lost his nerve when he saw the first troop carrier coming around the bend. He ran with Arthur and Marcos through the trees. Marcos motioned Arthur and Chris behind a clump of bushes. They hid and watched as four burly metal tanks passed them. Each was covered with metal-clad bionic men. Arthur noted the boxlike shape of the tanks and the way the armored stormtroopers filled the seats and held onto the sides. The bionic giants didn't look quite as frightening in the light of morning as they had the night before, but Arthur was not about to stand up and wave at them. The carriers roared their way along the road and finally vanished from sight. Their roar died away slowly.

Arthur, Marcos, and Chris ran through the trees, dodging briars and low-hanging limbs. They pushed through to the path that led to Malua's cabin. Arthur noticed he and Marcos still had their empty mugs. Ambrose, Mr. Lucas, Amos, and Lance were coming down the path.

"We heard the tanks and thought those things might have gotten y'all," Lance drawled.

"No," Arthur said, "but we got a good look at them. There were four of those vehicles."

"Four," Ambrose said thoughtfully. "This is grave news. The Steel-Hearts seldom venture out after sunrise, especially in such numbers."

"You think they're looking for us?" Lance asked.

"I don't know," Ambrose said, "but we should be careful of them."

When they arrived back at Malua's cabin, Malua and Angie were sitting beside a fire eating breakfast. Angie's hair was a tangled mass of blonde curls.

"Angie," Chris said. "I love your new hairstyle."

"I know," she said. "It looks terrible."

"Do you guys have shampoo here?" Arthur asked.

"Do we have what?" Amos asked.

"It's a kind of soap," Arthur said. "You use it to wash your hair."

"We have oil," Amos said.

"Not exactly what I had in mind."

Malua made a kind of hard, chewy bread for breakfast. The group talked and laughed as they ate. Chris still looked gloomy, but at least he was talking. Arthur hoped his dark mood was beginning to lift. He had not seemed like himself for a while.

After everyone had finished eating, Ambrose's men and Mr. Lucas harnessed and saddled the horses while the others filled the saddlebags. The group said their good-byes to Malua as they climbed back into the carriage. This time Angie sat in the front beside Mr. Lucas. As the carriage began to roll, Arthur looked back at Malua. The old black man stood waving in the mossy shade beneath his trees. He was still waving to them when the path turned, and they lost sight of him.

Mr. Lucas's carriage bounced out onto the main road. Heavy tracks left by the Steel-Hearts' tanks imprinted the dirt.

Chris—sitting by Lance on the carriage's rear seat— cast a sad glance over his shoulder at the place where the "doorway" had been. No one said anything.

The buggy rattled over flat rocks and washed-out holes that the rain had left. Trees full of moss watched silently as the carriage passed.

The group passed through the graveyard they had seen two nights before. The place looked different in the friendly light of a sunny day.

"Wait." Ambrose lifted his hand. Mr. Lucas stopped the carriage. Amos and Marcos reined their horses.

"The Steel-Hearts passed through here," Ambrose pointed to the heavy tracks in the grass. "They may have ridden to the ore mines in the hills, but they might still be in the village. Wait here until I return for you."

Ambrose rode alone through the gate in the broken fence and disappeared over the hill. He returned a few minutes later.

"We need to go to the market," Ambrose said, "We have only enough food for a day or two, and it may be a while before we pass this way again."

"What about the carriage?" Angie asked.

"Leave your carriage here," Ambrose said. "It will attract too much attention. We'll come back for it."

"Shouldn't one of us stay here with it?" Arthur asked.

"I will watch over it," Amos said. "These villagers have little love for Steel-Hearts—even transformed Steel-Hearts."

"Very well," Ambrose said. "Is there anything we can bring you from the village?"

"Nothing," Amos said. "Just be careful."

They left Amos with the carriage and followed Ambrose through a gate, over the hill, and into the village of crude huts Mr. Lucas and his students had seen two nights before. Ambrose led the group. He was standing tall and looking very much like a son of King Arthur.

The people looked up. Men dropped their baskets and ran from the orchards. The children stopped playing in the dirt streets and ran toward the newcomers. The women came to the doors of the huts where they worked and ran after their children and men.

Ambrose had come almost to the village's first building when the crowd reached him. People were packed in around him, jabbering excitedly about "the Pendragon." The men were darkened by sun and hardened by work. They were covered with dirt and sweat from the orchards and fields. The women were handsome and strong and most of them were wrapped in shawls. The children were healthy and full of life and energy.

Most of the people, judging from Ambrose's descriptions of the races, were *Bre'ons*—great-great grandchildren of the Britons who had been stranded there along with King Aurelius, Ambrose's royal ancestor. Some, however, had pale hair, catlike green eyes, or a general look of unearthliness.

Probably Elvish, Arthur thought. *Or Bi'ons.* He made a mental note to ask Ambrose about it later.

The people were talking at once, smiling, and laughing. Ambrose took a little, pale blonde girl onto his shoulders and carried her as they walked to the center of town.

"Show us a miracle, Son of Arthur," one of the men cried.

"Miracles?" Ambrose said. "Your children are healthy, and you have a rich harvest. What more do you ask?"

"Free us from that daemon," one of the men said.

"Angar!" a woman cried. "You should not say such things."

"Why not?" the man said. "We're in the presence of the great Pendragon. What could possibly happen to us?"

"The day of your freedom is almost at hand," Ambrose said. "How I know this, I cannot say, but I know it. You must be patient for a little while longer."

"It's always later with this one," one of the men said.

"Always just around the twist. Pah! I have no use for dreams."

There was grumbling and some shouting. The crowd thinned out as men stomped back to their orchards, women went back to their houses, and children went back to their play. A blond, Elvish-looking man took his daughter from the saddle before Ambrose and walked away.

A young couple, an old couple and their three grandsons, and a young woman remained.

"What do you ask of me?" Ambrose asked them.

"Only that you remember us on the day the New Camelot is established," the older woman said.

"What is your name?" Ambrose asked.

"Aurelia," the woman said.

"It is a good name," Ambrose said.

"Where are you going?" the younger man asked.

"Into the forest," Ambrose said.

"That is wise," the older man said. "The Steel-Hearts have been restless and cruel of late—more so than usual. They dragged two of our young men away to work in the mines this morning."

"That is unfortunate," Ambrose said.

"At least it was not the island," one of the men said.

"If you have the power to destroy them," the younger woman said, "why do you not use it?"

"I do not use the power," Ambrose said. He placed his hand on the hilt of his sword. "It uses me. We are in the grip of forces that we cannot see. Their purposes would seem strange to us, yet I believe the forces of light are greater than the forces of darkness. The will of our Creator-Lord will prevail."

"But what good is that knowledge when we do not know what the will of the Creator is?" the young woman asked.

"Peace, Ginna," the older man said. "There is some comfort in believing in that Ultimate Good, though not always as much as we would like. We must be patient, as he says."

The old couple sent their grandsons away. One came back with bottles of drink. Another had a bag of dried meat and some homemade soap.

"I'm glad to see that soap," Arthur said.

"Hope they've got some razors in with that stuff," Lance said. "We're starting to look pretty nasty."

The youngest came back with a pile of quilts. Ginna and Ioan, the young couple, left momentarily and came back with lanterns, clothing, and some other odds and ends. Ambrose thanked them all graciously. Ginna had tears on her cheeks as she gave them an embroidered blanket.

"This was a gift from your mother," Ambrose said. "She is dead. You do not have to give this."

"It is all I have to give," she said. "If you honor me at all, you will take it."

"Very well," he said. He bent down in the saddle and kissed her forehead. " We will treasure your gift."

"I thank you all," he said to the eight villagers. "You have been my friends and I will not forget you. May the peace of our Creator-Lord abide with you."

They returned to the carriage. Amos was still waiting there. Arthur and the others packed away the supplies the villagers had given them and climbed back into their seats. They rode until the path was divided into two paths going different directions. The tracks of the Steel-Hearts' troop carriers led down the left path, a wide and desolate highway. Ambrose said the path led to the Steel-Hearts' ore mines and factories in the black hills. He led the group down the right path, a narrower, greener trail.

The first part of the path was well traveled. Grass had been worn away from hard-packed dirt, and the brush had been cut away from the path.

After about forty-five minutes' riding, the trail led onto a long, wooden suspension bridge. The bridge was supported, above and below, by heavy timbers. Ambrose led out onto the bridge, his horse's hooves thumping against the heavy wood. Mr. Lucas followed with his carriage. The uneven timbers made the ride bumpy. Through cords of rope and heavy timbers, Arthur, Angie,

Lance, and the others could see the river below.

"In your tongue, it would be called the Emerald River," Ambrose said. The river was aptly named. The water had a greenish tint. It splashed over weathered gray stones and into deep, gray-green pools full of watery secrets.

Arthur was surprised to find himself tingling with expectation, with a sense of impending adventure. Every sense in him was alive and drinking in the things around him; drinking in the sunlight, the water, the green of the trees and the cool of the air. He was in a world where beings of myth and legend walked side by side with ordinary men and women. Anything could happen in this place. *Anything.*

The river was out of sight soon, but the sound of running water could be heard through the trees beside the road and, every now and again, the snaking riverbed was visible through the trees. The path, obviously, had been cut parallel to it.

The magic of the day held for Arthur as Ambrose drove the company into deeper and deeper places. The paths they took became narrower and steeper. They led through thickets of trees and abandoned buildings. They passed an empty village of bleached stone where an *Elvish* tribe had once lived. Ambrose guided Mr. Lucas and his friends on horseback to a road covered with weathered bricks. The bricks were cracked in some places, and parts of the old road were overgrown with vines or buried in rotting leaves or straw.

"This was once the main road of a great *Elvish* nation," Ambrose said. "Now it is all but forgotten and great parts of it have been destroyed by the *Elvish* to keep the Steel-Hearts from using it. The part we will use is intact, though. This road will take us where we are going."

The road led past ruined villages, ruined dwellings, and ruined statues.

Time and again, the same question was asked: "What happened to this village?"

Time and again, Ambrose gave the same answer: "The Steel-Hearts destroyed it."

The trees grew taller and taller. They almost shut out the sun in some places. Through gaps in the trees, Arthur and the others could see a flat-topped mesa that towered above everything else.

"That is where we are going." Ambrose pointed to the hilltop. "We should reach it before nightfall."

Once, when they had stopped for lunch, a dark shadow brushed across the ground.

"Look!" Angie said.

Arthur looked. A young man in a loincloth flew overhead. He had long, bird-like wings and down-like hair covering most of his body. He soared out of sight before anyone could get a good look at him.

"One of the *Seraf*," Ambrose said in explanation.

"Should we be worried?" Lance asked. "He could be scouting for Samhain."

"He is of no danger to us," Ambrose said.

"He didn't have any arms," Lance said. "How would you tie your shoes?"

"They have a single thumb on the top of each wing," Amos said. "And they have long, graceful feet."

"Maybe so," Lance said. "Seems like it would be hard to go to the bathroom. I mean you'd get it all over you."

"Lance," Angie said.

"Some people can ruin anything," Chris said.

They watched the sky in the hope of seeing another flying man, but they saw no more of the elusive *Seraf* that day.

6./The Fall of the Old Kingdom

Nightfall found Arthur and his group sitting with Ambrose and his entourage around a snapping, popping campfire. They were on a hilltop covered with empty stone buildings that had, long ago, been carved by Elvish tools. Some of the buildings were falling apart, but most were still strong. Their empty windows spied on their visitors like hollow eyes. A few yards from where the visitors had decided to make camp, the ground tumbled away to a steep slope of grass, scrub brush, and bare slabs of stone. At the bottom of this slope was the Emerald River. Gentle winds made slight ripples in the surface of the gray-green waters. Beyond the river was a forest of trees that went all the way to the glowing red horizon. The sky overhead was grayish purple and fading to black. A few stars had already appeared.

Arthur looked at his watch. 1:45 P.M., it said. The day before, the sun had set at 6:30 P.M. Therefore, the day on this world lasted only about nineteen hours. Yes, there was no getting around it. Wherever this place was, it was certainly not Earth.

Amos, Marcos, and Ambrose prepared some sandwiches of dried meat, herbs, and rough-cut bread. They poured out cups of a dark liquid that tasted like slightly sour grape juice. Some kind of table wine, maybe. The food was passed around. Ambrose lifted up a prayer to the Creator-Lord, and dinner was served. As they were eating, a burst of light lit up the sky along the horizon.

Everyone turned and looked in the direction of the glare. It had died down but still reflected against the sky.

"What was that?" Lance asked. "It looked like an oil fire."

"It is A'Vilian, the island in the lake near Thanatos," Ambrose said. "It burns every night and spouts up great flames."

"When we passed near it two nights ago," Mr. Lucas

said, "I thought I smelled burning human flesh." The others turned and looked at him. "I smelled it during my time in the military."

Ambrose nodded at what the teacher had said. "Flesh burns there," he acknowledged. "It has burned there every night since Samhain entered this world."

"Where did he come from?" Angie asked.

"From the island, child," Ambrose said. "At the time Samhain set foot on the island, the land was green and covered with grass and trees. But when he came, destruction followed him as a gale of fire." Ambrose chewed on his sandwich.

"How did he come to the island?" Arthur asked.

"As I once told you," Ambrose said. "The island was once known as A'Vilian, the Island of Doors. In your world, it was called Avalon."

Mr. Lucas looked up suddenly.

"Avalon? Of course."

"Wise men known as Worldsmen dwelled on the island and traveled freely through doors, windows, and tunnels that led to other worlds. They learned great secrets of science and medicine that revolutionized life here. They taught and recorded these secrets for the people of this place and in other worlds as well. Many of the Worldsmen visited more primitive worlds to act as teachers and healers. Merlinus Ambrosius, my namesake, was one of them."

"Merlin the magician?" Arthur asked.

"Yes," Ambrose nodded. "A visitor from another world who could vanish through time and space at will."

"According to the legends," Arthur said, "He perceived time backwards so he knew everything that was about to happen. I see where that came from now."

"Yes," Ambrose said. "His knowledge was quite remarkable to the men of your world. He and others like him blended with the men of those earlier eras and assisted those whose hearts seemed the most pure. It was one of the Worldsmen who brought my young ancestor and his mother here to protect them against the invasion that finally destroyed Camelot. He opened the doorway between worlds and allowed them to pass through the Valley of Winds."

"So they came here on purpose?" Lance asked.

"They did not know where they were going," Ambrose said. "Only that the king had sent them to a place of refuge, a place that the court magician would lead them to. He brought them here.

"They lived in peace for four generations, but there was one world the men were warned against ever entering. The world was closed to them and guarded by enchantments. Any who were caught trying to enter that world were, by the laws of the Worldsmen, put to death. One foolish man, no one will ever know who, succeeded in opening the door to that forbidden realm. And when he opened the door—a horrific, fire-filled abyss—Samhain stepped through. He had been chained to a rock in a place not unlike the G'hinna—the hell—of my fathers' religion. He emerged from the abyss and possessed the shell of the man who had summoned him. There were flames, monsters, and unspeakable horrors snapping at his heels.

"One of the Worldsmen plunged into the lake, once beautiful and blue, that surrounded the isle, and placed an enchantment upon it so that none of the fire or the things of the isle could cross the waters. Samhain, because he inhabited a human shell, was not bound by those enchantments.

"The daemon's next step was to claim this world as his realm, his kingdom to rule. No human has yet been able to oppose him. Those who try are consigned to the island. Within the outer walls, he has built a factory complex, the forge where his slaves shape molten metal into weapons of war. Those who are disobedient are cast over the inner walls into the abyss from which Samhain emerged."

"Why hasn't anybody sent him back through?" Arthur asked.

"Many have tried," Ambrose said, "but he has been too strong for them."

"Maybe so," Lance said, "but you'd still think he would

have closed the doorway if there was any chance of somebody sending him back through. Why doesn't he?"

"No one knows for sure," Ambrose replied. "Some say Samhain wants to keep the island of fires and daemons as a threat to his enemies. Indeed, the people of this world would rather die than set foot on that abominable isle. They have seen thousands of their kinsmen and neighbors driven across the lake into the gates of the island, and not a single soul has returned from that tortured place. Some say they can recognize the tortured screams of their loved ones amid the inhuman cries and howls of the daemons."

The fire crackled.

"There are others who say Samhain does not seal the doorway to the daemon-world because he lacks the power and the knowledge."

"I thought you said he could open doors between worlds," Arthur said.

"His sorcerers have a limited ability to manipulate the portals," Ambrose said. "Their experiments yield unpredictable and often disastrous results. Only the Worldsmen of A'Vilian had mastered the art of opening and closing the doorways to other places and times, but most of their knowledge was lost to the flames on the night when the doorway to the daemon-world was opened.

"There were, however, a few Worldsmen who were not on the island on the night of its fall. These Worldsmen formed secret orders and passed their secrets from father to son, from teacher to disciple. Samhain has, over the years, caught and tortured many of the Worldsmen but none of them betrayed any secrets."

"How many Worldsmen are there now?" Mr. Lucas asked.

"Only one," Ambrose said sadly. "Me. I am the last."

"Can't you pass your knowledge along to others?" Arthur said.

"I was only an apprentice when my teacher was slain," Ambrose said. "Much of our knowledge has been lost, but there are those who assist us."

"Those of my order are dedicated to preserving the

knowledge of the Worldsmen," Marcos said. "We are the keepers of the libraries."

"You were talking about the reasons Samhain didn't close the door to his own world," Arthur said.

"Yes," Ambrose said. "There is one other reason given for Samhain's not closing the door to the daemon-world once and for all. You see, Samhain neither eats nor sleeps, yet he has lived much longer than any man. There are those who say he draws his strength from his former realm. Somehow, they say, a stream of enchantment like an umbilical cord connects Samhain to the world beyond that door. According to this reasoning, then, if Samhain were to close the door to the daemon-world, he would literally be severing his own—as you would say it—lifeline."

"Thus there are three reasons given for Samhain allowing the doorway to his home world to remain. Any or all of these reasons might be true."

Another gust of fire erupted from the island. It hung over the trees like a great, clawed hand.

Everyone had finished eating.

7. /Dreams Dark and Light

Chris found himself alone in his room. He didn't remember how he had gotten back home, but felt a strong sense of relief that he had. His room was dark and the window was open. A night breeze stirred the curtains.

"Chris," someone said. "Hey, Chris." It was a girl's voice.

Chris went to the window and looked out. He was on the second floor. Standing on the dew-slick lawn beneath his window was a girl. She was partly hidden by the shadows of the oak trees that surrounded the house, but Chris knew who she was—oh, he knew. She was still wearing her cheerleader uniform, the same uniform she had been wearing the night she died. He could see the bloodstains.

"Stacy," Chris gasped. "What are you doing here?"

"I wanted to talk to you," she said.

"But you can't be here," he groaned. "You're dead."

"I have to talk to you," she said. She was more insistent this time.

"Okay," Chris said. His heart was pounding. "Okay. I'm coming." Something felt wrong about this—wrong and evil. Seeing Stacy again should have brought a feeling of joy and love, but it didn't. His mouth dry, Chris made his way down the stairs, down the hall, and to the door. His hands trembled as the turned the bolt, then the knob. He opened the door.

Stacy was there, her back to the light and her face in the shadows. Standing behind her was the figure of a man. He was nearly seven feet tall with burning red eyes. Stacy took a step forward. The pallid light from inside Chris's house fell across the pale, water-shriveled face of a corpse. There was a knife in her hand.

Chris didn't remember sitting up, but apparently he had. He was sitting up and gasping. A crackling fire burned in a circular pit in the center of a dark room. The ceiling overhead was dome-shaped, and the others were lying around him. Chris was certain he had screamed his throat raw, but the others were still fast asleep on their pallets. They hadn't heard. The screams had vanished down the black tunnels of the nightmare with nary an echo. Chris wished the fear had gone with it. He moved closer to the fire, pulled his knees up to his chest, and trembled. A wolf-like howl pierced the darkness.

***

Arthur smiled in his sleep.

It was night, but glowing stones lit up the forest with their gentle blue haloes. Mounted on the necklaces, belts, and tiaras of a thousand graceful dancers, the translucent crystals glided among the trees like disembodied spirits. The dancers were small, slender, and fair-haired. They sang in another language, but the words were pure and hauntingly sweet. The people were Elvish. They had to be. Their tilted blue eyes reflected the crystalline glow of the stones.

A gentle wind rippled tall, soft grass on the floor of the forest. It sighed in the trees that were over a hundred feet tall. A clear, silvery stream snaked amid the trunks of the trees. The people danced along its banks and sang, their crystalline adornments reflecting like fireflies in the face of the water. All of them knew the words as though the song had somehow been born into them.

Arthur was there in the forest with the people. He walked barefoot on the tall, damp, cool grass. The forest was dark yet bright with the glowing stones. Angie, Lance, and Mr. Lucas were in the forest with him—and Ambrose Pendragon was there. The vagabond king towered over the Elvish people like a spire. Then he bent down, and they placed some kind of jeweled crown on his head. He was their king; a Bre'on king of the Elvish. It did not make sense. Yet it did.

Arthur and his friends flowed along the stream with the Elvish dancers. A little Elvish girl took him by the hand and led him. Her hand was small and fragile. Ambrose, standing on the stream's bank, smiled mysteriously at Arthur, at his young friend.

Arthur walked over to the edge of the stream. He and his friends and some of the Elvish people stood and gazed into the waters. The surface was like dark silver. A shimmering portrait of Arthur and those around him gazed up from the mirror-like pool.

Ambrose's face tensed in pain for a moment. He leaned forward and a single teardrop fell to the surface of the water. Ripples clouded the reflection below, distorted it.

Something moved in the water. Was it a reflection, or was someone down there?

The Pendragon plunged his hand into the water, plunged it in nearly to the shoulder. Then he pulled, drew his hand out—his hand and someone else's. He kept pulling until he brought out a bare arm, a head, and finally a whole body. A teenage girl in a red-and-blue cheerleader uniform—strangely dry—stood knee-deep in the stream holding Ambrose by the hand. Arthur recognized the girl instantly.

"*Stacy*," he whispered. Then he woke up.

8. /Ghost Town

"Do we have time to look around this village?" Lance asked at breakfast.

"Yes," Ambrose said. "We will have all the time you need. We will be staying here for a while."

After breakfast was over, Arthur, Lance, Chris, and Angie went to explore the buildings. Marcos and Amos went with them while Mr. Lucas and Ambrose stayed back at the fire. They said they had things to discuss.

The teens walked down a narrow street between rows of deserted buildings. The buildings had smoothly flowing lines and arched windows and doorways. Many buildings had been sheathed in a kind of white plaster that had made them look like ivory. Now the plaster was cracking away like a dried husk. It crunched beneath the feet of the newcomers. Where plaster had fallen away, ugly patches of gray brick showed through. Though they had been beautiful once, many of the buildings looked like decayed teeth. In some places they had been scorched by fire. In other places, they were pocked with black craters. Samhain's people obviously knew enough about science to make bombs—unless they had assaulted the Elvish with some manner of sorcery.

Arthur peered through the dark window of a building.

"What is it?" Angie asked. The others turned and looked.

"Nothing," Arthur answered Angie. "Just seeing what was inside. Nothing in there but a few blackened ashes... just like all the other buildings."

"I guess when the Steel-Hearts destroy a place, they *really* destroy it," Chris said.

"This looks like a well," Lance said. He was looking down the mouth of a big tube that went down through the street. The others looked. Their faces reflected darkly on scummy, green water some thirty feet below them. The water sat in some kind of stone bowl at the bottom of the shaft. There seemed to be an open space around it.

"This looks more like a—what do you call it?" Chris asked. "It's a well with a big open space at the bottom."

"A cistern?" Arthur said.

"Yes," Chris said. "Exactly. That's what I think this is."

"Yes," Marcos said. "They provided water to those on the surface."

They hadn't walked a hundred yards when they passed a second cistern. This one was underneath a roof that was held up by four heavy posts. Near this second cistern were a weirdly shaped piece of metal—now partly melted—and a stone hearth.

"This probably used to be a blacksmith shop," Lance said. "That metal thing was an anvil. It's shaped different, but I bet that's what it was."

The others nodded.

After a little more walking, they found a building full of shattered, smashed statues. Crushed, burned, and blackened arms and legs, fingers, parts of faces, and trunks lay amid piles of rubble. Mouths almost seemed to gasp for air. Lifeless fingers of stone seemed to clutch the air. The carved face of a crying child, a face half blackened by soot, looked too real to ignore.

"Those poor Elves," Lance shook his head. "You can almost feel what happened to 'em here."

"None of it seems real to me," Chris said. "Elves. Steel-Hearts. Pendragons. This place is depressing, though. Let's get out of here."

They walked back out into sunlight.

They passed another cistern full of scummy, green water. Then they came upon a building with a staircase just inside the doorway. Stone stairs led downward into darkness.

"What is that?" Chris asked. "It looks like the entrance to a subway."

"Yeah, Chris," Lance said. "I'm sure the Elvish carved subways in their rocks."

"Let's see what's really down there," Arthur said.

Arthur, Lance, Chris, and Angie started down the steps.

The stone stairs were hard and rough and tinged with green lichens. Arthur led the others as they dropped down into damp, earthy darkness. Echoes of footfalls whispered eerily from somewhere far below the ground.

The bottom of the stone staircase was some thirty feet below ground level. Arthur and the others found it more by touch than by sight. Their feet raked against a floor of coarse stone. On the right, the staircase was set against a smooth, hard wall. To the left and front, Arthur, Chris, Angie, and Lance got the impression of a great open space, a big, cavernous tunnel. They stood in near-darkness, but they could see little splashes of light at even distances along the walls of the tunnel further down.

"Where's that light coming from?" Lance asked. "Have they got some kind of lights set up down here?"

"Let's find out," Arthur said.

Arthur, Chris, Lance, and Angie shuffled through the darkness. They moved slowly, dragged their feet, and kept their hands out ahead of them so they wouldn't run into anything.

"Why didn't somebody think to bring a flashlight?" Chris sighed.

"I've got my smartphone," Arthur said. "Give me a minute to turn it on."

"My battery ran out last night," Lance said.

"That's why I mostly keep mine turned off," Arthur said. "At least the camera and flashlight still work."

Lance started out ahead of them.

"Wait," Angie said. "You could fall down a well in the dark."

Lance waited as Arthur's smartphone powered up. The blue-white light lit the path ahead of them as they walked toward the first of the light-splashes. When they got there, they could see that the light was pouring out of a round alcove in the wall. In the bottom was a scummy, green pool of water. Light washed down through a shaft overhead. They thought it might have come from some artificial power source, but the light was from the sun. It was obviously shining down the shaft from an opening at the surface.

"This is one of those cistern-things," Angie said.

The others nodded agreement.

"This is what they look like from down here," Arthur said. "Is this a sewer system?"

"Maybe they were set up to trap rain," Angie said.

They looked around a little bit more, but found they could see very little.

"Maybe we better go back and get some lanterns from camp," Chris suggested. "We don't want to drain Arthur's battery."

"He's right," Angie said.

They returned to camp and told Ambrose and Mr. Lucas, about the tunnels they had found.

"Yes," Ambrose said. "The Elvish are known for their underground worlds. Their tunnels often go on for miles."

"Can we have a lantern?" Lance asked.

"May you have a lantern," Mr. Lucas corrected.

"Right," Lance said. "Well, mayent we or not?"

The lamps the villagers had given Ambrose's party were stored in Mr. Lucas's carriage. Ambrose unpacked three of them. The lamps were simple in construction. There were no switches, no knobs to turn, no wicks to light.

"These are Elvish lanterns," Ambrose said. "All one must do to have light is lift the shade."

Ambrose slid up a shade that surrounded the lantern. A blue glow radiated out of a shimmering piece of rock. The rock was enclosed in a transparent tube.

"The glowstones are the secret of Elvish lights," Ambrose said.

Arthur remembered his dream: Glowing stone necklaces lit the forest with a gentle blue light. He wondered if this dead village might somehow be speaking to him in his dreams.

"The Elvish mine the glowstones in secret places along the Green River and in hidden caverns," Ambrose was explaining.

"Do you want to come with us?" Lance asked.

"Yes," Ambrose said.

A few minutes later, the entire group of them descended the rough, greenish stairs into cool, earthy darkness. The blue-white glow of the lantern brightly illuminated everything within a ten-foot radius of the glowstone. The blue light showed everything reasonably well within thirty feet and played out at about sixty feet. In the blue glare, Arthur and the others got an idea of the true shape of the tunnel. It seemed that the hand-carved cavern was about fifty feet wide and almost thirty feet high in the center. Stone beams supported it. There was no determining the length of the tunnel. It led as far as the light would shine in either direction.

"It's bigger than most subway tunnels I've seen," Chris said. His voice echoed in the hollowness.

"See those light spots that show up ever so often," Arthur pointed down the tunnel.

"What are those?" Mr. Lucas asked.

"We think they're cisterns," Arthur said. They walked down the tunnel toward the nearest one.

"They're in round, hollowed-out pockets in the wall," Chris said. "There's water at the bottom. They're open to the sky at the top. They look like wells from up above."

"Yes," Ambrose said. "The Elven-folk used the cisterns to collect rain water and to store water from their underground rivers in places where people would have easy access to it."

"You think we'll see any of them underground rivers, Ambrose?" Lance asked.

"Yes," Ambrose said. He pointed to the debris littering the edge of the tunnel ahead of them. "Broken pottery and a skiff. The pots were once used to carry water from the river to those cisterns you saw. A certain level was maintained every day. The skiffs were used to traverse the underground rivers. There must be one nearby."

"One of my science teachers showed us pictures of a big, underground lake in Kentucky he went to," Angie said. "I always wanted to go there."

They walked about a hundred meters. For a while they

encountered nothing but skiffs and broken pottery. Then they heard gurgling echoes and sighs—like water splashing—and it was growing louder. The stone floor gave way to a platform of stone blocks and pilings. The platform led into the mouth of a second tunnel that ran at a right angle to the first. Steps—damp and covered with lichens—led downward.

"There," Ambrose said.

The light of the lantern brushed across a rippling surface that cast rippling reflections on the walls. The second tunnel was filled with water. The river was about twenty feet across, and it still flowed. Waves—blue in the lanter's glow—splashed across tiled walls. A thin layer of scum had built up on the tiles that were just above water level. Something splashed in the water.

"Was that a fish?" Lance asked.

"Probably," Ambrose said. "These waters were full of them until the Steel-Hearts filled them with poison. The waters are only now beginning to live again."

"Are the fish any good?" Angie asked.

"Yes," Ambrose said. "But most of the creatures you'll find in these underground rivers are colorless and blind."

"That's the way Mr. Russell said the fish and salamanders were in that place in Kentucky," Angie said.

"She had a crush on Mr. Russell," Lance said.

"I did not!" Angie protested. "Leave me alone."

"I thought I heard something," Arthur said.

"Probably an echo," Lance said. "HEY!"

"Hey...hey...hey... hey... ," the tunnel answered back. Lance's voice returned, filled with watery distortions.

"Be quiet!" Chris snapped.

"Afraid I'll wake up the monsters?"

"That's not funny, man," Chris said. "Not here."

"We oughtta call you 'Chicken-Man,'" Lance said. "You're scared of everything."

"Neanderthal," Chris said.

"It's a bird," Lance said. "It's a plane. It's CHIIIIIIII-IIIIIIIICKEN-MAN!" Lance's voice reverberated weirdly through the dark tunnels around him.

"Back off, Lance," Arthur said.

"Sorry," Lance said. "Just playing around with the reverb."

Quietness.

Arthur stood with the others on the stone platform and looked as far up and down the dark, flooded tunnel as the Elvish lantern's light would let him. In the blue glow, he could dimly make out openings. They looked like doorways, windows, and balconies. There was a whole underground world waiting to be explored, and Arthur felt it calling to him.

"Is there any way we could explore this river?" Arthur asked. "Maybe we could fix some of those skiffs."

"We should be able to patch some of the skiffs easily enough," Ambrose nodded. "Some of them were not badly damaged."

They all talked quietly and decided they would patch some of the boats, but they would do it later. There were other tunnels that could be explored on foot. They spent the whole morning walking by lantern light through the dark, damp tunnels beneath the village. The dark passages led for what must have been miles.

The tunnels were dark mazes with more tunnels leading out in all directions. Sudden shadowy staircases led to tunnels deeper and deeper underground. In some places, water dripped through cracks in the ceiling and left puddles on the floor. One of the tunnels farthest underground had about six inches of water on its floor. It reflected the ceiling and made the tunnel seem twice as large.

Tunnels led to tunnels that led to tunnels. Some of the tunnels were lined with rooms. Some rooms were empty. Others were full of broken statues or ash heaps left from fires. Underground streams and rivers wound through the tunnels via troughs in the stone floors. Marcos explained that the Elvish had a sophisticated system of dams, floats, levers, and pumps that kept their tunnel system from flooding. They also had vents to prevent the buildup of poisonous gases.

One of the deepest tunnels ended in a waist-high guardrail with nothing beyond but a dark, empty hole. Everyone stood by the rail as Ambrose held his lantern out into space. The lantern's glow showed a stone ceiling some twenty feet overhead. There seemed to be a hazy wall some fifty feet to the left, but no one could be sure. In all the other directions—right, straight ahead, and down—all they could see was empty space. The hole was wide and, for all practical purposes, bottomless. Lance and Marcos both thought they could hear water flowing far below, but no one else heard anything. Amos tossed a rock out into the pit, but no one heard it hit bottom.

At what appeared to be mid-afternoon, Ambrose, Mr. Lucas, Arthur, and the whole group found their way out of the subterranean catacombs and into daylight. They were all the way across the village from the spot they had chosen as camp. They spent nearly thirty minutes walking among buildings of weathered stone and finally reached camp. Ambrose and Marcos made a quick lunch of sandwiches and a kind of root tea and everyone ate.

That afternoon, Mr. Lucas, Ambrose, Arthur, and the others dragged four skiffs out of the tunnel and into camp so Amos and Marcos could repair them. The skiffs were made out of a primitive plastic resin that came from boiled tree sap. They were easy enough to patch. Amos started a nice, hot fire and melted some shattered splinters from other skiffs in a metal cauldron. He placed jagged sheets of Elven plastic over the holes in the boats and sealed them into place with molten plastic resin. The others assisted. Amos gave them instructions. They had to be careful not to burn holes in the boats and not to breathe the fumes too deeply.

***

Hours later, the work was finished and the group was waiting for the patches to firm up so the boats could be tested. The sun hung just above the horizon. Amos had dumped what was left of the melted plastic, and Ambrose was scraping a dried crust of plastic out of the bottom of the cauldron. Marcos was starting to prepare supper. That was when they heard the sound.

It was a roaring, metallic sound, and it was growing louder. It was not the low rumble of a tank, but the high-pitched whine of an engine. Arthur and Chris looked at each other.

"Is that a motorcycle?" Chris asked.

"Is it the Steel-Hearts?" Angie asked.

"I don't think so," Ambrose said. He kept on scraping the cauldron, calm as ever. "The rotohorse and rider are no danger to us."

The whine of the engine grew louder and louder until something shot out of an alley and into view. It was an angular metal beast with two wheels, and a man clinging tightly to its back.

"It *is* a motorcycle," Chris said.

"Not quite," Arthur said, "but it's a pretty fair facsimile."

The machine roared through camp. It swept through the edge of the campfire. The rider stuck out a boot and kicked a boiling pot through the air as Marcos yelled at him. He brought his mount to a level halt a few inches from where Ambrose sat calmly scraping the cauldron. He sprang from the machine. The rider was a young man with a narrow, v-shaped face, pale blond hair, and catlike green eyes. His arched eyebrows were joined in the middle. He wore chain mail, leather, body armor, and a belt of fur.

"You have no business in the place of my ancestors!" he cried. "Get out!"

"I would offer you some tea," Ambrose said, "but you seem to have spilled all of it."

Arthur noticed Amos was about to laugh at the rider. Then his expression changed. Arthur followed the big man's gaze to a wicked knife and a strange metal cylinder, both of which the rider carried on his belt.

"I am Ambrose Pendragon, son of Camelot," Ambrose stood. "These are my friends. They travel with me. You have said that this place is the home of your people. You are large for an Elf. Explain."

"I am Rael," he said. "Son of Dran of the Bre'ons and Laradril of the Huntaara Elvish."

"A bi'on," Lance said.

"Hold your tongue, whelp," Rael snapped, "or I will cut it off."

Ambrose held up his hand. "The young one meant no offense. We are friends of the Elvish. We came here for refuge."

"You call yourself a Pendragon of Camelot. Is it you that the rumors speak of?"

"It is."

"Then you have come to take the throne of Samhain?"

"He will fall."

"At what time?"

"At the time of the Father's choosing. The time was written of in the prophecies of the seers of my ancestors. When that time will come, I know not."

"Let us step away to ourselves, that we may speak in trust."

"There is nothing you can say to me that may not be said before these as well."

Rael looked around at Amos, Marcos, Mr. Lucas, and the young people from Earth.

"I do not keep council with children and commoners." He walked back to his rotohorse. "Damage nothing," he said, "or you will answer to me."

He leaped onto the back of his vehicle, twisted a cylinder, and roared out of camp. Ambrose watched him shoot between the buildings and out of sight.

"There goes a very stiff-necked young man."

The sound of the rotohorse slowly faded to nothing.

9. /Come Forth

The sky turned a blazing orange as the sun sank below a sea of dark green trees. Tired from the day's activities, the group sat around the fire and quietly ate their dinner.

Arthur looked down at his watch. 1:31 P.M.

We've been missing for two days, fifteen hours, one minute, and twenty-five seconds, Arthur thought to himself. The thought of home seemed distant, though. It almost seemed like a dream. Either home was a dream, or this was a dream. Arthur couldn't decide which. He took a bite of sandwich and chewed it thoughtfully.

"Are you okay?" Arthur heard Angie speak, but did not realize she was speaking to him. "Arthur?"

"Yeah. What is it?"

"You looked worried," she said. "I just wondered if you were okay."

"Fine," he said. "Under the circumstances. This whole experience is like a dream. I keep wondering when we're going to wake up from it."

"Speaking of dreams," Angie said, "I had the strangest one last night. Stacy was with us here."

"Here in the village?"

"Yeah. I think so. And there were other people around. I think they were Elvish."

"That's...really strange." Should he tell her he'd dreamed about them too?

"Sometimes I can't remember what she looked like," Angie said, "or remember her voice."

"That's normal," Arthur said. "That's what the grief counselor told us, anyway."

"Sometimes I'm afraid I'll forget her completely," Angie said.

"You won't," Arthur said. "None of us will. She's a part of us."

Arthur noticed Ambrose was staring at Angie and at him. The tall *Bre'on* king didn't say anything. He gradually turned his eyes away and went back to eating.

Amos picked up one of the patched skiffs and started out of camp. "Let's test our handiwork," he said. Marcos picked up another skiff and followed.

"Where are you going?" Chris asked.

"To the river, I assume," Mr. Lucas said. "The underground river." He followed the brothers as they left camp.

"They will test the skiffs for leaks," Ambrose said. "If they find none, we can see some of the river tonight."

"Tonight?" Chris echoed.

"Why not, my friend?" Ambrose smiled. "Why not?"

Arthur finished his sandwich. Ambrose Pendragon made him another one. Angie finished her sandwich but told Ambrose she was too full for seconds.

Ambrose poked at the fire with his sword. The flames were dying.

"You had a friend named Stacy?" Ambrose asked.

"Yeah," Angie said.

"And you lost her?"

"Uh huh," Angie said. "We were in a car wreck. I lived, but she didn't. Sometimes I think I should have died, too. Why should I get to grow up and have a life when she never will?"

"That is not for us to say," Ambrose said. "Life is a gift. The Father takes who he chooses and gives life where it pleases him."

"Well, sometimes it doesn't seem very fair."

Ambrose didn't say anything. He just went back to poking at the fire with his sword. The fire snapped and popped. The flames were burning brightly. They reflected in Ambrose Pendragon's eyes. For a moment the man called Pendragon sat without moving.

"I think we were about to explore an underground river," Arthur said. "Do you think the boats are ready, Ambrose?"

"If they are not," he said, "they will be soon. Gather the last two, and let's go."

A blue Elvish lantern glowed around them as they

walked through the streets of the dead village. Ambrose, Arthur, Angie, Lance, and Chris walked down stairs of stone into an underground world. Once again, the air smelled damp and earthy, and their voices and footsteps sent weird echoes skipping through the darkness. Marcos, Amos, and Mr. Lucas were waiting for them when they reached the river.

"You're right on time," Mr. Lucas said as they approached.

"First time for everything," Lance said.

They carried the four Elvish boats Amos had repaired down the wide stairs that led to the underground river. Cool water splashed up against the bottom step.

"This is amazing," Angie said.

"It will be amazing," Arthur said, "if we can get into those boats without getting wet."

Marcos was barefoot and his trouser legs were rolled up. He stood in the water and held the boats steady for the others.

Lance and Angie climbed into the first boat. It held them easily. The boat was wide, flat, and pointed on both ends. They looked a bit like leaves.

"We carved some branches into oars," Mr. Lucas said.

Lance found one of the makeshift oars and pushed his boat off. The water sloshed up against the dingy walls of the tunnel and the sides of the skiffs.

"You mustn't go too far," Ambrose said. "Marcos has the lantern."

Arthur and Chris climbed into the second skiff. It was surprisingly stable to be so light.

Ambrose and Marcos climbed into a third boat. The others let them get ahead of them because Marcos held the only lantern.

Mr. Lucas climbed into the last skiff. Amos shook the water off his feet and climbed carefully in behind him.

The light of the lantern lit the smiling faces of friends, the water, and the tunnel ahead. The shouts and comments of Angie, Marcos, and all the others came back in ringing echoes, made weird by the dark tunnel. Running, splashing water sent back hissing, sighing, sloshing sounds from the darkness ahead.

The tunnel curved steadily. Arthur couldn't see more than twenty or thirty feet ahead. The passage was about twenty feet wide and the roof of the tunnel was about the same distance above them. The walls and water glowed pale blue in the lantern light.

"What's that up ahead?" Arthur asked.

"That thing in the wall?" Lance said.

"Yeah."

"I don't know. Looks like some kind of porch or balcony."

The boats sloshed nearer.

"Statues," Angie said. "They're all broken."

"Work of the Steel-Hearts, no doubt," Arthur said.

There were feet and legs standing in the doorway of the balcony. Above the knees, nothing remained. There was rubble piled around the ruined statues. Figures, part of an ear, and a wavy surface that might have been stone hair were all that could be made out in the shattered plaster. The three pairs of trunkless legs caught the blue lantern light and threw fuzzy shadows on the tile wall behind them. The shadows moved as Marcos' boat passed them with the lantern. The tunnel made a sharp left, nearly cutting off Marcos' lantern as he rounded the turn. The other boats rounded the corner. The tunnel started curling gradually to the right.

Odd paintings decorated the walls in some places. There were also pecks, bare spots, and black smears where the Steel-Hearts had unleashed the energies of their weapons.

Oars splashed, and wet sounds reverberated into darkness and back.The boats drifted past another balcony full of smashed and burned statues. They drifted past several more balconies. All of them had been vandalized, desecrated.

"They ... desecrated an entire culture," Angie said bitterly. "A beautiful, graceful culture."

Ever so often, fluted pillars ran along the walls. Some of

these, too, were cracked and burnt.

The tunnel ended in a wall. Waves pounded against it and bounced back at the boats. Arthur felt warm water spray his face. He struggled with his wooden oar to stop his boat.

"Whoa," he said. "End of the line, people."

"This can't be the end," Angie said. "Who'd build a tunnel that doesn't lead anywhere?"

"It probably led a lot of places," Lance said. "We just got in at the wrong end."

"Ambrose?" Marcos said.

All eyes went to Ambrose Pendragon. The lean man seemed locked in a trance, his eyes boring into the stone of the wall. He gripped the hilt of his sword. He paused for a moment. A word formed on his lips.

"Open."

" *Openopenopen*" the tunnel answered back.

There was a scraping noise as the wall began to fall. The dark mouth of another tunnel appeared over the top. The wall fell beneath the waves and vanished as the waters swallowed it. Waves slapped the sides of the boats, flinging up droplets of water. Cool spray hit Arthur in the face.

A new tunnel yawned before the boats, a tunnel like none yet seen. It was dark but colored lights glowed in the distance. The passage echoed with strange and wonderful sounds: the fragile ringing of glass upon glass, chime upon chime, hammer upon anvils. Flutes seemed to play.

"Let's go," Arthur whispered.

"Yes," Mr. Lucas nodded. "Indeed, let's."

Unlike the plastered walls of the passage behind them, the walls of this tunnel looked like rock. The new tunnel was wider and taller, even, than the other. Ambrose, Lance, and Angie entered first. The others, in their boats, followed them in. They looked all around.

"Wow," somebody whispered.

"Turn off the lantern," Mr. Lucas said.

Marcos dropped the shade of his lantern. Strange tunnel lights glowed in the dark. People watched from among the rocks—people frozen for all time, people of colored stone. The statues had breath and life. The plaster and stone ghosts of the Elves of Huntaar smiled at their long-awaited guests. Elven workmen hammered without movement upon anvils that never felt a blow. Crystal sweat clung eternally to their foreheads. Elvish children played under a rainbow-colored sun. Young women picked shimmering flowers from fields of sparkling emeralds, rubies, and topaz. The haunting music of flutes flowed past Elvish herdsmen in their fields.

They're exactly like the people I dreamed about, Arthur was thinking. Exactly!

They heard a scraping noise followed by a slam. It had come from behind them.

"The wall," Lance said.

"I guess we're stuck in here," Arthur said.

"Ambrose opened the way for us before," Marcos said. "Why do you think he cannot do it again?"

"Good point."

Crystal chimes hung out into the water where they were played by waves. Some of the rocks, like the glowing lamp that Marcos held, had a radiance all their own and a rainbow of colors. The tunnel widened on the left where a waterfall splashed down a staircase of glowstones into a deep, round pool. Butterflies of gold lit on leaves of shining green. Fountains spewed over handcrafted Elves who hid beneath big, metal leaves. Misty, hand-painted mountains were etched against the walls. The tunnel seemed to fill a world ... a universe.

The tunnel grew narrower. Arthur paddled past a singing choir. Haunted voices sung the songs of people long dead. The roof went higher and higher. It became a black dome hung with glowing yellow stars like a million million fireflies. Each star, when the light hit it just right, looked like a tiny winged person. Golden cherubim guarded the rear door of the chamber. They stood on either side of a great arch on which was carved the whole history of the Elvish in tiny, intricate images and symbols. The tunnel beyond the arch was dark.

"The water's running faster," Mr. Lucas said. "Be

careful, everyone."

The others stopped paddling. The current carried the boats along faster and faster as they entered the door beneath the arch. Darkness swallowed them up. The tunnel sloped downward, and the water picked up speed.

"I hear something," Angie said. "It sounds like rapids."

"Or falls."

Arthur tried paddling against the current to stop his boat, but found that he couldn't.

"It's all right," Ambrose said.

The boats rounded a bend, and the world dropped out from under them.

"AHHHHHHHHH!"

The boats weren't dropping in a complete fall. They were sliding, churning, turning, bumping, splashing down a chute full of water. They plunged down, down, and down through a dark world filled with water and fury that soaked them all to the skin. Their screams filled the darkness.

The tunnel leveled off, and the boats drifted almost to a stop. Where were they now? They could hear water sloshing beneath them. The sound of the echoing waves told them they were in a huge, empty chamber.

"Is everybody okay?" Lance asked.

"I'm wet," Chris said.

"Marcos," someone said.

Marcos lifted the shade of his lantern, and soft, blue light illuminated the four boats with their soggy passengers. They were floating on a sea of black.

Castaways, Arthur thought. We look like a bunch of castaways.

"That was fun!" Lance said.

"Glad you liked it," Chris said gloomily. "I think I wet my pants."

Angie pushed wet hair out of her eyes.

"There's something glowing ahead of us," Lance said. "Maybe more of those stones."

"Yes," Ambrose said. "Paddle in that direction."

"What is this place?" Arthur said. "I don't see the sky so

we must be underground. This must be some kind of cavern full of water."

"It is," Ambrose said. "I had heard there was a lake beneath the mountain." He paddled his boat toward the glowing shape ahead. Arthur paddled after Ambrose. The splashing of the waves echoed in the huge chamber.

As their eyes adjusted to the darkness, a domed building with arches and columns took shape ahead of them. Elvish glowstones lit a set of steps at the building's entrance. Some glowed from beneath the water. Ambrose paddled through an arch into a narrow harbor. He steadied himself on a rail and climbed out onto the steps. He waited as the others followed.

"Do you know what this place is?" Chris asked.

"Yes," Ambrose said. "I think I do."

"Well, what is it?"

"You will see."

Ambrose climbed the steps and stepped through the front entrance. The others followed. They walked down a short tunnel and stepped through an arch into a large, round chamber. In the center of the room was circular pool. A narrow bridge led to a stone table that stood in the center. Pictograms decorated the sides. Ambrose drew his sword, laid the blade flat on the table's stone surface, and closed his eyes. "Extinguish the lamp," he instructed.

Marcos dropped the shade. Except for the glow of the stones behind them, the chamber was completely dark.

"You said you knew what this place is," Lance said.

"Yes," Ambrose said. "You will see, but you must be quiet now."

The group obeyed. After a moment of standing in total darkness and silence, Ambrose began to sing. Strangely, the words of his song did not translate into English. The melody was deep and mysterious and filled with longing. Lights began to appear in the dome overhead. Arthur thought, at first, that he had imagined them, but they began to grow brighter. The dome grew bright and filled with golden skies. Imagery from another world appeared in the arched doorways around the room. It was a world of spiked mountains and glistening seas. The dome changed colors and the golden world vanished. The sky turned blood red, and the doorways showed a lava plain. Volcanic cinder cones burned on the horizon. The smell of burning sulfur floated on a hot wind. An enormous birdlike shape glided overhead. It looked like a pterodactyl. The beast screamed and began to circle. The dome changed again. This time it transformed into a night sky with a crescent moon. Dark tree-shapes appeared around them and night insects began to sing.

"The moon," Arthur said, suddenly realizing. "That's our moon!"

"It's a doorway," Chris said. "We're home. Come on!" He ran toward one of the arches. The others looked to Ambrose. He shook his head.

Chris ran through the arch and vanished among the tree-shapes there.

"Chris," Arthur said. He started to follow.

"He will be all right," Ambrose said, "but our job here is not done. Step up to the edge of the pool."

The images on the dome began to fade. As the room grew darker, the depths of the pool grew clearer. Arthur could see lights shining far below the crystalline surface and knew it was much deeper than he had imagined.

"What's down there?" Lance asked as he squinted into the depths.

"Some see the future there," Ambrose said. "Others see the desires of their hearts. What do you see?"

As Arthur stared into the depths, he felt a lump form in his throat. His eyes began to water. Embarrassed, he fought to hold back the torrent of tears that poured from his soul. Lance, Angie, and even Mr. Lucas, he noticed, were struggling to hold back tears of their own. Tears glistened in Ambrose's eyes too. *What's wrong with us?* Arthur watched as Ambrose leaned out over the edge of the pool and let the strange and sudden tears fall into the waters below. As if drawn by instinct or participating in some strange ritual, the others did the same. As their tears struck the surface, the waters flashed bright and then grew dark. Arthur felt a tingling sense of déjà vu as he saw a figure rising from the depths. His heart began to pound in his chest. He watched, frozen, as Ambrose knelt down on the narrow bridge and plunged his hand beneath the surface. When he drew it back out, Arthur could see that he was holding someone else's hand. A bare arm, glistening with water, appeared. A head and shoulders broke the surface. It was a woman. Water splashed from her body as Ambrose knelt down and lifted her to the bridge beside him. She gasped and coughed and pushed the hair back from her face. Though his logic fought to deny it, Arthur already knew whose face he would see.

"Stacy?" Lance and Angie gasped at once.

"Am I alive?" The girl fought to catch her breath. "Where are we?"

"You're not going to believe it," Lance said.

"Are you cold?" Angie asked.

"A little," she said. She turned to Ambrose. "I know you...don't I?"

"All of your questions will be answered in time," Ambrose said.

"How long was I gone?" she asked.

Ambrose went back to the table that stood at the center of the pool. As he picked up his sword and sheathed it, the room grew dark.

"Let's go," Ambrose said. "Chris is waiting."

Fading images rippled along the walls as they left the domed room. Arthur, Lance, and Angie crowded around Stacy. Mr. Lucas was clearly delighted to see her too.

"Who is she?" Marcos whispered.

"Someone they loved and lost," Ambrose told him.

"Yes," Amos said. "I can see that."

"What did he mean by that?" Stacy asked. She was shivering from the cold.

"Here," Mr. Lucas said as he wrapped his coat around her.

"Thanks, Mr. Lucas."

Ambrose led them in a direction they had not gone before. Rock-hewn stairs led upward through a crack in the earth. Following them, they found themselves standing beneath a starry sky at the base of a mountain. Chris was waiting there, a stricken look on his face.

"It wasn't real," he said. His voice was raw with pain. "None of it was real."

"It was not a doorway," Ambrose said. "Not for us, anyway. It was only a window."

"Why did you do that?" Chris snapped.

"Hey," Lance said. "Look who we found."

Chris gasped. "Stacy?"

"Yeah," Lance said. "Can you believe it? It's like a dream."

Fear clouded Chris's eyes. "Don't say that."

"You act like you haven't seen me in months," she said.

"We haven't," Arthur said.

"How did you get here?" Chris demanded.

She frowned. "I'm...not sure."

"What's the last thing you remember?" Arthur asked.

"Do you remember anything about an accident?" Lance pressed.

"Accident?" Stacy said. "The last thing I remember, we were leaving Pizza Hut. Then I was in this other place. I was starting to wonder if my old life was a dream, but here you all are. Maybe I'm dreaming now."

"Something's wrong here," Chris said. "Something's not adding up." Tears came to his eyes. "You're not Stacy. Who are you?"

"Hey," Arthur said. "Take it easy."

"No," Chris pulled back. "You're all blinding yourselves to the truth because you want it to be her. She's probably not even human."

Dead silence. Shocked stares. Stacy stood open-mouthed and speechless with the rest. Mr. Lucas put a hand on Chris's shoulder.

"No," Chris jerked away. "Don't look at me like there's something wrong with me. If somebody you just happen to miss shows up on an alien planet that happens to be run by an evil sorcerer, you don't just accept it like nothing happened." He backed away from them.

"You are wise to be cautious," Ambrose said, "but this is no dark enchantment."

"Is she part of the prophecy?" Marcos asked as he turned to Ambrose. "A second maiden. A twin of the spirit."

"Yes," Ambrose said. "She is why we came here, but I did not know it until now."

"How did you do this, Ambrose?" Arthur placed a hand on Stacy's shoulder. "Making plants grow is one thing, but how could you or anybody else bring somebody back from the dead?"

"Dead?" Stacy said. "I'm dead."

"I am only an instrument," Ambrose said.

"An instrument of what?"

"An instrument of a power more mysterious and wonderful than you could possibly imagine. This is only a taste. Do you understand?"

"I'm not sure."

"This is only the beginning," Marcos said.

"The beginning of what?"

"The putting right of things gone wrong."

"This is a lot to take in," Arthur said.

"Just go with it," Lance said. "She's here. We're here. Just go with it."

"I'm dead," Stacy said. "Wow. It all makes sense now."

"We're dead, too," Arthur said. "That's it, isn't it?"

"No," Chris cried. "It can't be!"

"You are not dead," Ambrose said. "Only displaced."

"Displaced," Arthur said. "What does that mean?"

"I have told you," Ambrose said. "You are here to fulfill a destiny."

"Right," Arthur said. "A destiny."

"Let us get back to our campsite," Amos said.

The others agreed. They climbed the winding stairs that led up the side of the mountain. Blue lantern light lit the way ahead of them.

"What kind of place is this?" Stacy asked. "What are all of you doing here?"

"Mr. Lucas took us out for a carriage ride," Arthur said. "We passed through some fog and ended up here...wherever here is."

"Let's just say we ain't in Kansas anymore," Lance said. "Not exactly Oz either."

"And I'm dead?"

The others nodded reluctantly.

"How's my mom? And Paul?" Paul was her stepfather.

"Okay," Arthur said. "Under the circumstances."

"They weren't too upset?"

Nobody knew how to answer.

"Of course they were upset, child," Mr. Lucas said after a long pause. "They loved...love you."

"But they're all right now?"

"Fine," Arthur said. He thought about how tired, how shattered, Mrs. Perry had looked the last time he'd seen her. And Paul looked like he'd lost his own daughter. Arthur saw the house in his mind, a sad and lonely place with a "For Sale" sign out front. "They're just fine."

The walk back to camp seemed like a dream. Arthur wondered for a moment if they were still inside the Elvish chamber experiencing some kind of vision. He wondered if Stacy would vanish at any moment, and started to reach for her hand. That was when he realized Lance was already holding it. Angie walked close behind them, and Chris lagged behind the others, a tortured expression on his face. Stacy was still with them when they made it back to camp. Amos stoked the fire as the others made their pallets. They sat around and told Stacy everything about their adventures so far—about the werewolf, the Steel-Hearts, and all the rest.

Arthur noticed Ambrose standing at the edge of camp. He looked lost in thought. Arthur left the others and approached him.

"Ambrose," he said. "I'm sorry to disturb you."

"It's all right," Ambrose said. "What's on your mind?"

"What is she?" Arthur asked. "A ghost? An angel?"

"She is...." He thought for a moment. "...a possibility,"

Thanks, Arthur thought. *That tells me a lot.* He waited a moment before speaking. "Will she still be here tomorrow?" he finally managed to ask.

"Yes," Ambrose answered without a moment's hesitation. "She will be here."

"Is she real?" he asked. "Is she here to stay?"

"That has yet to be determined," Ambrose said. "Would you love her any less if you knew she was only here for a while?"

"No." Arthur cleared his throat. "No, of course not."

As the group settled in for the night, Chris withdrew to the edge of camp and pulled his blankets up around his neck. Arthur, Lance, and Angie arranged a sleeping place for Stacy. The fire crackled in the firepit and sent a warm glow around the room. The teens sat and talked until they began to nod off.

"I think we better go to bed," Stacy finally said. "I'll see you in the morning." She pulled off her shoes and rolled off her socks. Yawning, she lay down and pulled a blanket over her body. Lance kissed her goodnight and tucked her in. Chris watched from a distance and rolled his eyes.

***

Chris Castle lay awake most of the night. When he finally drifted off to sleep, he dreamed he was walking through a graveyard at night. Wisps of fog clung to the air like ghostly webbing. Chris stopped at one of the graves and stood over it. The inscription on the stone didn't make any sense, but Chris knew what lay beneath the mound of damp earth at his feet. He tried to walk away, but found that he had grown roots.

The mound began to pulse as though something were breathing beneath the dirt. A bloodless hand pushed up through the dirt and clawed blindly for Chris's foot. Chris fought madly to pull himself free of the roots that held him. He twisted and pulled and ... woke up. He sat up, propped himself against a stone wall, and softly sobbed as his friends slept on.

10./Haunted Forest

Arthur woke up lying in a pile of blankets. He had gotten used to waking up in the strange world he and his friends had somehow been transported to, but he continued to hope he'd wake up in his own bed at home. Scientific explanations didn't matter. He just wanted to be home. Arthur heard movement and sat up in time to see Stacy Knight dropping an armload of wood onto the fire. *Stacy!* He stared at her in amazement. Sensing his gaze, she turned and smiled.

Arthur pulled on his shoes. He looked around the room at his sleeping friends and noticed Chris was missing. Stacy hugged Arthur as he approached the fire. She acted as though she had not seen him in months. Arthur held her in return and wondered if she was back to stay. What had Ambrose meant when he'd said it was yet to be determined?

"Have you seen Chris?" he whispered as they separated.

"No," she answered. "He was gone when I woke up. Do you want to talk outside?"

Arthur nodded. He got his coat and followed her down the corridor to the stone pavement outside the building's entrance. They walked to the edge and gazed down the hillside—it was covered with tall grass and gray hunks of rock—and into the green coolness of the river. Arthur's eyes crossed a stone bridge to a tall, deep forest of ancient evergreen trees.

"How are you?" Stacy asked.

"I'm okay," Arthur said. Standard answer.

"I still can't believe I'm dead," she said.

"Do you remember anything?" Arthur asked. "A tunnel? A light?"

"I remember the light," she said, "and I remember how I felt when they told me I had to go back. I didn't want to go."

"Who told you you had to go back?"

"I think it was...God. My dad was there, too."

Standard near death experience. Arthur wanted to accept it, but he felt a hint of suspicion nagging at the corner of his consciousness.

"You're not afraid?" Arthur asked her.

"Of death?" She shrugged and smiled. "Not after what I experienced. It was beautiful. I didn't want to come back."

"But what about your friends? Your family?"

She shrugged. "I just felt like everything would be okay."

Arthur nodded.

"How is everybody?" she asked.

"It's been hard," Arthur said.

"Is Angie okay?"

"Hard to say," Arthur said. "She's changed the way she dresses and gotten more artsy. I hope it's a good sign."

"Like she's not trying to copy me anymore?" Stacy said.

"Yeah," Arthur said. "Maybe."

"What about Lance?"

"He's coping. He wrote a poem about you last week."

"Lance?"

"Yeah, believe it or not."

"And Chris?"

"He's been downright weird since you...."

"Died?"

"Yes," Arthur said. "Worse since we came here."

"He's always been different," Stacy said. "Not in a bad way. He's just so intense. Deep and dark. I don't think I was ready for the kind of attention he focused on me."

"He smothered you?"

"He scared me. I felt like he watched everything I did. I didn't know how to deal with it. Once he asked to read all of my text messages, and blew up when I asked him why."

"I didn't know about that." Arthur sighed. "What about my brother?"

"What do you mean?"

"Were you really serious about each other?"

"I don't know," she said. "Lance never seemed serious about anything, but we always had fun together. I hope you don't think I was using him." She shook her head. "Maybe I was. I didn't think so at the time, but maybe I just wanted some relief from Chris. I hurt Chris, I used Lance, and Angie is better off without me. What kind of person does that make me, Arthur?"

"Human," Arthur said. "And I don't think Angie is better off without you."

"But you're not going to argue about the rest?"

"I think I'd better go look for Chris."

"Changing the subject?"

"Yeah. I always say the wrong thing."

"No, you don't." She hugged him. "Do you want me to go with you?"

"No," Arthur said. "Somebody needs to stay and tell the others where I'm gone."

"Where are you going?"

"Back down the hill," Arthur said. "The place Ambrose took us last night was some kind of portal. Chris may be trying to access it to get home."

"Can he do that?"

Arthur thought for a moment. "I don't think so. Not without Ambrose's sword." He and Stacy looked at each other.

"Oh, no."

They both ran back inside. They crept around the fire to where Ambrose was sleeping. Stacy pointed. The sword was impaled into the floor of the chamber. It looked as though it had been hammered through solid rock.

"How in the world?" Arthur whispered.

Stacy laughed softly. "At least we know Chris didn't take it."

They walked back outside.

"Maybe he got Amos to stab it into the ground for him," Stacy suggested. "He looks pretty strong."

"Through solid rock?" Arthur shook his head. "What kind of metal can cut through solid rock?"

"You're right," she said. "It's weird."

"Didn't King Arthur pull his sword out of a stone?"

"Yeah," she said. "Come to think of it. At least we know

Chris doesn't have it. Are you still going to look for him?"

"I think I'd better," Arthur said. "If I don't find him in thirty minutes or so, I'll come back and get the rest of you."

"All right," Stacy said. "Be careful."

"There's a sword in the carriage," Arthur said. "One of the villagers gave it to us. I think I'd better take it."

"You can't save everybody, Arthur."

Stacy's words stopped him in his tracks. Arthur turned and looked at her. He thought about asking why she had said it, but didn't. Instead, he went to Mr. Lucas' carriage and found a short sword in a scabbard tucked beneath the seat with some other provisions. He strapped it on, waved goodbye to Stacy, and started down the stone steps the group had climbed the night before. The view from the hillside was lovely, even with the ruins of the Elvish civilization scattered amidst the exposed rocks and brush. Far below, the Emerald River skirted the base of the mountain and twisted away into the forest. About halfway down the mountain was a break in the steps where a road girdled the mountain. This was the path the group had taken the night before. Arthur turned left onto the road in an effort to retrace their steps. Ambrose had led them through the dark, and Arthur hoped there weren't any branching paths he had failed to notice. As he started to walk, Arthur noticed shoeprints in the dust. Most were pointed toward the steps—they had left those the night before—but one set was pointed in the direction he was going now. Chris had been there. Arthur was sure of it. He had tried to find his way back to the underground chamber.

Arthur thought about his conversation with Stacy as he walked the narrow path. He knew he should be happy to have Stacy back, but the more he thought about it, the more he realized he was afraid, though he was not sure why. Maybe it was the fear of losing Stacy again, or maybe he was starting to question his sanity. Maybe it was her account of the afterlife—if that was really what it was— that unsettled him. If heaven meant forgetting about your closest friends, what kind of heaven was that?

Arthur could not remember how far the group had walked in the dark, but after walking for about ten minutes, he came to a stone doorway that had been carved into the hillside. Arthur suddenly realized he hadn't brought a lantern. He pulled his smartphone from his belt and switched on the light. That, at least, still worked in this place. He took a few steps into the passage and stopped. The way ahead of him was blocked by a slab of stone. The underground chamber was sealed. Arthur looked around for other openings, but found none. He saw more footprints in the dust and knew Chris must have done the same. Arthur was wondering where Chris would have gone when he realized the doorway was closed to him. Then he looked across the river and saw a marvelous structure winding through the tops of the trees there. It was a treehouse or maybe a whole village of them. Boards and pieces of metal and stone were lashed to some trees by heavy vines and chains and pieces of knotted rope. Rope bridges connected the trees and, in one of the largest trees, Arthur saw the remains of a large structure. There were smaller houses in other trees, but this one seemed like the focal point. Arthur felt a thrill of fear and wondered if there might be someone living there. If the natives of that place did not want to be disturbed....

No. The treetop estate looked deserted. The roofs of some of the buildings had fallen in. Arthur wanted to get a closer look, but had no way to cross the river. He looked down and saw an arched stone bridge at the bottom of the hill. A set of steps lay only a few yards ahead of him. Arthur went to the steps and started down them. He wondered for a moment if he should go back to the village and get the others, but decided to go ahead alone. He only wanted to take a look. If he actually found anything, he could still go back. Arthur reached the bottom of the hill and stepped out onto the bridge. The structure felt solid beneath his feet. Arthur didn't know what technology the people of Huntaar had used to build the bridge, but it looked strong enough to bear the weight of an automobile. He wondered what they had used it for. Chariot traffic, maybe?

Arthur put his hands on the smooth wall of the bridge and peered over into the cool, green waters that rippled and roared some twelve feet below. The water, though greenish, was remarkably clear. Arthur could see fish swimming, and far, far below, a mossy floor of rocks and sand. Even with the water's magnification, the river looked much deeper than he had expected.

Arthur crossed the bridge and found an overgrown path on the other side. The road had been paved with bricks, but trees had pushed up through the cracks in places and underbrush crowded the edges. Arthur walked in the direction of the treehouses. After a moment, he felt that he was being watched. He heard movement above him and spun around. Chris was standing on a bridge, watching him from the treetops. Arthur tried to read the expression on his face, but Chris just stood and stared.

"How'd you get up there?" Arthur asked.

Chris pointed to the tree the bridge was lashed to.

"That tree's hollow. There are steps inside leading up here."

"Are you serious?"

Chris nodded. Arthur examined the tree. There was a wild growth of bushes on one side of the base.

"There's a doorway down there," Chris said. "You have to claw your way through those bushes to get to it."

Arthur pushed back limbs and wriggled between leafy shrubs. Leaves hit him in the face. They got into his mouth and scraped his eyes. Finally Arthur stepped through a man-sized hole in the tree trunk. He breathed a sigh of relief and brushed himself off. Then he looked up. Morning sunlight poured through an opening some fifty feet up. The inside of the tree was a dark tube. Chris stuck his head through the opening and cut off half the light. "There are handholds and footholds in the wall," he said.

"I've got to be crazy for doing this," Arthur mumbled to himself. He started climbing. After a few seconds, he looked down. The bottom of the tree was twenty feet below. Arthur's knees suddenly felt weak. He hated high places.

Finally, Chris helped Arthur out of the tree and onto the rope bridge that led to the tree house. The floor of the forest was about fifty swinging, empty feet below them. The bridge looked to be a good bit higher than it had looked from down below.

"It would kill us if we fell from here," Arthur said as he clung to the ropes.

"Cheerful thought," Chris said. "Look at this view."

In one direction, they could see the river through a wall of twisted limbs and green leaves. In the other three directions, tall, ancient trees went on forever. A crisp wind swept over the bridge, made it swing. Leaves danced fifty feet below.

"Is everybody out looking for me?" Chris asked.

"Just me," Arthur said. "Most of them were still asleep when I left. What were you thinking? It's not safe to wander around here alone."

"It may not be safe back in camp either," Chris said. "Our enemies may be closer than you think."

Arthur wondered what he meant, but did not ask. "What were you trying to do? Get back into that chamber?"

"I thought it was worth a look." Chris gestured around him. "This place is a prison. Can you blame me for checking the bars?"

"Where do you think we are?"

"Last night," Chris said, "you asked Ambrose if we were dead. He says we're not, but I don't know if I believe him."

"This isn't my idea of heaven," Arthur said. "Not with those silver-eyed zombies and werewolves running around, anyway. And I always pictured hell as being a lot hotter. I could be wrong."

"Stacy's here," Chris said. "Stacy or somebody that looks just like her."

"And you don't believe it's really her?"

"No, I don't. It looks like her, acts like her, but, in my experience, dead people stay dead."

"Jesus didn't."

"Don't bring religion into this," Chris said. "This isn't

Jerusalem, and Stacy isn't the Second Coming. We have to approach this logically."

"Logic doesn't exactly apply here," Arthur said. "Not the logic we know."

"You do have a point," Chris admitted. "I keep trying to come up with a logical explanation for all this, like maybe we're all a part of some weird lab experiment. But none of it makes any sense. I don't know. Maybe this is a dream. Maybe if I just jump off this bridge, I'll wake up in bed." He put his hands on the rail and looked down.

"Don't!" Arthur said.

"Don't worry." Chris sighed. "I'm not gonna jump. It looks too real."

There was a pause.

"Why don't we put logic on the back burner for now," Arthur said. "After Stacy's funeral, you said you wished, more than anything in the world, that you could tell Stacy you were sorry for the things you said about her and the way you treated her."

"You've got to be kidding," Chris said. "I was grief-stricken when I said that. I wasn't thinking straight. I'm not apologizing to her unless she apologizes to me first. Stacy and Lance did some pretty low things."

"Maybe you did things that pushed her away," Arthur said.

"No," Chris said. "Don't blame their behavior on me. What they did was low!"

"Lance has apologized to you over and over. I don't know of anything else he could do. I know it takes time, but you've got to let it go eventually."

"Why did you come here, Arthur?"

"To look for you."

"You found me. You can go now."

"I'm not going back to camp without you."

"Then you're going to be here for a long, long time."

Stacy's words returned to him with stinging force: *You can't save everybody, Arthur.*

***

Arthur and Chris met the rest of the group as they were

walking back to camp. "What did you think you were doing?" Mr. Lucas demanded. Chris listened in sullen silence as the teacher rebuked them for leaving camp.

"We found a set of treehouses," Arthur told Ambrose. "There were bridges connecting them. Do you know who built them?"

"That would have been a Seraf dwelling," Amos said.

"Yes," Ambrose said. "I gather that you saw no sign of the Seraf themselves?"

"It looked deserted," Arthur said.

"That is fortunate," Amos said. "The sky-fliers can be fiercely protective of their nesting places."

"I'd like to see it," Angie said. "Do you think it's safe?"

"It's safe," Chris said.

Ambrose led the group as they walked along the grassy path that skirted the mountain's edge. They came to the doorway Arthur had seen earlier.

"Is this where we came out last night?" Arthur asked.

Ambrose nodded.

"It's closed now," Chris said. "It doesn't lead anywhere."

"The Elvish portals are protected," Ambrose said. "There are not many left, and very few know how to operate them."

"Look," Lance said suddenly as he pointed beyond them. "Is that the treehouses?"

"Yeah," Arthur said. "That's them."

"It is a Seraf settlement," Marcos said.

"What's left of one," Amos said. "I'm surprised the Steel-Hearts left it there."

The group walked down the path and took the worn steps down the hillside to the waiting bridge. Lance held Stacy's hand as they made their way across the heavy stone arch. Arthur saw Chris glaring at them. Everyone stepped off the bridge and into the trees, becoming aware, for the first time, how really huge and how very old the forest really was. Many of the trees around them were more than a hundred feet tall and gnarled with age.

"This place must be at least as old as the village," Angie said. "It feels ancient, as old as time."

"Yes," Mr. Lucas whispered. "You can almost smell time here."

Arthur felt small as he walked with his friends beneath the branches of ageless trees. He thought of stories his mother and teachers used to read him, stories like *Jack and the Beanstalk* where giant plants led to strange new worlds in the sky, or stories about little people who lived in trees and came out only if you believed in them. They shuffled through centuries of brown leaves. Knotted roots stuck out in some places.

"How'd football season go this year?" Stacy asked.

"Curtis Academy knocked us out of the playoffs again," Lance said.

It seemed strange to speak of such things under such unusual circumstances. Arthur thought, at first, that it seemed disrespectful to talk, laugh, or yell in a forest so big and old as this one. But no. No. Somehow, now, Arthur knew that this was a happy forest. The children of the Elvish people had once played here. They had sung and laughed and lived beneath the trees, and the trees had been happy. The silent giants missed those people of long ago and longed, always, for someone else to come and enjoy their shade, to climb in their branches, to eat of their nuts and fruit. Something, some tingling intuition in Arthur's heart, told him that this was a forest that liked to give. After a moment's walking, they stood beneath the treehouses.

"That's amazing," Angie said.

"Kind of makes you think of the days when we were going to make the biggest tree house in the world," Chris said. It was the first pleasant thing he had said in a long time.

"I remember the time we tried to build a two-story," Arthur said.

"Yeah," Angie said. "They made me get up there and walk across their sorry second floor. They told me I'd be the head of their club if I did it."

"We had to test the floor," Arthur smiled.

"That was very wicked of you," Mr. Lucas grinned. "Did

the floor pass the test?"

"Nope," Lance said. "She fell through it and broke her arm. We had to carry her books for a month."

Ambrose laughed. "I bet they didn't use you to test any more treehouses," he said to Angie.

"How do you get up there?"

"The entrances are usually hidden," Amos said.

"There's a hollow tree," Arthur said. Arthur started through the brush. "It's over here."

"How did you know it was there?" Angie asked.

"Chris found it."

"How did you find it, Chris?" Lance asked.

"It wasn't that hard," Chris said. That was all.

Arthur reached the base of the tree, but saw no sign of the opening there. He walked all around the trunk, but the tree was solid.

"Are you sure that's the right tree?" Angie asked.

"I thought I was," Arthur said. "Chris?"

Chris just shrugged.

"You're sure you didn't see anyone?" Amos asked.

"No," Arthur said. "The place was deserted."

"Let's get some breakfast," Lance said. "I'm starving."

As the group started back to camp, Arthur noticed Chris lagging behind the others.

"You didn't see anything else, did you, Chris?"

"Not a thing." He smiled, but it was not a friendly smile.

11. /The Sign of the Sword

"This will be our last night in the village," Ambrose told the group as they sat around the fire. "Tomorrow we will return to civilization and the dangers that await us there."

"Do you think Samhain is still looking for us?" Arthur asked.

"Perhaps," Ambrose said. "We will have to be careful of the Steel-Hearts, but they are easily enough detected. It is Samhain's enchanters that pose a greater threat. They have the power to twist the mind, to warp your perceptions."

"But you can protect us from them," Lance said. "Right?"

"His enchantments have no power over me," Ambose said. "I am immune to them, but I can only protect you as long as I am with you."

"Unless you take the Oath of the Sword," Marcos added.

"I was getting to that," Ambrose said. "I can extend my immunity to Samhain's enchantments to all of you, but only if you pledge yourselves to me as knights of the new Camelot."

"Why didn't you do that in the first place?" Lance asked.

"You did not know me," he said. "You did not know who I was or if you could trust me. We have spent these past few days together. We are strangers no longer. You know almost enough to trust me, but there are other things you must understand. Watch."

Ambrose raised his sword high and brought it down, point first, into the stone below. The tip of the blade sliced easily through the stone. Ambrose plunged it halfway to the hild and then released his hold on it.

"Now," he said. "You saw how easily my blade penetrated the stone. Try to remove it."

They looked at each other.

"Which of you is strongest?"

Lance and Chris looked at each other. "I am," they both said.

"Very well then," Ambrose said. "Step forward."

"Beauty before age," Lance said as he stepped up.

"Not so fast," Chris said. He shoved past Lance and gripped the sword by its handle. Planting his feet, he pulled as hard as he could pull. His face reddened, and veins stood out in his temples. Finally, he released his hold. "Fine," he said, "but you can't do it either."

"Wanna bet?" Lance said. "Watch and learn." He stepped forward and took hold of the blade. Like Chris, he strained without success to pull the blade free.

"Anyone else?"

"Sure," Arthur said. "I'll try."

He was no more successful than the others had been.

"Let Amos do it," Lance said. "If anybody can pull it out, he can."

"I have tried," the big man said, "but to no avail."

"Come, Amos," Ambrose said. "Let them see. Perhaps today you will succeed."

"Hah," Amos said. "Do not tease me." He stepped forward, gripped the handle, and pulled with all of his might. His mighty muscles bulged, and sweat appeared on his forehead. He twisted and strained, but the stone refused to give up the enchanted blade.

"Now," Ambrose said. "Behold the sign of the sword." Using only two fingers, he gripped the sword and easily pulled it free.

"No way," Lance said. "That's got to be some kind of trick. He's got us hypnotized or something."

"No," Ambrose said. "It is no trick. It is a sign. Do you know the story of Arthur and Excalibur?"

"When the sword first appeared, it was stuck into an anvil," Arthur said. "On the anvil was an inscription that said only the future king would be able to pull the sword free."

"Exactly," Ambrose said. "The mightiest of the knights tried to withdraw the blade, but only Arthur, a young page at the time, was able to pull it free."

"And when he was wounded and near death," Angie said, "the Lady of the Lake took the sword from him, and he was taken away to Avalon. According to legend, he would one day return."

"Yes," Ambrose said. "You have heard the story."

"Is that the same sword?" Lance asked.

"It is."

"But how can that be?" Arthur asked. "Excalibur never had the kinds of powers this one does."

"Arthur was a warrior," Ambrose said. "The sword served him by giving him powers befitting a warrior. I am a healer and a teacher. My enemies are not flesh and blood as Arthur's were. I fight darker and more sinister forces, and my blade protects me from them."

"How did you get the sword?" Arthur asked.

"One night I was traveling through the countryside. I fell asleep in the forest and dreamed I saw a woman in white floating on the night breeze. Her clothes swirled about her like fog. She led me to a lake. The water was like glass. She told me to step into it. Believing I was dreaming, I stepped into the waters and walked until I was waist deep in them. The lady came to me then. She reached beneath the water and drew out a gleaming sword.

"Take hold of it," she said. I did. And she said, "I declare that you are Ambrose Pendragon, son of Arthur, heir to the throne of Camelot. With the power of this sword, you shall break the hold of Samhain's forces and restore the kingdom of your ancestors.'"

Ambrose paused in his narrative.

"Then what happened?" Lance asked.

"I awoke," Ambrose said, "and knew that I had been dreaming. Then I noticed that my clothes were wet, and that the sword had been plunged into the ground beside me."

"So, it really happened?" Angie asked. "You saw the Lady of the Lake?"

"I did."

"Who is she?" Arthur asked. "What is she? One of the Worldsmen like Merlin?"

"We do not know who she is," Ambrose said. "Only that the Elvish have spoken of her since ancient times. Some have wondered if she might be an angel, a message from the Father. Others believe she is a different kind of being entirely."

"Does she still live in the lake?" Angie asked.

"The waters of the lake have been poisoned," Ambrose said, "polluted with blood and death. She wanders the night winds now with no place to truly call home. Her spirit cries for the restoration of the lake and the reclamation of A'Vilian."

"So what is this Oath of the Sword?" Lance asked.

"If you will pledge your service to me and to the kingdom of Camelot," Ambrose said, "the power of my sword will overshadow you and shield you from Samhain's enchantments."

"Fine," Lance said. "Sign me up."

"There is something else you must know," Ambrose said, "a condition of the covenant."

"Here it comes," Chris said.

"You must never, under any circumstances, pass through the gates of Thanatos. If any of you who are of the sword shall, of your free will, enter through the gates of that wicked city, you forfeit the pact, and my sword will no longer protect you. All who lay their hands to the sword are mine, but all who enter into the gates of Thanatos— they belong to Samhain. They are his to toy with, his to test, his to torture, his to destroy. This is the Law of Choices. It was written on the foundations of the city before the first brick was laid. Do you understand this?"

"Yeah," Lance said. "I understand."

"Very well then," Ambrose said. "Approach and kneel on one knee."

"Yes, sir."

"Lance Richards, I declare you to be a knight in the kingdom of the New Camelot." Ambrose touched the sword to each of Lance's shoulders and to the crown on his head.

"Who else will take the oath?"

Arthur, Angie, Stacy, and Mr. Lucas stepped forward. Ambrose took each of them through the ceremony as he had Lance. Chris stood and watched.

"Now, Christopher Castle," Ambrose said. "Will you take the oath also?"

Chris hesitated.

"Well," he said. "Okay. I guess."

"You must be certain about this."

"I'm...," Chris began. "Okay. Fine. I'm certain."

"Approach, then," Ambrose said. "Kneel as you saw your friends do." Chris stepped forward and dropped down onto one knee.

"Christopher Castle," Ambrose said. "I declare that you are a knight in the kingdom of the new Camelot." He completed the ritual. "Sleep, well, everyone."

***

Chris looked around at his friends as they slept around the fire. So naïve. So trusting. He pulled on his shoes, stood, and pulled his coat around his shoulders. He crept around the others and started outside.

"Where are you going?" Amos asked. Chris gasped. The big man was standing just outside the door.

Chris swallowed hard. "I have to go to the bathroom."

"You may pass."

"Thanks."

Chris stepped out into the cool night air. He reached beneath his shirt and pulled out a necklace with a glowing Elvish stone affixed to it. Moments later, a cloaked figure emerged from darkness. Chris swallowed hard and took a step back. The figure pushed back his hood, and starlight fell upon his angular features. It was Rael, son of Dran.

12./ Harsh Realities

"I'm going to miss this place," Arthur said as everyone sat around the fire eating breakfast.

The air had a cool, crisp autumn feel to it and the sun was bright. For three days, Arthur, Mr. Lucas, and the others had camped with Ambrose and his men in the village. Dressed in hand-sewn Bre'on garments Prisca had fashioned for them, Arthur and the others from Earth looked like typical New Logres villagers. And they had had fun. With a friend they loved, a friend they thought they had lost forever, they had explored tunnels, walked in the forest, and fished in the river. They would miss the village, but leaving didn't make them sad. They would be leaving with Stacy.

They spent the morning tidying up. Ambrose let the offworlders clean up while his men took turns harnessing and saddling up the horses. One of the empty rooms had a basin, and they had set it aside as the scrub room. Perhaps that was what Elvish had used it for also. Bathers took turns rubbing themselves with soap that felt like sandstone, toweling off, and drying themselves on blankets. Sharpened blades functioned as razors. Clothes were soaped down and rinsed in the river and dried out on rocks.

The frontier life took getting used to, especially for Angie and Stacy. There was no shampoo and there were no hair rollers. Angie's naturally wavy hair didn't take as much styling as other hairstyles might, but she still spent a long time in the makeshift bathroom.

"Why does it take girls so long to get ready?" Lance asked her.

"We have to slow down for the curves," Angie said.

Chris snorted. "Shouldn't take you long, then."

Arthur saw the stricken look on her face. "He was joking, Angie. You look great."

"Stacy looks great," Angie said. "I look like a twelve-year-old boy."

"You have an athletic figure," Arthur said.

"Yeah," Lance said. "Like one of those little gymnasts."

"Don't dig yourself in any deeper," Chris said.

"Oh, be quiet." Lance frowned. "You're the one that hurt her feelings."

At mid-morning, Ambrose and his men mounted their horses. Mr. Lucas and his young neighbors climbed into the carriage. Mr. Lucas slapped the reins on the backs of his stallions. They started walking, their hooves making their now-familiar clippety-clop sounds on the brick street beneath. The carriage and horses rolled among empty buildings that seemed like friends. The road out of the village looked different by day. The outer edges of the village were grown up with young trees and tall grass that had hidden many of the buildings in the dark of the night when the group had first come to town. The buildings grew more and more sparse as the carriage and horses wound down the snaking mountain road. Tall trees crowded the edges of the road in places, and ruined bricks cracked under carriage wheels. Arthur thought the bouncing of the carriage would rattle his teeth out.

Ambrose gave orders to stop for lunch at mid-afternoon. Mr. Lucas pulled his carriage over at a wide spot in the trail. The place, though grown up with tall, pale yellow grass, had the look of a picnic ground. It had tall, well-spaced trees and there was a stone table big enough for the entire group to sit around. Marcos and Ambrose prepared a quick lunch.

After everyone had eaten, Ambrose thought it would be a good idea for all of them to walk around a little while before riding another few hours. The walking felt good. There were birds singing in the trees overhead. Angie and Stacy found a wide creek a few meters from the table. The water was brown and lazy. Stacy tossed a dried leaf into it and the leaf slowly and drunkenly pinwheeled away.

***

As the day wore on, the sky darkened and rain began to fall. The afternoon shower lasted about fifteen minutes, but the sky stayed gray. The air smelled sweetly of ozone. The horses plodded along through mud puddles and the carriage rolled. The little caravan crossed a bridge over a clear, gurgling stream. It passed ruined Elvish houses and statues that hid themselves in tall grass and young trees and vines. Brick streets still cracked beneath carriage wheels and, ever so often, a sapling tree would rake the underside of the carriage. The horses left Elven country and came back to forgotten trails made by Bre'on humans. The first ones were overgrown with grass and some were muddy. Others had clear wagon ruts and had the appearance of having been used more recently. The group crossed the Emerald River at dusk. After that, most of the trails they took were well traveled.

"We are just outside the village now," Ambrose said. "We will seek a night's lodging soon."

A few minutes passed. Then, through the dark forest, came a sound of shouting like people at a sports event.

"What's going on here?" Arthur asked.

"Madness," Ambrose Pendragon said.

No one asked Ambrose what he meant. They just rode in the gray of early twilight. The only sounds to be heard were those made by horses' hooves, carriage wheels, night insects, and whatever wild revelry was going on up ahead.

Ambrose Pendragon rode beside Mr. Lucas's carriage and his men rode ahead as they all emerged from the forest into the clearing where the village was. The huts that ran along the road were dark, but a great bonfire burned in an unplowed field. It threw flickering flashes of orange light over a crowd of people. It seemed that every person in the village and all the woods dwellers round about had gathered there.

Ambrose and his men on horseback rode alongside Mr. Lucas's carriage as they drew closer to the crowd.

"SAM-HAIN, SAM-HAIN, SAM-HAIN," the crowd began to chant. Arthur looked at Ambrose and shuddered. He had never seen a human face twisted with such fury and sadness.

Arthur peered through the crowd. The people were

gathered around something. It was a pile of wood and rocks. A man stood atop the pile. He wore a long robe and a cowl over his head. The cowl was like a black bag with eyeholes cut into it.

"SAM-HAIN, SAM-HAIN, SAM-HAIN," the crowd yelled.

The man drew out a knife. He held it against the sky. The bonfire behind him glowed wickedly around his shape.

"SAM-HAIN! SAM-HAIN! SAM-HAIN!"

"Hah!" someone yelled. A rangy figure on a runaway horse thundered through the crowd. People cried out, jumped out of the way. The horse sprang into the air, jumped over a heap of huddled bodies, and landed beside the pile of wood and rocks.

Arthur was aghast when he saw Ambrose Pendragon swing from the back of his horse onto the altar and put his sword to the robed man's throat. The robed man dropped his meager knife at Ambrose's feet, and the crowd went silent.

"Look," Mr. Lucas said. "On the altar."

As Arthur stood up in his seat for a clearer view, he suddenly understood Ambrose Pendragon's anger. A child lay on the altar. She was small and blonde and was probably about eight years old. The villagers had dressed her in a white robe, a sacrificial gown, and heaped wildflowers around her in preparation for her sacrifice.

The crowd and the hooded man stood frozen in the glare of the vagabond king. Ambrose glanced down at the child in white who lay tied on an altar. Her gown was smeared with the blood of others he had been too late to save. She was unconscious, probably drugged, but at least she was not afraid. Arthur realized, as Ambrose must have, that this was the same child he had picked up and held when he had been in the village three days before.

With a flash of his sword, Ambrose pierced the sacrificer's hood. The man cried out, but the sword had missed him. Ambrose tore the hood from the man's face and hurled it onto the blood-soaked altar. The man stood before Ambrose and trembled in mortal terror, but the look on Ambrose's face had changed. His rage morphed into disbelief and then to profound sadness. Like the child on the altar, the man who stood before him had pale blond hair, golden skin, and slightly Elvish facial features. The child bound at his feet was his own daughter.

Ambrose pointed toward the forest.

"Go."

The man didn't move.

"GO!" Ambrose cried. The man leaped from the altar, hit the ground running, and fled into the forest. Ambrose faced the crowd. They knew who he was. They had seen what he could do.

"What madness has taken you that you would do these things?"

No one dared to reply.

"Go home," the Pendragon told them. "There will be no more killing tonight."

Ambrose knelt down in the blood on the altar and carefully cut the ropes that bound the little girl. Then he took the child in his arms and walked over to the edge of the altar. A woman stood there sobbing.

"Is this your child?" Ambrose asked.

The woman nodded. Tears rolled down her face.

"Then take her," Ambrose handed the sleeping child over to her mother. "And do not ever allow anything like this to happen again."

Mr. Lucas had stopped the carriage. Arthur, Angie, Lance, and Stacy climbed off. Chris and Mr. Lucas stayed put. Amos and Marcos had climbed off their horses. Some of the villagers still wandered around in the darkness.

"Come," Ambrose told his traveling companions. "It has been a long day."

Arthur had thought maybe Ambrose would direct the group back to Malua's place, but he didn't. Instead, he led them down a long, twisting path through the graveyard. The stones glowed in the moonlight. The path ended in a gate. Ambrose climbed down from his horse and opened it.

The others rode through. Ambrose closed the gate behind him but was soon back on his horse and in the lead again.

They rode through a dense forest. Finally there was a twist in the path. The horses and the carriage emerged in a dark clearing. A big, boxlike building cast a square, hulking shadow in the starlight. An iron brazier stood on a pole beside the path. In the blue gloom, Ambrose drew his sword from his belt and aimed it at the brazier. Fire leaped up in it.

"What do we do now?" Chris asked.

"We wait," Ambrose said.

After a few seconds, they heard the sound of a bolt being drawn back. The building's heavy door creaked inward. A wedge of soft blue light fell upon the stones in front of the door. It widened as the door opened. In the door was a tiny woman in an ornate robe. Her reddish hair was swept back from a finely sculptured face. Her eyes were tilted on the ends and there was something alien in the sweep of her facial bones.

Amos went to the door. The woman threw her arms around him. Her hands were not visible, but the sleeves of her robe were long and fanlike, and they moved as though they were alive.

"She has wings," Angie whispered. "She's a Seraf."

"Karissa is only half Seraf," Marcos told her. "Her wings did not fully develop. She is flightless."

"Who is she?" Arthur asked.

"This is Karissa," Ambrose announced. "She is the keeper of this place. She is also Amos's wife."

13. /Amos' Story

"Talk about opposites attracting," Lance whispered as he watched the hulking Amos standing beside his small, birdlike wife.

"His stable is back here," Ambrose said.

Once the horses were unhitched, unsaddled, and happily munching hay in Amos's stable, Ambrose and Marcos led the others around the front of the building. There were stairs there and double doors. A spire rose from the peak of the roof.

"This is a church!" Lance said.

"Once," Ambrose said. "It has long been abandoned. Amos and Karissa live on the grounds and maintain it."

Amos rejoined the group.

"Where is Karissa?" Ambrose asked.

"She will join us shortly," Amos said. "She insists on cooking for us."

The big man opened one of the front doors and stood beside it as Ambrose, holding up his lantern, led the others inside. A big, empty chamber awaited them.

"Most of the furniture here was smashed by Samhain's army before they barred all chapels from those who would worship. Amos has salvaged enough wood to make the table and benches there ahead of us."

The lantern's light glowed across what looked like a long, sturdy wooden picnic table. It sat by itself in the middle of a big, empty room. The floor was made of chiseled stone. The ceiling was a maze of heavy timbers that hung far overhead.

Ambrose set his lantern on the table. The front doors opened. Amos stepped into the room, a frame of starlight around his massive, dark silhouette. He was carrying a flat, metal tray of bread, cheese, and fruits. His tiny wife carried a second tray. On this tray were a pitcher and some metal goblets.

"Thank you, Amos," Ambrose told his host. He walked

over beside the young woman and turned to Arthur and the others. "Come in, Karissa. I'm glad you finally joined us."

"The meal is hastily prepared, my lord," Karissa said. "If I had known you were coming, I would have prepared better."

"Anything you have prepared is an honor to us," Ambrose said.

"You honor us with your presence, Ambrose."

Amos and Karissa set the trays down on the wooden table. Ambrose took Karissa by the shoulders and kissed her on the cheek.

"I've missed you, Karissa," he said. He turned to the others. "Karissa has been a friend of Camelot since the day I received the sword and heard the calling of my ancestors."

"If not for her, I would still be riding with Samhain," Amos said.

"Please," Karissa said. "Let's just eat."

Food was passed around and everyone sat in the blue near-darkness and ate. Very little was said for several minutes.

"So," Angie said. "How did you two meet?"

Amos and Karissa looked at each other.

"It is a long story," Amos said. "The village where my brother and I grew up was destroyed."

"Steel-Hearts?" Arthur asked.

"No," Amos said. "The raiders were human: pitiful, lawless creatures who traveled around the countryside preying on the weak and unprotected. They raided our village, killed my parents, grandparents, and cousins. I swore that I would avenge them all, but I never got the chance.

"A short time later, those raiders were foolish enough to ambush a party of Steel-Hearts."

"What happened?" Lance asked.

"The Steel-Hearts slew them without hesitation or mercy. When I learned of it, I wanted to become one of them. I admired their strength. Even more than that, perhaps, I coveted their total lack of emotion. Their hearts were steel, and their silver eyes wept no tears. Intent on joining them, I journeyed to Thanatos and swore my loyalty to Samhain. Within months, I had been reborn. My heart of flesh was cut out and replaced with a steel pump. My muscles were augmented with implants, and the humours of my body were replaced with chemicals brewed by Samhain's alchemists.

"My brother chose a different path. He joined the people of the library and became a scholar. For a long time, I did not see him. I did not want to. Human attachments led to vulnerability. One day my regiment was ordered to attack the library. When I saw that my brother was among those to be executed, my soul was stirred within me. I struck down as many Steel-Hearts as I could and hid my brother from them. The vengeance of my former comrades was fierce. When they left, they believed they had slain me. When the survivors saw that a spark of life remained within me, they discussed among themselves whether they should help me or extinguish me. Among those survivors was a young woman, half Bre'on and half Seraf. She was known to be both wise and kind, and, in the end, it was her voice that prevailed. At Karissa's insistence, the scholars drew upon the wisdom of the Worldsmen to save my life and restore as much of my humanity as they might. When she learned of Ambrose Pendragon and swore her allegiance to him, I trusted in the wisdom that had spared my life and swore my allegiance to him as well."

"It is a good story, my brother," Marcos said.

"Yes," Ambrose said, "but there is more I must tell you before we sleep tonight. Our time is limited." His face shone grimly in the blue glow of his lantern. "Do you remember when I told you Samhain would have you killed if he realized who you were?"

"I think I remember something about it," Arthur said. "It was just after we got here."

"Yeah," Lance said. "It was over at Aquila's place. You said we were some kind of danger to his power or something like that."

"Yes," Ambrose said. "You are a tremendous threat to him."

"How?" Stacy asked.

"Because you are from the Land of the Fathers, the world with twenty-four-hour days, one moon, and four seasons in its year. You come from the world of King Arthur."

"What's so threatening about that?" Chris asked.

Marcos looked like he was ready to jump up and down with excitement.

"You are a threat," Ambrose said, "because the seers and wise men of the Bre'on race prophesied long ago that others would come, as my ancestors did, from the Land of the Fathers. It was foretold to them that these others would be young, even as Arthur Pendragon was young when he drew out the sword and took his throne. It was also predicted that these young ones from the World of the Fathers would herald a great age of upheaval, of the restoring of things to their proper order. It is this that Samhain fears."

"Well, I don't think he has much to fear from us," Chris snorted.

"You are wrong, Chris Castle," Ambrose said. "You are a much greater danger to him than you can possibly imagine."

Ambrose took a bite of bread, chewed it, and washed it down with water.

"Samhain has convinced many of the people that all the stories of your world, of King Arthur, and of the God of my ancestors are no more than empty lies dreamed up for the amusement of children. He claims that the Bre'on are of this world and that there are no other worlds.

"But you...," Ambrose pointed to Arthur, to Lance, to Stacy, to Chris, and to Mr. Lucas. "You are living proof that the World of the Fathers exists."

"But will anybody believe it?" Chris said.

"Many will not," Ambrose said. "But wisdom vindicates her children and truth burns pure when placed in a furnace with lies."

"Wonderful," Chris said. "Now he's quoting fortune cookies."

"Chris!" Stacy said.

"Those who have been loyal to me will accept the truth from you," Ambrose said. "I have told Amos and Marcos, Aquila and Prisca and Malua who you are and they have accepted it."

Amos and Marcos nodded.

"Tomorrow I will go and speak to people in the village," Ambrose said. "Some of them will join us. Many will not. For those who do join us, I will appoint a special place and a special time where all who serve the Pendragon may meet and be made strong. I will not be there to lead you to that place."

"Why?" Lance asked. "Where are you going?"

"You will have your answers at the hour you need them," Ambrose said. "Not before."

"Typical," Chris mumbled.

The meeting broke up. Ambrose took the Elvish lantern he had taken from the table and walked over to the outside door. He held the lantern up as Arthur and the others filed out of the building into the cool darkness of night. The forest, deep and black, looked peaceful. The sky overhead was gray-black with only a sprinkling of stars to light the night.

Blankets were taken out of Mr. Lucas' carriage. Amos and Karissa pulled other blankets out of trunks. Arthur, Chris, and Lance laid blankets on a stone floor and spent the night in the library of the church. Old books and scrolls stood against walls all around them. A fire burned behind a grate.

Chris didn't go to sleep for a long time. When he finally was able to drift off into a light slumber, he had a nightmare. In the dream, he was lying in bed in a dark room when he saw two red lights—eyes—moving toward him. The two eyes kept drifting closer as he lay under his covers, too afraid to move. Finally Chris could make out the shape of a face—Stacy's face—and the cold glint of a silver knife. Gasping for breath, he woke up. The others slept on.

14. /By Steel Boots Trampled

The next morning's breakfast looked normal enough. The white cream in the goblets was very likely milk but, in a world like this one, it could just as easily have been the milk of a dragon as the milk of a cow. The white, spongy thing was certainly a slice of bread, but was the yellow jelly smeared on it honey or was it something else?

Arthur and his friends didn't bother with questions when Amos woke them and led them to the big empty chamber, to the wooden table where they had met the night before. They just followed the hulking cyborg to a table already loaded with food.

Arthur and the group found only Mr. Lucas waiting for them in the big, empty chapel. Ambrose, Amos, and Marcos were nowhere to be seen.

"Where's Ambrose?" Stacy asked.

"Ambrose is in the village," Mr. Lucas said. "He and Marcos and Amos rose quite early and rode into town hoping to catch workers on the way to their orchards."

"Rush hour traffic, huh?" Arthur smiled crookedly.

"When's Ambrose coming back?" Angie asked.

"He thought he would be back sometime this afternoon," Mr. Lucas said. "But he wasn't sure of it."

The young people found places on the benches that ran on either side of the wooden table. Mr. Lucas was seated on a stool at one end of the table. The chapel looked different in the light of morning. Wooden shutters had been thrown back, and the doors were open so the sun could shine in and the fragrance of the morning could drift in on the wind. The high ceiling, with its maze of wooden beams, didn't look as mysterious in the light of morning as it had the night before. The morning light also showed the scars. There were shattered bricks, black patches, and melted spots on the walls where religious artifacts had been destroyed. The Steel-Hearts had torn every symbol of holiness and goodness from the sanctuary room. Only wood and stone remained.

After they had eaten breakfast and helped Karissa scrub the dishes, Arthur, Lance, and Stacy, and the others wandered around the field that surrounded the church. It was a field of tall, green grass and flowers. In the edge of the forest that stood just beyond the clearing, Chris found a green, mossy spring that gurgled up out of a hole in the ground. The spring cut a clear, snaking creek through the straw-covered floor of a needle-leaf forest. Amos led his young friends to a small, round pond that lay a few meters from his house. He caught some fish by using a lightweight harpoon to spear them. Karissa soaked the fish in wine, rolled them in meal, and fried them with spices and diced hot peppers. They smelled great and tasted even better.

Ambrose had told Amos not to wait for him, but to go ahead and eat lunch when he felt like it. So Amos, Karissa, Mr. Lucas, and the young people were already sitting in the sanctuary room around a table full of food when Ambrose and Marcos walked in.

"How'd it go?" Arthur asked. He could tell by the expression on Ambrose's face that things had not gone well.

"Most of them had hardened their hearts and would not hear me," Ambrose said. "They would rather sacrifice their little sons and daughters to daemons than side with me and risk angering Samhain." He paused. He looked around the table at Arthur, at Chris, at Angie, and at the others.

"Last night most of you made a pact with me. That pact had a single condition. What was it?"

"Don't go into the city of Zandos," Lance said.

"Thanatos," Angie corrected.

"You are right," Ambrose said. "And what will happen if you should enter through the gates of Thanatos?"

"Your sword can't protect us," Arthur said.

"Good," Ambrose said. "You must never forget this."

Ambrose, Amos, and Marcos rode back into town after lunch. At mid-afternoon, Arthur, Stacy, Lance, and the others got bored.

"Let's go to the village," Stacy said. "I want to go hear

Ambrose."

"I was just about to suggest that," Arthur said.

"Sure you were," Lance ribbed.

The group helped Mr. Lucas harness up his horses and climbed into the carriage. Mr. Lucas slapped the reins on the backs of his horses.

***

"...And your loyalty is tested at times such as this. Though Samhain has kept you, in his wickedness, from worship in churches, there is no law that prevents you from worshipping in secret places and in your own hearts. The day will come when you must bring your faith before his eyes and risk the edge of the sword."

Ambrose was standing on the rickety porch of the village's trading post. Fifteen or sixteen people were standing around him when Mr. Lucas and Arthur and the others climbed out of the carriage and, quietly as they could, made their way to where their friend spoke. Amos and Marcos stood toward the back of the crowd. Marcos raised his hand in greeting as the teacher and his young neighbors stepped up.

Grumbling came from the crowd, some question about the laws Samhain had set up.

"You will obey those laws which do not transgress the laws of the Father Above which have been revealed to the hearts of men since the beginning. You will pay taxes. You will go to the places where you are allowed to go, and you will stay away from those places where you are not allowed to go. These laws you will obey.

"However, you must not blaspheme or honor the rites of daemons, nor must you bow before Samhain, nor may you commit immoral acts in temples. You know the acts I speak of, for many of you have done them. You must not sacrifice your children nor your brothers, sisters, nor parents to Samhain nor to his gods. These laws you will not obey, for they are laws against the mouth of the Father. You have always known this."

The crowd grumbled. Samhain's name was mentioned.

"That day is not yet come," Ambrose said. "The day of

Samhain's fall will come soon enough, but it is in days such as these that your loyalty is tested; for all are faithful in times of peace and convenience, but true subjects are shown faithful in the wicked days."

"It is easy for you to speak of these things, Pendragon," a tough, weather-worn man shouted at Ambrose as he shook his finger. "Your powers will protect you, but you get the rest of us killed. May your Creator pity anyone foolish enough to follow you." With these words said, he turned and walked away from the crowd. Eight others followed him.

"He has said that it is easy for one with powers such as mine to talk of surrender," Ambrose said. "Yet there will come a time when even I must lay down my sword and be led away captive, and you will be left to decide which future you shall have."

Ambrose spoke to the seven villagers who stayed behind. Among them were Ginna and Ioan, the same young couple who had stayed before; Aurelia, three middle-aged men, an old woman, and a girl about thirteen years old. Ambrose talked with them for nearly an hour. He didn't sound at all like a king lecturing subjects. He was a friend talking to friends.

"The gates of Thanatos lie only a short walk from here," Ambrose said. "You have been forbidden to enter those gates, but seven days from now—the length of one week on the World of the Fathers—just as the sun begins to set, all of you and others who hate the evil of Samhain and support me will gather before those gates and pronounce the end of Samhain's reign."

"Are you trying to get us all killed, my lord?" Ioan asked.

"If our ruler asks us to die," his wife Ginna said, "then that is what we must do."

"You will not die," Ambrose said. "Not on that day. Not if you remain true. But you must gather at those gates no matter what shall arise between that time and this."

"We will be there," Ioan said.

***

The sun was starting to set. It was an orange ball hanging over the horizon. A man came thundering into town on horseback. This was the same middle-aged man who had led so many people away such a short time before.

"Pendragon," he said. "I need to talk to you."

"He doesn't want to talk to you," Marcos said.

"Please," the man said. "I need your help. My daughter...."

"You didn't trust me before," Ambrose said. "Why do you come to me now?"

"Please," the man cried out. "I need you." Tears spilled from his eyes. He dug into his face with his fingers.

"I will go," Ambrose said.

"I'm going with you," Marcos said. "I don't trust him."

"I don't either," Amos said.

They ran to their horses.

Arthur looked at the weathered man on the horse. For a split second, he thought he saw a horrible smile crawl across his face. Then the look was gone. Ambrose, Amos, and Marcos followed him as he rode away.

Just as the sounds of their horses' hooves had faded, two hulking Steel-Hearts stepped out from behind the trading post.

"RUN!" Arthur yelled. He shot toward Mr. Lucas's carriage. Three more cyborgs stepped from between two buildings. Everyone in the street had scattered. Arthur was cut off from the carriage. He turned around to run. Chris slammed into him. Both boys tumbled into the dirt.

People were screaming and running. Lance counted nine bionic stormtroopers. Then another one appeared. Then three more. Then two more. A metal spine whistled toward Lance. He ducked.

"Ahh!" Stacy fell, a heavy needle buried in her back.

Mr. Lucas grabbed a shovel and smashed one of the storm troopers across the face. It didn't even react. Then two needles hit the teacher in the back. He fell to the ground.

Lance gathered Stacy into his arms, tried to pick her up.

An armored leg kicked his feet out from under him. He almost fell on Stacy, but managed to catch himself on a knee and dodge a kick aimed at his face. Then a needle buried itself in his shoulder. Lance passed out.

Arthur made a flying leap, grabbed the roof of the trading post's porch, and swung up onto it. A bionic arm knocked a roof support in half. The roof fell and Arthur rolled off into the dirt. He rose to his feet. A needle cut across his back, sliced through the shirt. He felt a burning in his veins and a deadness. His legs fell out from under him. Arthur dropped to the ground and lay paralyzed. He tasted sand. It ground against his teeth, but he couldn't spit it out. His mouth was going numb. He saw metal feet closing on him. Suddenly an explosion showered him with dirt and left his ears ringing. A second blast hit as his consciousness faded.

15. /The Bargain

"Arthur! Arthur, are you all right? Arthur!"

The voice belonged to Chris. Arthur felt hands digging into his shoulders, shaking him. He forced his eyes open. Needles of light burned them, and he squeezed them shut again.

"Arthur?"

"Be...all right in a minute," Arthur whispered, and he hoped it was true. He shielded his eyes with his hand and opened them slowly. Chris was standing over him. Angie was kneeling beside him. She was silently crying.

"Where are we?"

"The village," Chris said. "We were attacked. Don't you remember?"

"The Steel-Hearts," Arthur said. "Ambrose?"

"He's not back yet," Chris said.

Arthur squinted at the sky. The sun was still halfway over the horizon. Arthur realized he hadn't been out for more than a few minutes. He rolled over onto an elbow and looked around.

"He's all right," Chris told someone.

Lance was standing and talking to some other people. One of them was a young man with blond hair, a v-shaped face, and body armor. It was Rael, the angry young man they had seen in the abandoned Elvish village. Arthur didn't recognize the others with him. He just knew he didn't like their looks.

The most striking member of Rael's motley group was a tall bird-man, one of the Seraf. He had wings instead of arms and fine down instead of hair. Even his eyebrows were bushy down feathers. A tall and rather masculine-looking girl stood beside the bird-man. Her hair was close cropped and cut at jagged angles. A boy with shaved head and a ponytail over his right ear, a black-haired youth with a baby face, and a girl with flaming red hair and a headband completed the group.

Rael, the red-haired girl, and the bird-man held smoking metal tubes—weapons of some sort—in their hands. Five rotohorses lay on the ground behind them.

"They saved us, Arthur," Chris said. "They've got weapons. They killed some of the Steel-Hearts."

"Are you all right, Arthur?" Angie asked. She gently brushed some of the dust out of his hair and off his back.

"I think I'm okay," Arthur said. He rolled slowly to his feet and felt a little dizzy. He looked around and saw black powder marks on the ground and raw gashes in the earth. A dead storm trooper lay a few meters away. With its armor torn open, it looked like a turtle that had been run over by a car. Arthur felt his stomach flop. Two other storm troopers lay a few feet away. The things were hideous, but he still felt sorry for them.

The village streets, now littered with broken wood, blood, and bodies, were mostly abandoned. Several dead bodies lay on the ground, but coats and blankets covered most of them. A few weeping villagers were dragging away their dead.

Arthur spun around and noticed Mr. Lucas lying flat on his back on a piece of rough cloth. He was only a few feet from where Arthur had been lying. The teacher's eyes were closed. His face looked pinched.

"What's wrong with him?" Arthur demanded.

"He must've got a stronger dose of that poison than the rest of us," Lance said. "They got him with two needles instead o' one."

"They will recover," Rael said. Even with the translation spell in force, he still had an odd, lilting accent.

"Rael?" Arthur asked. Chris nodded.

Arthur massaged his head and found his hair full of dirt from his fall. He didn't care much. He just wanted to lie down. His head hurt. He felt dizzy. Then he realized he hadn't seen Stacy.

"Where's Stacy?"

Nobody answered.

"WHERE'S STACY?" Arthur grabbed Chris by the shirt.

"They...took her," Chris said.

"Took her where?"

"We were too late to stop them," Rael said.

"Where is she?"

"Thanatos."

"Why would they take her and not us?"

"I don't know," Lance said, "but we've been talking about how we might be able to get her out. Rael's got a map of the whole city's layout." Arthur noticed that the tall, short-haired girl was holding out a sheet of parchment with a design etched on it.

"The Steel-Hearts captured one of Rael's friends, too," Chris explained. Rael thinks maybe we can rescue both Stacy and his friend before the sun goes down."

"We don't have much time," Rael tossed his head toward the horizon. "Nightfall is coming."

"Rael says Samhain's curse only takes effect if we get caught in the city after dark," Lance said.

"That's not what Ambrose told us," Arthur said.

"Ambrose is gone," Chris said. "Lord knows when he'll be back. And his magic sword doesn't seem to have done us much good anyway."

"We're not dead," Arthur said. He massaged his aching head. *No, we're not dead. We just feel that way.*

"The sun ain't down yet," Lance said. "And Samhain don't usually show his face in the daytime. And it's always at night that they put people on the island. Now if we can ride in, get Stacy, and ride out without Samhain's people catching us, we'll be all right."

"Sounds like suicide," Arthur said. "You saw what just a few of his cyborgs did to us."

"But Rael and them have those guns," Lance said. "We can do it, man!"

"Your friend will be here," Rael said. He traced his hand along the etching of Thanatos. He dragged his index finger through the front gate, down a side alley, up a street, through another alley, and into the heart of town. "This is where he executes his prisoners. There are cages in the maze beneath the platform. Will you go with us?"

Arthur and the others looked at each other.

"Arthur's right," Angie said. "It's risky. And Ambrose didn't say anything about nightfall."

"It's the only chance we've got," Lance said. "Do you want to lose Stacy again?"

Rael and the redhead climbed onto a rotohorse. The others—the bird-man, the bald man, the tall girl, and the baby-face—sprang to their own mounts and brought them to roaring life. Rael motioned to Arthur and the others.

"Let's go," Chris said.

Lance climbed onto the back of the rotohorse driven by the bald man with the ponytail. "Come on!" he yelled.

Chris climbed on with the baby-faced, black-haired boy. Angie climbed on with the red-haired girl. Arthur didn't move.

"Are you coming?" Chris said angrily.

Arthur hesitated before climbing onto the back of the bird-man's rotohorse. "I'll go," he said, "but this is all wrong. You've treated Stacy like dirt ever since she came back. I can't believe you're so hot on rescuing her now. What's really going on here?"

"I don't have to explain myself to you," Chris said as the red-haired girl pinched down on some kind of control lever. The roto bearing Rael, son of Dran, shot out ahead of the others. It threw up dust and rocketed down the road that led out of the village. One by one the other rotos followed. The roto driven by the bird-man was the last to pull out. Arthur grabbed the saddle beneath him as the machine jerked forward. He clung for white-knuckled life to the seat of the bird-man's roto. If he let go, Arthur knew he would fly off the machine and his head would splatter against the ground like a melon dropped off a truck.

Arthur felt sick and miserable. He was groggy from the Steel-Heart's drugged dart, sickened by the speed of the bird-man's roto, and disgusted with himself for not standing up to Chris. When had his friend become an antagonist? Arthur wondered if he had ever really known Chris at all.

Rael's rotohorse led the others through a forest trail, past the ancient graveyard that lay near the village, past the trail that led to Malua's cabin, past the point where Mr. Lucas's carriage had first brought Arthur and his friends to the strange and dangerous new world. The rotohorses plummeted at breakneck speed into the darkening forest. After five minutes spent negotiating hairpin turns, they emerged on the bank of a vast lake—flat and mirror-like— that spread itself nearly to the horizon. Sidelong rays of orange sunlight danced evilly against the deceptively calm waters. Arthur had seen the lake before, yet he scarcely recognized it. A single rocky isle broke the watery expanse. This was the Island of A'Vilian, the island where all hope ended. A ferry glided silently across the expanse between the rocky island and the shore ahead of the riders. It was moving toward a flat-topped hill with a city on it: Thanatos, the city of death.

Arthur was forced to remember the dream he had dreamed days ago. Motorcycles and four-wheelers had roared out of the woods, passed a lake, and driven into a big amusement park. The dream had been fun, filled with laughter and good times. Now real life had become a twisted, evil parody of the dream.

The rotos left the road and shot down into a forest trail that twisted to the left, to the right, and to the left again. Finally Rael led the gang, his people and Arthur's, around a blind curve, and Thanatos sprang into full view. Perched on its mound like a dark temple, the city towered over everything. With its high walls and shimmering towers, it looked like a basket of cobras. Nothing living grew within a hundred yards of the mound in any direction. The sides of the hill on which the city sat were completely encased in brick that rose up to merge with the city's high walls. The walls were curved inward and the only breach in them was a front gate with a long, slanted bridge/ramp leading up to it. Arthur looked around for guards but there weren't any. The gates of the village were wide open and completely unguarded. *"Step into my parlor," said the spider to the fly.*

Rael's rotohorse was the first to reach the foot of the ramp. The red-haired girl who was driving pulled the machine to a halt. The bald man and Lance, who were riding double, stopped beside them. The tall girl, riding alone, and Chris and the baby-faced youth, and Arthur and the bird-man sat still on rumbling rotohorses and scanned the city with their eyes.

"No guards," Arthur said. "It's a trap."

"No," Rael said. "It's never guarded. They don't expect us."

Arthur, Baby-Face, Lance, Chris, Bird-Man, and the others all looked at each other.

But all who enter into the gates of Thanatos, they belong to Samhain.

Ambrose's words burned through Arthur's brain.

"If all who enter those gates belong to Samhain," he said, "He wouldn't want to keep anybody out. He'd want them all to come in."

"What?" Lance said. "I can't hear you."

Arthur felt a strange fear wash over him. There was a ringing in his ears and some power seemed to be gripping his throat.

"Samhain wants us to come in," Arthur whispered. He could barely make himself talk. He felt dizzy, like he was going to pass out. What was happening to him?

"What?" Lance yelled. "I can't hear you over the bikes!"

"He wants to own us," Arthur gasped. The others looked back and forth at each other with blank expressions. Arthur knew they could not hear him.

"Come!" Rael yelled.

"No," Arthur said. With one last burst of strength, he shifted his weight and tumbled off the saddle of the bird-man's rotohorse. He hit the ground with bone-jarring impact.

Lance, the bird-man, and some of the others started to jump off their bikes and help him.

"COME!" Rael yelled. He jerked his head toward a sun that sat just on top of the horizon. "There's no time!"

Arthur forced himself to sit up. The others all stared at him.

"I'm not going," Arthur forced himself to say. His voice seemed to get stronger. "It's a trap. I'm not going in there."

"He's chickened out on us," Chris said. "Let's go. We will help Stacy. Arthur's too scared."

"Are you all right, man?" Lance asked.

"Please, Lance," Arthur said. "Don't go in there. It's a trap."

"You may be right," Lance said, "but I can't abandon Stacy. I'll see you when we get back. Pray for us."

Rael's bike sprang out ahead of the others and plowed up the slanted ramp into the city's gates. The female driver's red hair flew behind her like the burning tail of a comet. Rael sat on the back of the rotohorse's saddle and waved the others after him with his left hand.

Four rotohorses growled in protest as they were forced up the ramp. Arthur pushed himself to his feet and watched the thundering machines as they vanished, one by one, into the gaping jaws of Thanatos' only entrance. Part of him wanted to go with them, but he knew in his heart that he had been right not to. Why couldn't they see that?

And why was Chris suddenly so eager to save Stacy? Had Rael promised him something else?

Arthur looked at the sinking sun. The bottom edge of the alien star was sinking into the forest. Arthur fixed his eyes on his digital watch and saw the seconds as they rolled past. Seconds turned to minutes.

"Come on," Arthur whispered to the city gates. The sun was almost down and neither Chris nor Lance nor any of the others had returned from the hilltop city. Arthur was feverish with anxiety and indecision. Should he stay put and wait for his friends? Maybe he should have gone into the city, tried to help them. Or what would happen if he ran back to the village and got help? Maybe Ambrose, Amos, and Marcos had made it back. Mr. Lucas, at least, should be awake.

Arthur paced the packed earth and watched the sun's orange disk as it dipped lower and lower. Finally he made up his mind. He would run back through the forest to the village. It was clearly the only smart thing to do.

Arthur turned back toward the dark forest. He picked up his right foot and broke into a run. The forest trail Rael had led Arthur and his friends in through was narrow and dark. Arthur slowed his pace as he neared the dark path. Weird sounds of night animals were starting to make themselves heard. The trail looked lonely—menacing, even. Arthur tensed his muscles and got ready to run down that trail so fast he would knock a hole through anything that got in his way.

"Arthur!"

Arthur stopped and swung around. His heart pounded. That voice had come from inside the city.

Arthur stood still and listened. The only sounds he could hear were the sounds of night animals and the sound of his own hard breathing. He looked at the sun. A rim of orange clung to the far edge of a gray sky. In only a few minutes that rim would be gone. Arthur stood frozen with indecision. Should he go into the city or shouldn't he? Had he really heard his name called or was it just a noise that sounded like his name?

Just as Arthur had convinced himself that he hadn't really heard his name at all, there was another shout. "Arthur!"

Arthur jumped straight up and spun around again. This time he knew he had heard his name.

He looked at the little edge of sun that hung on the horizon. His brain spun with the burning weight of the choice he had to make.

Arthur held his breath and charged up the ramp that led to Thanatos's gate. His feet pounded against the wooden timbers as he ran. Over the side of the ramp, Arthur watched the ground fall farther and farther away with each step. At last he reached the top of the ramp and bounded into the gates of Thanatos.

All who enter the gates of Thanatos, they belong to Samhain. They are his to toy with, his to test, his to torture,...and his to destroy.

Arthur pushed the face and voice of Ambrose Pendragon out of his mind. He looked around him. He thought at first glance that Thanatos had to be one of the most stunning places he had ever seen. In a quick look around, Arthur took in crystal spires, polished white domes that looked like polished ice, fountains flowing with wine, streets of sparkling silver, towers of gold, statues that seemed to breathe, and arched walkways that wound through the air. Crowds of people walked around like they were in a daze. No one even seemed to notice Arthur.

Arthur scanned the crowd frantically, searching for a face he recognized. He saw men with pointed hats. He saw people who wore purple feathers and big earrings. He saw creatures of indeterminate species and gender.

"Lance!" Arthur yelled.

His voice didn't carry far over the noise the crowd made. But Arthur heard other voices that did carry. They were mechanical voices. He whirled to see two seven-foot Steel-Hearts moving through the crowd toward him.

Arthur turned, cut through a crowd of people, darted into an alley, and ran for his life. He pounded out of the alley, his footfalls echoing behind him, and lost himself in the crowd of people he found there. The crowd was much thicker and Arthur felt like he was drowning in people...and such people. Some of them wore robes and masks. Some had pointed ears. One man had horns. Some were Seraf, bird people like Rael's friend had been. A crowd of them were thickly bearded and fanged. Arthur was shoved past a tank of people who had flesh-colored fish tails instead of legs and gills on their throats. Merfolk. He briefly made eye contact with one of them, a girl a little bit younger than he was. She smiled a sad smile.

The crowd swept Arthur along. He couldn't seem to plow through the mass of bodies. If he stopped moving, he knew he would be trampled. The crowd was full of the smells of soured sweat and perfume.

Finally, the river of people thinned, spreading out as they reached a stone amphitheater that had been hewn out of the hill Thanatos had been built on. A raised platform stood in the middle of the bowl. Arthur could just make it out over the heads of the people. Some kind of ceremony was going on. Scantily-clad dancers moved with savage grace as a macabre orchestra forced alien music from strangely-shaped instruments. They blew on pipes, plucked strings, and pounded on the tight faces of their drums.

"I'll never find the others in this place," Arthur thought to himself. He started to leave, but his eyes were drawn to one the dancers.

"Angie?" he gasped. The girl on stage certainly looked like Angie, but the hairstyle and make-up made it hard to be certain. She was covered with tattoos and there were jewels glued to her bare skin. Her figure was still slim, but it had a roundness it had not had before. The body was that of an adult woman. It could not be Angie...or could it? The resemblance was strong, and Arthur was both horrified and attracted by what he saw.

He had to get a closer look at her. He had to see if it was really Angie he was seeing. His legs carried him down into the amphitheater bowl seemingly of their own will. Arthur moved through the crowd, hardly noticing that the mob opened up before him. He got closer and closer to the center of the amphitheater bowl, closer and closer to the stage. Sweat clung to his body. He had to see more. The girl's illustrated body gyrated. Her hips shook. The jewel in her navel vibrated hypnotically from side to side. Her bare arms clutched at the sky. The women cast aside their veils, showed more and more skin. Closer. Closer.

The sky had turned dark. Only the last rays of dusk hung over the horizon. Lights were shining in the city of Thanatos. Elvish lamps glowed all around the amphitheater.

Arthur lumbered closer and closer to the raised platform where Angie's double was dancing with the others, to those perfect bodies writhing in painful grace. His heart was pounding in rhythm with the drums of the musicians.

A wind swept over Arthur's sweaty form, and he realized night had fallen. He had to get closer to the stage. What was it about nightfall he was supposed to remember?

Arthur moved closer and closer. People were obviously

moving away and letting him by. All of the women on the stage were looking right at him. The one who looked like Angie was standing still. The others were motioning toward him. Arthur sprang up onto the platform with them. Voices howled all around him.

Then everything stopped. Arthur felt as though he had suddenly been jolted awake. His mind cleared. He was still standing on a platform with a crowd around him. Angie—strangely transformed—was still there but the other dancers were gone. There were no musicians. In their place were Chris, Lance, the bird-man, the redhead, the bald man, the tall girl, the baby-faced youth, and a bruised and battered Rael. All of them were standing at frozen attention with their feet planted and their hands at their sides. Stacy was not with them.

Arthur tried to look behind him. His head wouldn't turn. He couldn't look up either. He tried to turn around, but his feet were held by the gravity of a thousand planets. He tried to say something, but his vocal cords were gone. Something held his hands in place, too.

Then someone stepped out of the crowd behind Arthur and sprang up onto the platform. It was a blond man with an Elvish, V-shaped face, and body armor. *It was Rael, son of Dran.*

There with the others was a second Rael, the battered, bloody Rael he had seen earlier. There were two of them. Then the awful truth ripped through Arthur like a bullet: The Rael who had led them into Thanatos was an imposter—probably Samhain's shape-changing henchman. They had been tricked.

The blond man's face melted and hair sprang up all over his body. It was the werewolf, the one they had met that first night. The creature pulled out a long, curved horn made of bone and blew into it. As the eerie sound echoed over the arena, the curtains at the back of the platform opened, and a gigantic figure bounded into view. His skin looked blackened and mummified. His head was bald, and his eyes were glowing, burning lights. His body was encased in something that looked like liquid gold and one of his hands was missing.

"Sam-hain," the crowd began to chant. "Samhain. Samhain. SAMHAIN. SAMHAIN. SAMHAIN. SAMHAIN. SAMHAIN. SAMHAIN."

Arthur could hear his heart beating in his hollow ears as the chanting grew louder and louder.

"We meet at last," Samhain croaked. He gestured toward his henchman. The werewolf raised his arms. His body melted into green slime. Part of it oozed off into the floor and puddled up. Then the slime took shape and hardened. A giant, green snake was coiled up where the shape-shifter had stood. Its ugly head—its lidless eyes and smiling, lipless mouth—was raised about six feet from the stone floor of the platform. It swung toward Arthur and stopped a few inches from his face. Arthur fought down terror as his breathing tore at his throat. He tried to pull away, tried to close his eyes, and tried to scream. It was all to no avail. All he could do was stand frozen to the floor and wheeze.

"Come," Samhain said.

A thing in a ragged robe drifted onto the platform like so much fog. It held an executioner's axe in skeleton's hands.

"You choose," Samhain said. "Worship me, and you will die easily. Dishonor me, and you will visit my island."

Three rotting succubi, female demons with long hair and corpse faces, crawled out of the crowd and stood on the platform with Samhain and his henchmen. Red Elvish lamps glowed behind them.

Samhain grabbed some dust from the executioner's rotting robe and tossed it to the floor of the platform. The dust moved as it changed into spiders and scorpions. As the first ones spread across the platform, more and more of them grew from the dust. Arthur saw them crawling up Angie's bare legs, crawling on the feet of his brothers and comrades. He felt something on his shoe and fought to look down. His neck wouldn't bend. He felt something tickling his socks. He heard Lance half-scream. Lance, he knew, would be screaming his throat raw if he could, but all he could do was moan and whine like someone trapped in a nightmare.

A succubus crawled toward Arthur on its hands and knees. Its rotting face was covered with warts and holes where bones showed through dried, leathery skin. It grinned at Arthur with yellow, decaying teeth. Arthur's heart pounded in his chest. He was gasping in pure terror, praying for an end to the nightmare.

Spiders crawled on Chris's arms as he wheezed and cried and moaned and tried and tried to move. Angie moaned through closed lips. Tears poured from her eyes. Arthur could tell by the spasms shaking her body that she was trying to move, trying to shake the spiders and scorpions away, but she had no control over her muscles.

The shape shifter still held the form of a huge, green python. It slid around the platform. He moved behind Arthur. Arthur felt the hair on the back of his neck stand up. The head of a snake—a head fully the size of a dog—dropped onto his shoulder and looked into his right eye.

Spiders clung to Angie's hair and face and chest.

Rael tried to jerk away from a succubus that stood a few inches from his face.

A man with fangs was holding a torch a few inches from the face of the big, short-haired girl from Rael's gang. The girl was sobbing terribly, tears spilling down her cheeks.

Rats were crawling on the red-haired girl and the baby-faced man.

Arthur couldn't see anymore. Spilling tears and pounding blood blurred the world beyond. Arthur's head spun as his every gasping breath burned through his raw throat. Fluid in his ears distorted every sound. He whined and sobbed and gasped for breath. Muscle spasms wracked his body as he tried to move, but he couldn't move. He couldn't even make himself fall.

Suddenly, across a wall of fear, a voice spoke:

"Enough."

Arthur, his friends, and Rael's battered gang dropped to the floor like so many marionettes with their strings suddenly cut. They lay there gasping. Their hearts clenched and unclenched painfully, quickly. The scorpions and spiders crumbled to dust.

The crowd moved aside and Ambrose Pendragon stepped through. He stopped at the steps of the stone platform.

"What are you doing here?" Samhain cried. "You have no place here."

"I have come for my knights."

"They came here, and they are mine now," Samhain chuckled. "You came here. You are mine, too."

"No," Ambrose Pendragon said. Arthur and the others were never so glad to hear a voice. "The language of the curse says that those who enter through the gates of the city are yours, Samhain. I did not enter through the gates."

"There are no other ways," Samhain said.

"There are ways to all places," Ambrose said, "... for the last of the Worldsmen."

People from the crowd—men with feathers, succubi, horned men, women with snakelike pupils, and all the others—seemed to yell at once.

Samhain seized the curved horn from his henchman. With his single leathered hand, he raised it to his mummified lips and blew into it. A loud blast of sound ripped through the air and echoed all through Thanatos.

Steel-Hearts poured into the amphitheater bowl from all directions. Their boots clanged against stone stairs. The crowd screamed out their excitement.

Ambrose Pendragon seized the hilt of his sword. A nimbus of pure white light surrounded his body. It was as though he had been transformed into a star. The Steel-Hearts covered their faces and fell back. Even with his eyes clenched shut, Arthur could still see the light. It seemed to X-ray his very soul. The feeling that crept over him was a weird combination of glowing, peaceful warmth and total terror.

Samhain took a step back. Arthur was sure he saw fear flash over the daemon's rotted face.

"You have no power over me, Samhain," Ambrose Pendragon said coldly. "You have nothing."

Samhain stood nearly a head taller than Ambrose Pendragon but, face to face with the king of Camelot, the walking death looked no more threatening than a big, angry prune.

"Good to see you, Ambrose," Lance said. "Chop him up and let's get out of here."

Ambrose shook his head sadly.

"You still don't realize what you've done, do you?" he finally said. "You gave up your lives when you came here. You gave yourself to Samhain. That cannot be reversed. It is the Law of Choices. You broke our pact. Now the price must be paid."

Arthur felt his heart sink. He stood, weak and sickly, with the others. His heart pounded in his chest. Was there really nothing Ambrose could do?   The spiders and scorpions had turned to dust when Ambrose had first appeared. Arthur wondered if they would be back with maggots and worms and even worse things. He wondered if he and his brother and friends would end their lives on an alien planet on an island called A'Vilian?   Sweat drenched his palms. His heart pounded. The whole world went silent.

"You've managed pull my young knights into your realm," Ambrose pointed his finger at Samhain's ugly head. "They're yours now, but I can't live with that. I offer you a trade. How much is my life worth to you, daemon? What would you trade for the life of the man who could destroy you?"

Samhain looked at his Steel-Heart army, an army rendered helpless by the glow of Ambrose's bright blade.

"This is the trade I offer you," Ambrose said. "My surrender to you for the lives of your prisoners."

The evil one smirked. "For you, I would trade them all."

"Then let it be as you say," Ambrose Pendragon said. He turned to the crowd. "Samhain has agreed to release you all in exchange for my surrender. Yet, by the Law of Choices, you have bonded yourself to the city and to my enemy. I, however, though I have come into the city, do not belong to Samhain. I am free to leave this place at will. Yet I choose to stay, so that you may go. For the requirements of the Law of Choices to be satisfied, a joining must take place. You must bond with me by becoming one with the sword."

"Is he talking to us or to everybody?" Lance whispered.

Ambrose drew his sword from the sheath at his hip and lifted it to the sky. It glinted in the light of stars and glowing Elvish lamps. Ambrose Pendragon stepped up onto the platform where Samhain, Arthur, Angie, Lance, Chris, Rael, Bird-Man, and the other prisoners stood. The skeletal executioner and the succubi and the fanged man watched him warily.

"Some of you have made a pact with me and you chose to break it. You will have a chance to make a new pact, a pact stronger than the first. But others will go before you."

"Ambrose," Lance said. "Are you really gonna stay here?"

"I am," he said.

Arthur, Angie, Chris, and the others stood silent. Somehow Ambrose was giving himself up to save them. Arthur burned with shame and fear at the same time. He wanted to cry out and beg Ambrose not to give himself up, but he was even more afraid of Samhain. If Ambrose did change his mind, there would be no way out for him. Ambrose Pendragon was his only chance.

Ambrose turned and faced the silent crowd in the seats and on the terraces of the amphitheater. Hundreds of faces stared back at him. Sorcerers, witches, succubi, Elvish pleasure-givers, slaves, fanged men, bird men, men with pointed hats, women who wore feathers, people in strange robes, creatures that scarcely looked human.

"Samhain has said he will release all prisoners in exchange for my surrender. If you want to walk out of Thanatos tonight, come now and feel the touch of my blade."

A tall, scantly clad woman with wild hair and heavy make-up stood. A dark-skinned, lean man with big earrings came out of a crowd. An old woman in a robe stood up. A young, muscled blond man stood. A merman with a water-filled helmet and a hovering chair drifted down the stairs, never touching them. Movement came from different places around the amphitheater bowl. Silent, their heads hung low, the people made their way toward the stone platform where Ambrose Pendragon stood. One at a time, they came before Ambrose. He touched their heads with his sword.

"Leave this place," he said to each one. "My people will come to you and tell you what to do next. Peace be with you."

One by one, the people nodded. One by one, they walked away, climbed the amphitheater steps past frozen Steel-Hearts, and left the city. Samhain stood silently, like an ugly statue, and watched everything through burning, yellow eyes.

Ambrose turned to Rael and his group.

"What of you?" he asked. "Will you touch my sword and be freed from this place?"

Rael and his people had been talking among themselves.

"We will do as you say," Rael said. "You obviously control this place." He looked at Samhain. "...And we do not side with losers."

Ambrose laid his sword on Rael's head.

"Peace be with you, Rael, son of Dran," Ambrose said.

The bird-man stood before Ambrose.

"You are the Pendragon of which the *Bre'ons* have spoken?"

"I am."

"I am...honored," the young Seraf said. "My name is Shreeokh. In your tongue, it means 'brother of the sky.'" Ambrose touched him with the flat of the sword.

"Peace be with you, Shreeokh."

"And with you, my lord."

The tall, short-haired girl came forward.

"My name is Vita," she said simply. The baby-faced, black-haired young man felt the touch of the sword. His name was Pax. The bald man with the ponytail lowered his head and accepted the sword's touch and the freedom

Ambrose offered. His name was Jess. The red-haired girl came. Her name was Pyras.

"What now?" Rael asked.

"Wait there," Ambrose said. "And bear witness."

Ambrose turned to Arthur, Lance, Angie, and Chris.

"Children of Earth," he said, "World of the Fathers. Your coming to this world was foretold by prophecy and you have a role yet to fulfill. As a sign to the people of this world, you will bear the powers of my sword. You will pass these abilities to Lucas and Stacy as I pass them to you, for they are also of Earth.

"Come now and make a pact unlike the first. The first pact was a promise. The second is a rebirth. With the power of the sword, you will finish what I began. Come."

Arthur and Lance stepped slowly toward the tall man.

"Ambrose," Lance said. "They've got Stacy here, too. You've got to help her."

"She was never here," Ambrose said. "She is waiting for you outside the gate."

Lance stumbled back and almost fainted. Arthur caught him and steadied him. The news about Stacy relieved him, but it was only then that he understood the full extent of Samhain's deception.

"I'm sorry, Ambrose," Arthur said. That was all he could say, but it seemed like far too little.

"Arthur tried to talk us out of going," Lance said, "but we went anyway."

"They tricked me, too," Arthur said.

"It is well that you admit your errors. You make no excuses. I am pleased."

Ambrose lifted up his sword.

"Your hearts are pure, but your plans were misguided," Ambrose said. "Beware of wrongful paths to pure goals. Arthur and Lance Richardson, like the Arthur and his knights of old, wield the power of the sword, do good, and preserve the spirit of Camelot until it becomes a reality. Look into the skin of my sword."

Arthur looked. In the sword's gleaming surface, he saw his own face. In a way he couldn't describe, he saw something more. He saw himself—everything about himself. He saw every dark fantasy, every act that he had ever burned with shame over. That was only the beginning. When he thought about sins, it was the things related to sensuality that Arthur always thought he would be the most ashamed of. Then he saw the cruelty, the selfishness, the things he had done and said and forgotten about. He had hurt people and enjoyed it. Nervously, he looked around at the others.

"They did not see," Arthur heard Ambrose say. "Only we know. But look now."

Arthur looked. Instead of his own reflection, he saw Ambrose's. "What just happened?"

"You will understand later," Ambrose said. "Now lower your head as I place my sword upon you."

Arthur lowered his head. He felt the flat of the sword upon his head. The weapon only rested on Arthur's head for a second or two. He had expected warmth, a magical charge, but all he felt was the smooth metal.

"My powers to you, your curse to me. Be free now."

Ambrose went through the same ritual with Lance. He didn't seem to notice the line of people. He didn't seem to realize the urgency. He spoke with Lance as though he and Lance were standing on a mountain somewhere watching a sunset. Ambrose touched him with the sword.

Angie came up. With her metal brassiere, red loin cloth, bracelets, jewelry, and tattoos, she looked like she'd grown up in Thanatos. Only hours before, she'd looked like a clean, well-scrubbed high school freshman from a nice family. She couldn't look Ambrose in the eyes so she just stood with her head down.

"I was going to disguise myself," she said, her voice just above a whisper. "They started putting their clothes on me. I saw myself in the mirror, and I didn't look like a little girl anymore. I was so tired of looking like a little girl. Now I look like a freak. They destroy people by giving them what they want."

"Yes," Ambrose said. "They do." He lifted her chin, wiped the smeared make up from around her tear-filled eyes. "I can free you of the spell this place has put on you, but you will have to bear the marks until the time has passed. Lower your head, Angelina."

Ambrose touched her with the sword. He kissed her forehead, and she slowly moved aside as Chris stepped forward.

"What did they promise you, Chris Castle?"

"A portal back home." The others could barely hear him.

"Come, then. Feel the touch of my sword."

Chris stepped up warily. He gazed down into the depths of the sword. His face twisted with horror and rage.

"Oh my God!" he sobbed. Stumbling backwards, he screamed and slapped the sword away. Blood oozed from a nick on his arm. Chris leaped from the platform. He landed on stone stairs, fell, stumbled to his feet, and ran.

"STOP!" Ambrose called to him. "You don't know what you're doing!"

"Leave me alone!" Chris yelled over his shoulder. He dashed up the steps of the amphitheater, dodging frozen Steel-Hearts.

"Come back!"

Arthur bolted after Chris. He sprang from the platform and hit the stairs running. He hadn't gone more than a few yards until Chris was out of sight. He spun around. Ambrose was calling him back.

"Don't you want me to go after him?"

Ambrose shook his head. "Not this time. The decision is his, and he has made it. It was foretold."

"What'll happen to him now?" Angie asked.

"He might be caught by Samhain and be killed," Ambrose said. "Or he might be caught and transformed into one of Samhain's monstrous servants." Ambrose looked profoundly sad. "Or he might be condemned to wander the streets of the city forever, never finding his way out. To those under the curse, the city is much larger inside than it is outside."

Ambrose scanned the group before him, his eyes brushing across the faces of Arthur, Angie, Lance, Rael,

Vita, Pax, Pyras, Shreeokh, and Jess. He looked tall and solemn in the blood-red glare of the Elvish lamps. "You must leave soon," he said. "The power of the sword will hold the Steel-Hearts immobile until you are safely away. I must die tonight, but the name and cause of the Pendragon line and of the Worldsmen must continue. You must be my sons and daughters, my princes and princesses.

"In seven days, you must gather all who support us at the place I spoke of in the village. Goodbye, my friends." He raised his sword high above his head. It gleamed in the red light of the lamps. Then, with lightning speed, he brought the sword down, tip first, and impaled it into the stone platform.

Slish! Metal hissed against stone. Ambrose plunged the blade nearly to its hilt. The stone had gripped it and no hand but Ambrose's could draw it back. Ambrose turned to Samhain.

"I have laid down my weapon, and I surrender myself to you."

Samhain sprang over to the sword and tried to pull it out of the platform. It was wedged tight and no evil hand could move it. The daemon strained against the blade for what seemed like minutes. Finally he stopped. He looked at the succubi, the fanged man, and the executioner.

"Take him," he croaked, pointing a jabbing finger at Ambrose. "Put his hands on the block."

The succubi seized Ambrose by the arms, hissing and laughing as they dragged him to the dark-colored block that stood in the center of the platform. The executioner stood beside it, his dark and tattered hood drifting like fog. His skeleton's hands held the axe ready.

The succubi laid Ambrose's hands on the block.

Arthur felt his heart pounding in his chest. His teeth were clenched together. He wrung his hands.

"You'll never raise a sword against me again, *Bre'on*," Samhain said. "Do it."

The executioner raised his axe and brought it down hard.

A scream ripped through the air and echoed out into

the forest. Arthur's knees nearly buckled under him. A gorge formed in his throat as tears burned his eyes.

Just then lightning seared the heavens, and rain began to fall.

"Take him to the island" Samhain said. "Cast him to the abyss."

Arthur, Lance, Angie, Rael, Vita, Pax, Jess, Shreeokh, and Pyras watched as Samhain's creatures forced the tall, lean man to his feel. He trembled from the shock of his injury as they dragged him away.

Samhain's yellow eyes glared at the speechless friends of the man called Pendragon. A smile formed on his mummified lips.

"Run," he said.

They did.

16. /Refugees

Arthur, Angie, Lance, and the others ran for all they were worth. They left the amphitheater, ran through dark and empty streets, through an alley, and into the big courtyard by the main entrance. Fountains ran with blood and gargoyles sat crouched on the ledges of buildings.

They passed through the gates of Thanatos in a dead run. They ran down the ramp with its rough, heavy timbers like railroad crossties, finally reaching the hard-packed earth below. Arthur hit the path running with all the others around him. All, that is, except Shreeokh who had taken to the storm-lashed skies.

Wind howled through the forest and whipped the trees around. Lightning flashed and turned everything white for an instant. It left a flash-picture on Arthur's retina. Lightning flashed again. Cybernetic voices rang through the air. They heard the sounds of machinery coming through the gateway behind them.

"The troop carriers!" Arthur yelled. "Get off the road!" The forest lay beyond them. Rael passed Arthur up. His long legs carried him into the woods and out of sight. Arthur, Lance, and Angie ran with Rael's gang into the forest. The cool shadows of wind-tossed trees settled over them.

"Where's Stacy?" Arthur asked suddenly. "Ambrose said she would be waiting."

"I don't know," Lance said. "Stacy!"

There was no answer.

<THEY ARE ESCAPING.> A stormtrooper's mechanical voice carried through the forest.

"We've got to go," Angie said. "They're coming."

"STACY!" Lance called.

"Run!" Arthur cried. Angie tripped over a log and fell into a briar patch.

Arthur and Lance pulled her to her feet. Her cape had shielded her bare, tattoo-covered arms and legs from the worst of the thorns, but she still cried out as they tore free.

Arthur watched as Rael's group vanished through the trees. "Come on," he said.

"Forget them," Lance sighed. "It's easier to hide three people anyway."

Thunder still rumbled in the sky overhead, but no rain came. They ran until the cyborgs seemed to be well behind them. The woods got thicker. Arthur, Angie, and Lance came to a thicket of young pine trees that grew so close together they almost shut out the sky. Straw shrouded the branches like brown blankets and gouging, painful sticker vines grew all through them. There was a little clearing in the middle of the thicket, but it was knee-deep in thornbushes. Arthur carried Angie through it.

For what seemed like hours, Arthur, Angie, and Lance pushed through the dark maze, nothing but the most pallid starlight to guide them. Even when their eyes had fully adjusted to the darkness, there were places of pitch darkness. They held hands as they walked through them. Walking through that forest that night was like walking through depression.

Arthur drove himself on because there was nothing better to do. Over and over again, he thought about Ambrose and Chris and about the hideous images that mapped Angie's body. He felt sick with shame over the way they had left Ambrose behind. In his mind, he saw the pale shattered form of his friend being dragged away by Samhain's henchmen. He was too great a man to end up like that. And Chris. Chris was the only kindred spirit Arthur had ever had. He loved *Star Trek*, read Tolkein, and hated P.E. When Arthur thought about facing that loudmouthed bunch at Summerstown High without Chris, he felt his eyes cloud. A lump formed in his throat.

Finally they reached an older part of the forest where the trees were taller, and their trunks were not as close together. Nobody spoke a word. They dragged their feet through drifts of brown leaves and straw. After a few minutes' walking, they came to a crack in the floor of the forest and heard water rushing down below. They had come to a creek. It was a shallow creek, but still too wide to cross. There were tall bluffs on each side of the water and narrow, muddy banks on the edge of the stream.

"This is probably the creek we were crossing when the werewolf jumped us," Lance said.

They started to walk the edge of the creek.

"Where are we going?" Angie finally asked.

"Amos' house, I guess," Lance said. "Anybody got any better ideas?"

"No," Arthur said. "That's where everybody was."

They walked up and down the high banks of the creek, looking over the edge of the bank for a place where the creek was narrow enough to cross.

"There," Lance said as he pointed downward. The water was only about three feet across. It wouldn't take much effort to jump. A few yards ahead of them was a notch in the bank left by the wash of water. Arthur and the others braced against the sides of it and climbed down to the level of the water. With tall bluffs on either side of them, they started the dismal trek along the edge of the creek.

Arthur took a step and his shoe sank into the mud. He groaned as he pulled it out.

"Just be glad you've got shoes," Angie said. Her sandals were covered in ornamentation, but they didn't give her feet much protection.

"Shh!" Lance said suddenly. Everybody got silent. The booming of cyborg voices echoed from somewher downstream.

"We've gotta move!" Lance said.

Arthur jumped the chilly, fast-running waters of the creek and scrambled up the opposite bank. Lance and Angie followed. Lance climbed the bank first, then pulled Angie up after him. They all ran into the darkness, determined to leave the super-strong, silver-eyed zombies behind.

After they had walked for hours, Lance found a dried-up ditch filled with straw and roots. He said it was a dried-up branch of the creek. In one spot, tree roots covered with green moss, old leaves, and straw formed an almost-roof over the ditch. It was like a small cave.

"You think we should spend the night here?" he asked the others. "I have no idea where we are."

"Me, either," Arthur said. "And I'm really starting to get tired."

"Do you think we'll freeze to death?" Angie asked.

"Not if we snuggle," Lance said.

Under other circumstances, snuggling with a girl as cute as Angie would have been a welcome prospect, but the little den was cold, damp, dirty, and uncomfortable. Arthur lay with the back of his head jammed against hard, knotty roots and thought how horrible everything had turned out. He managed to drop off to sleep a couple of times.

In the light of morning, Arthur saw Angie, Chris, and Mr. Lucas walk up to him, smiling. They were dressed in everyday, twentieth century clothes. Angie was wearing a sleeveless shirt, and there weren't any tattoos on her arms. He asked them about Ambrose. The dream vanished, and Arthur woke up in the cave. His back was really starting to ache. He managed to doze off a second time, and dreamed he saw the glowing eyes of the Steel-Hearts peering into the cave at them. Even after he woke up and knew it was a dream, he was still afraid to open his eyes or move for several minutes. Finally, he stood up, stuck his head out of the ditch, and looked out into the forest. In the light shed by the bright band in the strange world's sky, he saw nothing but trees. Arthur sighed, crawled back into the hole, and tried to get comfortable.

Morning was forever in coming, and none of the group waited until high sun to get up and about. They were all trudging through the forest at the pale light of earliest dawn. The sky was gray and foggy and the world seemed thankfully unreal. Angie kept her cape pulled tightly around her body, and Arthur could almost believe that her tattoos had vanished with the darkness of night.

They found a road that looked familiar, and followed it to Aquila's and Prisca's sunken home. There was no one home. The door was unlatched, so they went in and borrowed heavier clothes for Angie. They knew Prisca would not mind.

"Look at this," Angie said as she laid aside her cape. The dancer's costume underneath looked like a combination of a swimsuit and a torture instrument. Angie's bare skin was branded with the bizarre imagery of Thanatos. Snakes slithered, spiders crawled, and skeletons rattled and laughed. There were other creatures that would have been more at home in the nightmares of lunatics than in any physical realm. Arthur and Lance didn't know how to respond.

"Go ahead and say it," Angie said as she pulled on a tunic. "They're hideous."

"Why did you let them do that to you?" Lance asked.

"They didn't look like that at first," she said. "At least, that's not what I saw. They were beautiful, and the needles didn't even hurt."

"That much real tattoo work would take weeks," Lance said, "but they did it in minutes. Maybe they're not real tattoos."

"They're real," she said. "And they won't ever go away. I feel like they branded my soul."

"No," Arthur said. "You saw what happened when Ambrose touched you with the sword. Your soul is clean. The tattoos are just remnants."

"They're scars," she said. She began to cry. Arthur and Lance tried to comfort her but found themselves fighting back tears too. They surrendered themselves to the pain for a little while, but quickly they pulled it together and pushed onward. They made it to Amos's church by noon. The building had been ransacked. The back door had been knocked off its hinges. Food and pots and pans were thrown into the floor of the kitchen. In the library and the study that had served as makeshift bedrooms, furniture had been broken into splintered pieces, and books had been torn from the shelves. Thankfully, there were no bodies.

Arthur, Lance, and Angie walked on into the edge of the

village clearing. They were hoping to catch sight of Mr. Lucas's carriage, Amos's horse, or anything they recognized there among the crude, wooden huts and fruit trees. All they found there were Steel-Heart troop carriers.

"What do we do now?" Lance asked.

"The Elvish village," Arthur said.

"How long will that take?" Angie asked.

"Without horses," Arthur said, "maybe two days. Does anybody have a better idea?"

Nobody did. The village was the only place left to go. Tired, weary, and footsore, they walked on for hours. At one point, they thought they saw Shreeokh, the bird-man from Rael's group, flying through the air above them, but they weren't sure.

They reached the heavy bridge over the Emerald River by mid-afternoon. They stopped and rested for a while, sitting on the bridge and looking down on the cool, mossy green water. Just the sound of the water was refreshing.

After about thirty minutes' rest, they pushed on. Nightfall found them still wandering along abandoned roads. They had passed two ruined villages and were walking on roads of weathered brick. A fog had sprung up suddenly, cutting visibility down to about ten feet. They hadn't had anything to eat all day and each step was a painful effort, but they drove themselves on. Night insects chirped somewhere across the fog. The river rushed through its bed somewhere not far distant. Then there was another sound, a low roar.

"What was that?"

"I don't hear anything."

The sound got louder ... louder.

"Sounds like a motorcycle."

"Or a rotohorse."

"Let's get off the road."

They hid behind a bush. The sound closed in. A blue-white light cut through the fog behind them. A lean figure came riding out of the swirling miasma.

"It's Rael," Lance said.

Arthur threw himself out of the bushes. The rotohorse

blew past him. Rael put on the brakes.

"Thank the blessed king," he said. "I have looked all over for you. We must take care. Steel-Hearts are everywhere. Are your brother and the maiden Angelina here with you?"

Lance and Angie came out into plain sight.

"Do you know where Stacy and Mr. Lucas are?" Arthur asked.

"Yes," he said. "They are in the village of my mother's people. They wanted to search for you, but we could not afford to lose any more offworlders. Shreeokh has been searching for you from the skies."

"I think we saw him earlier," Arthur said.

"If you are ready, I will take you to the village, but I can only take two this time. One of you will have to wait."

"I'll wait," Arthur said. "I'm the oldest."

"But you'll be by yourself," Angie said.

"It's okay."

Angie and Lance climbed onto the saddle behind Rael. The machine roared off into the fog, and Arthur was all alone. He did not know how long he would have to wait. The carriage ride had taken hours, but Rael's rotohorse could no doubt make the trip more quickly. Even so, Arthur did not relish the idea of waiting by a dark road on an alien world. The night was dark and foggy, and his imagination began to play tricks on him. More than once, he was sure he could see eyes gleaming in the starlight. He heard movement in the underbrush, but the sound faded after a while. It was probably some small animal. He hoped so, at least. After a while, his anxiety began to subside. It was almost pleasant to be alone. He had needed some alone time to gather his thoughts. This was not the place he would have chosen, but he welcomed it all the same.

In a thankfully short time, Arthur heard the whine of Rael's roto in the distance. Moments later, Arthur could see its cyclops eye cutting through the fog. When the vehicle finally arrived, Arthur lost no time climbing onto the saddle behind Rael.

Rael found a wide spot in the road to turn around,

pointed his vehicle back toward the village, and twisted hard on the throttle. The vehicle shot down the dark road like a rocket. The glare from the headlamp created swirling kaleidoscope images in the fog. Arthur clung tight to Rael's armored body as he negotiated twisting mountain roads without slowing down. Vine-draped ruins and toppled statues appeared in the lights as they blew past them. Arthur closed his eyes and had almost dozed off when he felt the vehicle brake to a stop.

Arthur opened his eyes and saw a heap of debris littering the mountain path ahead of them.

"What happened here?" he asked. "It looks like an avalanche."

"It was our doing," Rael said. "To block the troop carriers. It will give us time to escape into the forest."

"Can you get through it?" Arthur asked.

"Yes," Rael said. "Hold on." He turned onto a steeper, narrower path that connected the switchbacks. Arthur had to hold on tight to keep from sliding off the saddle. He was relieved when the rotohorse reached the next switchback and returned to the main road. They stopped three times to identify themselves to sentries as they made another loop around the mountain. Finally, they passed through a gate and rolled into the familiar village. The domed building they had camped in before was a welcome sight, a reminder of happier times. Arthur was warmed by the sight of Mr. Lucas' carriage sitting out front, but wondered how he would get it back down the mountain with the path blocked. The horses were tethered to posts outside. Arthur heard voices coming from the building. As he and Rael were about to go inside, Arthur noticed Marcos standing on the roof of the building. He was staring off over the trees through his tarnished metal telescope.

"Can you see anything?" Arthur asked.

Marcos jumped, nearly fell off the roof, and righted himself. "You startled me," he said.

"I'm sorry."

"It's all right." He waved his hand dismissively. "I am glad you are still alive, my friend. There are many strange happenings afoot. Look!" He pointed.

Arthur and Rael gazed out over the edge of the mountain and into the darkness beyond.

"I don't see anything," Arthur said.

"Precisely!" Marcos said.

"You're making no sense," Rael snapped.

"There is no fire in the sky tonight."

Rael gasped and looked into the darkness once more.

"Would you be able to see the glow from the Island through a fog like this?" Arthur asked.

Marcos shook his head. "I don't know."

"We have to know," Rael said. "This could be important."

Arthur squinted his eyes and peered into the mist. Suddenly he was standing on a levee overlooking a dark lake. A tall, rocky island lay before him. Arthur knew at once where he was standing. When he saw the city of Thanatos sitting silently on its mound, he knew he was standing in the same place he had been when he and his friends had seen the island and the city on that first night. A blanket of fog hung over the lake, but he could see the island clearly. It was dark. There was no fire, no heat, and no smell of burning flesh and brimstone. He could smell the tang of the forest though, and he could hear the lake's gray waters lapping against the shore.

Suddenly he was back in the Elvish village.

"Did you see that?"

"See what?" Rael's catlike eyes narrowed.

"Nothing," Arthur said. "I really need some sleep." He gazed back into the fog and shook his head.

"Eat first," Rael said.

Arthur smelled food cooking and realized just how hungry he was.

"Go," Rael ordered. "They're waiting for you."

Arthur stepped through the building's arched doorway. He could see the shimmering glow of the fire at the end of the corridor and could dimly make out the shapes of the people around it. Conversation paused as he stepped into the room.

"They're back," Arthur heard someone say. Someone leaped into his arms and nearly knocked him down. *Stacy?*

"They said you did it for me," she said. "You went into that place because you thought I was in there."

Arthur didn't know what to say. He had wanted to go after her, of course, but he had tried to talk the others into waiting for Ambrose to get back. He felt even worse when Stacy kissed him.

"I heard about Chris," she said. "I'm so, so sorry." The sight of her tears nearly broke Arthur down too. "Why do you think he did it? Why was he so afraid?"

"I don't know," Arthur said. "I really don't know."

"It's good to see you," Mr. Lucas said as he gripped Arthur's hand. "We feared the worst."

Arthur's stomach growled. The smell of fried fish was almost too much for him. Stacy dragged him to a place beside the fire. Vita and Pyras, two of the women from Rael's group, turned to him as he sat down.

"Please forgive us for leaving you last night," Vita said in her deep, gentle voice. "We were cowards. I was only worried about myself."

"After what happened," Arthur said, "I can understand that."

"We heard the Steel-Hearts behind us and feared a patrol had caught you," red-haired Pyras told him. "We watched them for a while, but didn't see you with any of the patrols, so we went on to warn the others in the village."

"You all talk too much," Prisca said, pushing past the others with a metal plate in her hand. "He is hungry. Feed him. Is it ready, Karissa?"

Karissa had some fish frying in a dish that stood up on tripod legs.

"It is very ready." Karissa smiled, but there was sadness in her eyes. She pierced a piece of fish with a fork and dropped it onto the plate. Prisca passed it to Arthur.

"Blow on it until it is cool," she said. "I will pour you something to drink."

Arthur nodded. A log in the fire popped and threw up

sparks.

"Marcos has seen something," Rael announced suddenly as he entered the room. "Or, more properly, he has seen nothing. There is no fire in the sky tonight."

The group went silent for a moment. Then they all began to speak at once.

"Hold it!" Amos said, cutting the air with his large arms. "Hold it!"

The group fell silent.

"We have to be sure about this," he said. "It could just be an effect of the fog."

It's not the fog, Arthur thought, but he said nothing. There was no way he could have been standing beside that lake, yet he was sure what he had seen had not been an illusion.

Shreeokh the Seraf stepped forward. "I will go and find out," he said.

"Be careful," Amos said. "Seraf are not immune to Steel-Heart weapons."

Shreeokh nodded. "I am all too familiar with Steel-Heart weapons."

"Then go in peace, my brother."

Shreeokh nodded to him and bounded toward the door, his wings outstretched.

"What do you think this means?" Angie asked the others.

"It could mean anything," Amos said. "These are strange times. It is hard to tell good news from bad anymore."

Lance sat down beside Arthur as he ate. "Some of them think Chris may have ratted us out."

"I saw the other Rael speaking with him," Jess, the bald man with the ponytail, said. "They had made some kind of arrangement."

Arthur swallowed and nodded. "I think Chris must have told the other Rael to take Stacy hostage. That's how they baited us into the city."

"There is not another Rael," Rael protested. The others ignored him.

"But why would he do that?" Stacy asked.

"I think they promised him a way home," Arthur said. "A portal somewhere inside the city."

"Yes," Vita said. "I heard him speak of it."

"The water is hot," Arthur heard Prisca telling Angie. "You must bathe."

***

Prisca led Angie back to the room with the basin. It had been filled with water. The old woman didn't try to bathe her this time. She simply nodded and left as Angie began to shed her clothing. Angie sat for a long time in the hot water and scrubbed off the makeup and perfume, the dried blood from the briar scratches, and the mud. Her throat tightened as she looked down at the horrible images covering her arms and chest. What would she tell her parents if she ever made it home?

"Angie?" The voice had come from the hall outside. She recognized Stacy's voice.

"I'm here," Angie said.

"It's me," Stacy said. "Can I come in?"

"Yeah," Angie said. She looked down at her body and sank lower into the water. "Yeah, okay."

Stacy stepped into the room and sat down on a stone bench beside the basin. She tried to make small talk for a little while, but her eyes kept wandering to the tattoos on Angie's arms and back.

"What did they do to you?" she finally asked.

Angie began to cry. "I let them do it," she said. "I wanted them to do it. I was tired of being everybody's little angel. Boring and plain."

"This is my fault," Stacy said. "I did this to you. You were never boring and plain, Angie. Nobody ever said you were boring and plain."

"But I lost the cheerleader election."

"Only by a few votes. You'd have gotten it next year. The upperclassmen always get preference. I should have told you that. I didn't think it bothered you that much. You've always done so well at everything."

"Grades," she said. "And art."

"And music," Stacy said. "All those instruments."

Angie shook her head dismissively. "You don't get popular because of things like that. They call you a nerd."

"Because they're jealous. I can't draw or play anything. I wish I could. And I wish my grades were better...had been better. I don't guess it matters now."

"Don't say that," Angie said. "You're going back with us."

"What if I'm not? What if I can't go back?"

"You have to go back," Angie said. "I don't think I could take losing you again."

"Of course you could," Stacy said. "You're stronger than you think you are."

"That makes me think of something else," Angie said. "Last night when Ambrose saved us, he traded himself for us, and I saw myself for the first time. When I saw my reflection in his sword, I saw everything. My whole life. Then my reflection was gone, and I just saw Ambrose. What do you think that means?"

"I don't know," Stacy said. "I heard he'd traded himself for you, but Rael didn't say anything about the sword."

"He said we had bonded with him. I'm trying to remember how he put it. 'One with the sword.' That's what he said. And he told Arthur he would wield the sword's power. Do you think he just meant Arthur or did he mean all of us? I don't feel any different, but what if he passed his powers along to us?"

"What if he did? How would you know?"

"I don't know." She held up her arm. "I wonder if I can make the tattoos go away." She focused on an image of a snake that coiled around her wrist. At first nothing happened, but then the image began to blur and shift. She concentrated harder, tried to will the image away, but no amount of concentration could make it invisible.

"You were doing it," Stacy said. "What happened?"

"It won't go away," Angie said. "All I can do is move it around."

"Can you change the image? Make it into something besides a snake?"

"I think so," she said. As she focused in, the image broke apart and reformed itself into a cloud, a flower, and finally into the face of Ambrose Pendragon.

"That's amazing," Stacy said. "Do another one."

There was an image of a laughing skull emblazoned on the back of her left hand. She willed it into the face of a noble lion.

"Pass me that sheet," she told Stacy. Angie stood as Stacy passed her the cloth. She wrapped it around her body as she stepped out of the basin. Then, a bit at a time, she moved her hand over the images beneath her skin and remade them. They flowed like watercolor paint beneath her fingers. She started with the ones on her arms, back, and shoulders. Then, shifting the cloth, she moved to her legs, feet, and torso. Stacy sat and watched as she reshaped the images into a tapestry of beauty, nobility, and hope. Symbols of death melted into symbols of life. Disjointed parts became a flowing whole. When the transformation was complete, Angie sank down onto the bench beside Stacy.

"That was incredible," Stacy said. "Like a dream."

"There's one more thing," Angie said. "Ambrose said we were to pass his power to you and Mr. Lucas the way he had to us." She raised her hand, palm out, toward Stacy.

"How does it work?" Stacy asked.

"I'm not sure," Angie said. "He had us make a kind of pledge. Do you pledge yourself to the kingdom of Camelot and the courage and virtues of—I don't know—a life of courage, virtue, and wisdom?"

Stacy touched her palm. "I do. I pledge myself."

They waited for a moment.

"Did it work?" Angie asked.

"I don't know," Stacy said. "I guess we'll find out."

Then, suddenly, they did.

***

Most of the people in the room were sleeping or talking in low tones. Lance was sitting on a blanket gazing into the fire. He was about to doze off when a burst of screaming guitar music jarred him awake. The sound was familiar, but where was it...? Suddenly he remembered. It was the ringtone on his phone.

Lance fumbled for his shoulder bag as people around the room began to wake up. Embarrassed, Lance jerked open his bag and started rummaging through it. Then he saw the light at the bottom of the bag. The face of the phone was glowing as music flowed from it. He pulled it out and touched the green button on the screen.

"Hello?"

There was no answer, but the face continued to glow. Lance was certain the battery was completely drained...or maybe not so certain. He opened up his list of contacts and punched Arthur's name. He waited and listened.

"Hello?"

"Hey," Lance said. "It's me. Where are you?"

"Outside," Arthur said. "How are you doing this?"

"I don't know," Lance said. "It just suddenly started working. What are you doing out there?"

"Waiting for Shreeokh to get back."

Angie and Stacy entered.

"Where's Arthur?" Stacy asked.

"Outside," Lance told her.

"Get him back in here," Stacy said. "We've got something to show you."

"Come in here," Lance said. "The girls want to show us something."

"He's got phone service," Angie suddenly realized. "That's impossible."

***

Arthur and Lance followed the girls into an empty room.

"All right," Lance said. "What's so important?"

Angie turned her back and stretched the collar of her tunic down on one side to expose her right shoulder blade. The tattooing there showed a field with flowers and trees. As she moved her hand over it, the flowers and grass began to sway in the wind, and a swarm of brightly-colored butterflies glided across her skin.

"How did you do that?" Arthur asked her.

"Ambrose gave us the power of his sword," Angie said. "I think that's what this is. I can't make the tattoos go away, but I can change them into just about anything. And I can make them move."

"So your body's like a canvas?" Arthur asked her. "Or a TV screen?"

"Yes," she said. "Exactly."

"Angievision," Lance said. "Sweet. If we get her fat enough, we can have a wide screen."

"And that's not all," Stacy said. "Look." She held out her arms and began to glow. Soft golden light flowed from her skin, her hair, and even her clothing.

"Wow," Lance said. "You can glow. What else?"

The glow faded.

"That's all," Stacy said. "I just glow."

"Have you tried focusing it?" Arthur asked. "Maybe you can generate heat or start fires."

"I can't do any of that," she said. "I just glow. I know it's not very useful."

"It's cool," Lance said. "Shekinah glory."

"What is that?" Angie asked.

"They talk about it at church," Lance said. "Don't tell me I've heard of something you haven't. It's like the light that comes from the presence of God."

"I know that light," Stacy said. "After the accident, I was standing in light. It was like being inside of love. Soaking in it. I wanted to stay there forever."

"Have either of you noticed anything?" Angie asked. "Any unusual abilities?"

"My phone just started working," Lance said. "Does that count?"

"It would have to be something like that," Arthur said. "Your battery was dead and there's not even a network here. There's no way you should have service, but you do."

"What about you, Arthur?" Angie asked. "Have you been able to do anything unusual?"

"No," Arthur said. "Not at.... Well, maybe. There was something."

"What?"

"When I first got here, Marcos noticed there wasn't any glow coming from the direction of the island. He wondered if something had happened to the fires, but the fog was so thick, we couldn't tell for sure. We couldn't tell if the fires had stopped burning, or if the fog was just covering them up. I stared out through the haze. One second I was straining to see, and the next second I was there. I was standing on the levee beside the lake we saw that first night. I could see the island and the city of Thanatos sitting on its hill. It was like I was really there. I could smell the forest and hear the waves lapping against the bank."

"And what about the island?" Lance asked. "Was there any fire?"

"None," Arthur said. "It was completely dark."

"What do you think it means?" Angie asked.

"I don't know," Arthur said. "I'm not even sure I was really there. I mean, it felt real, but who knows?"

"There should be a way to test this," Lance said. He stepped out the door. "Can you look back into the main room and tell who's sitting around the fire?"

"I don't know," Arthur said. "I'm not even sure I can do it again."

"Just try," Lance said. "Don't worry about whether it works or not."

Arthur stared at the wall and willed himself to be in the next room, but nothing happened. He concentrated on the wall and tried to picture the room beyond. His mind wandered for a moment, and he found himself wondering if Shreeokh had made it back yet. Suddenly, he was standing outside with Rael, Amos, and Marcos. They didn't seem to be aware of him, but their attention was focused on the skies. Arthur waved his hand in front of Rael's face, but he didn't react at all.

"Hey, guys," Arthur spoke the words in his mind, but they were swallowed by silence.

"He's coming," Marcos said as he peered through the battered tube of his telescope.

A dark, winged shape appeared against the glowing belt of weirdly shaped stars that made up the planet's gritty ring. As the flying shape drew closer, Arthur could make out Shreeokh's long, angular body. The Seraf glided in close, folded his wings, and dropped to the ground.

"It is true," he said. "There is no fire on the island tonight."

Arthur fell back into his body. He lost his balance for an instant and had to brace himself against the wall.

"Did you do it?" Lance asked.

"Shreeokh's back," Arthur said breathlessly. "He says there's no fire on the island."

***

When word of Shreeokh's return got around, everyone in the encampment gathered outside to hear what he had to say. When they heard his startling news, they all asked the same question: "But what does it mean?"

"That is not a question I can answer," Shreeokh said. "I only know that the fires no longer burn. The island is dark."

"Perhaps Samhain has been defeated," Rael said. "His reign is at an end."

"No," Marcos said. "There's more to come. The prophecies have not yet been fulfilled."

"You and your Bre'on prophecies," Rael said. "No disrespect to your king intended, but are you so sure?"

"There is to be a battle," Marcos said, "a showdown with the forces of darkness. Ambrose himself spoke of it."

"Maybe he fought the battle for us," Pyras suggested. "We saw him immobilize Samhain's soldiers."

"But that isn't what he said would happen," Marcos said.

"But the fires no longer burn," Rael said. "What if the city of Thanatos lies empty as well? If the evil ones have left this world...."

"They were still here this morning," Lance said. "We saw them looking for us."

"We need to know what is happening in Thanatos," Amos said. "I can go."

"Are you mad?" Rael snapped.

"No," Amos said. "You forget I was once a Steel-Heart.

There is a way in. A secret way. That is how Ambrose was able to reach you without falling under the city's spell."

"I thought he just used his magic sword," Lance said.

Karissa stepped forward. "The city is still a dangerous place, my husband. Even if you were able to get inside...."

"Arthur can tell us," Stacy said.

"How?" Amos asked.

"When Ambrose surrendered himself for us, he gave us his powers," Arthur said, "but not exactly."

Amos looked back and forth between them. "What do you mean?"

A hush fell over the crowd as Stacy raised her arms and began to glow. Light flooded the clearing and a soft wind blew through her hair. The sense of peace was undeniable. The glow faded.

Amos cleared his throat. "All of you can do this?"

"Not exactly," Arthur said. "That's what I was going to tell you. None of us has the same ability. Stacy can glow, and I can see things that are happening in other places. I'm not really there, but it feels like I am. I can see, hear, and smell everything that's going on around me, but I'm invisible to the people there."

Amos looked doubtful. "Are you sure about this?"

"A minute ago, I saw you standing here just as Shreeokh was coming back," Arthur said. "You and Marcos and Rael. None of you could see me."

"Pendragon said the outworlders would have his abilities," Rael said. "He said it would be a sign to others."

"So you could enter the city of Thanatos and see what is happening there?"

"I think so."

"I don't know about this," Lance said. "The last time we went to that place, it didn't work out so well."

"But I wouldn't really be there," Arthur said. "Not physically."

"That place is filled with evil enchantment," Amos said. "Are you sure you want to take this risk?"

"No," Arthur said. "I'm not sure. But I think we need answers, and I'm the only one who can get them for us. I can't think of a better way. It might not even work." Arthur fixed his eyes on the horizon.

"Listen, Arthur. I don't think...."

Arthur was in the city. Somehow he had landed in the amphitheater in the center of town. It was dark, empty, and cold. A layer of fog swirled just above the ground. The scarred block of stone where Ambrose had surrendered himself sat on the platform at the center. It was an altar, Arthur realized, an altar that had been soaked with the sacrificial blood of Samhain's enemies. Ambrose had driven his sword into the block and none of Samhain's men had been able to remove it, but now the block stood empty. The sword was nowhere to be seen. The block, Arthur suddenly noticed, was cracked.

What did it mean? No hand but Ambrose's could withdraw the sword from the stone, but what if the stone itself had been shattered? Would the enchantment still hold, even with the rock broken, or could any hand remove it? Someone had taken the sword, but who? That was the question. Could Arthur provide the answer?

Arthur started up the stairs. Maybe if he moved invisibly among the inhabitants of the city, he could learn something. Would his power allow him to walk unseen into Samhain's throne room?

A strange, sick feeling came over Arthur. Something about the city, something raw and savage, was pulling at him. He could feel it drawing him, and knew he had better leave before his judgment failed him. Perhaps he could gather his strength and return later. He concentrated on the Elvish village, on the hilltop where his physical body and his friends awaited him and tried to will himself back. His feet rose from the stone pavement beneath him, but something was clinging to him, drawing him downward.

Arthur looked down at the fog that surrounded his feet. Black tendrils of smoke clung to his ankles like ivy, and they were growing thicker. Arthur fought back panic and tried to will himself away. The pull at his feet grew stronger. Arthur heard—or maybe felt—a low roar. It was deep and rough, and it vibrated through the stone beneath him. He looked down. The oily tendrils had changed into hands. They had long, clawed fingernails, swollen joints, and slimy skin the color of obsidian. They were pulling him downward. Arthur saw his feet vanish into the stone. Icy cold burned through to the marrow of his bones. He spread his arms and wished himself back to the village, but the grip on his ankles grew stronger. The icy cold that gripped his feet crept up his shins as he dropped deeper into the stone. Inhuman laughter echoed far beneath him.

They're pulling me down to hell. He panicked as the terrifying thought went through him. The fog clung to him like quicksand as he fell in up to his waist. He silently prayed and fought against his fear. He had the power of the sword in him. If he could tap into that power....

Golden light flooded Arthur's vision, and warmth surrounded him. Suddenly Ambrose Pendragon was standing before him. The amphitheater was filled with people. Ambrose placed his sword on Arthur's head.

This is the past, Arthur realized. *I'm seeing the past.* The instant he realized it, the scene around him changed. The air around him reeked of sulfur, and it was so hot, he could hardly catch his breath. Steel-Hearts stood silently around him, their faces as hard as wind-blasted stone. Arthur reeled back when he saw that they were standing at the edge of a pit. There was no rail along the edge and, so far as he could see, the pit had no bottom. He heard a rumble and turned to see a platform with gears and pulleys being cranked out over the pit. Two figures stood upon it. One was Samhain's executioner. The other, Arthur realized, was Ambrose Pendragon. He looked small, weak, and broken.

Samhain stood imperiously at the edge of the pit with a crowd of his henchmen surrounding him. "This one dared to oppose me," he roared. "He dared to declare himself a king. He will now meet the fate of all who dream such dreams." He lifted the curved horn to his leathered lips and blew into it.

Something disturbed the crowd. Arthur wondered for a moment if his presence had somehow been detected. Then he realized they were looking up. He gazed upward and saw something, some bright and burning object, plunging from the heavens. It was heading straight for the platform. Arthur wondered for a moment if this was part of the execution process, but even the Steel-Hearts seemed surprised by it. He wondered if Samhain had prepared some extravagant spectacle to commemorate the death of his foe, but the daemon king seemed as surprised as the others.

Just as the object was about to reach ground level, Ambrose Pendragon sprang to life. He leaped from the platform, reached out with phantom hands, and grasped...his glowing sword. Arthur watched in stunned silence for what seemed like a full minute as the man and the sword dropped into the chasm and vanished from sight.

Arthur found himself back at the broken altar with Ambrose's glowing sword hovering above his head. A cloaked figure stood before him. Arthur couldn't see his face, but he caught a glimpse of its wrists.

"Go now."

Arthur felt a push. With no demonic hands binding his ankles, he tumbled backwards through the air. The city fell away. Treetops zipped past him as he soared over village and forest, finally slamming to a halt as his consciousness reconnected with his body. He gasped for breath and tried to focus his vision, but the world around him was blurry. He stumbled and nearly fell. Amos caught him as he steadied himself. His heart was pounding in his chest. He squeezed his eyes shut for a moment and caught his breath. When he opened his eyes, his vision was clear. Amos, Mr. Lucas, Lance, Angie, Stacy, and the others were all staring at him expectantly.

"Are you all right?" Stacy asked.

"Did you see it?" Marcos asked.

Arthur nodded. "I saw it. And I saw him."

"Him?"

"Ambrose," he said. "I saw Ambrose. He was in the city."

"Wait," Lance said. "Slow down. You're saying you saw

Ambrose?"

"Yes," Arthur said. "Well, first I saw the stone block. It was broken, and his sword was missing. Something tried to pull me down, but someone showed up and drove it all away. I couldn't see his face, but I saw his wrists. There were scars, like his hands had been severed and reattached. And he had the sword."

"If Ambrose is still alive," Rael asked, "why didn't he come back and tell us himself?"

"I don't know," Arthur said.

"The last thing he said to do," Amos said, "was to gather his subjects outside the gates of Thanatos. We can't very well do that if we're all huddled together on this mountain."

"What will we have them do once they're gathered there?" Rael demanded. "We need weapons, some kind of plan of attack."

"He has given them abilities," Amos said.

"The ability to glow? Body art that moves? What good will any of that do against cybernetic armies?"

"Military force cannot prevail against Samhain," Amos said.

"My mother's people refused to use violence against him," Rael said. "Look what it got them. Cities in ruins. People dead or enslaved. Ideals have no substance in the physical realm. You have said military force cannot prevail against Samhain, but what else is there?"

"What else, indeed?" Mr. Lucas sighed. "Are idealistic pacifism and militaristic pragmatism really our only options? My own people have struggled with that question often enough. My father served in my country's military. My grandfather was a member of a sect called the Quakers that did not believe in the use of military force. Both were men of honor."

"Then what would you have us do, Lucas?"

"Gather the people as Ambrose said. Arthur and his brother will use their abilities to coordinate our efforts. Marcos will assist them. The rest of us will act as emissaries, traveling from village to village."

Rael turned to him. "And when we have gathered them at the gates of Thanatos, what then?"

"Then we wait."

"And when they ask why we are gathering at the gates of that city, what will you tell them?"

"The truth," Lucas said. "What we're doing is an act of faith. If the Bre'on prophecies prove false, and Ambrose Pendragon is no more than a pretender to the throne, Samhain's forces will destroy us."

"Mind your words," Amos said. "Ambrose Pendragon is no pretender."

"Then we have a job to do, don't we?"

18. /Camelot's Last Stand

The week had seemed for a time as if it would never end. From their secret places, Arthur, Lance, and Marcos had directed the others on their journeys through dark forests, over mountains, into villages, and hidden strongholds. Arthur had kept constant watch for the Steel-Hearts but the hulking cyborgs had been surprisingly passive. He wondered, at times, if Rael had been right. What if the darkened island really did signal the end of Samhain's reign? He knew in his heart that it could not be that easy. He could feel the pressure building beneath the surface. It was only a matter of time before Samhain and his henchmen resurfaced. Finally the day came, the day Ambrose had set aside for the final showdown.

The sun was beginning to set when Mr. Lucas' familiar carriage appeared on the road that led to Amos' chapel. "There they are," Lance said as he saw it.

Stacy, Angie, and three people the brothers had never seen before were riding as Mr. Lucas drove. No longer trying to blend in, Lucas, Angie, and Stacy were wearing clothing from twenty-first century Earth. Tonight everyone would know that they were from another world.

Amos, Marcos, and most of Rael's group had already made it back to the chapel that was to serve as their secondary staging area. In only a few moments, they would ride together to the gates of Thanatos and make their stand. There would be no more running, no more hiding, no more staying just ahead of Steel-Heart patrols. Their faith in Ambrose Pendragon, the Bre'on prophecies, and the power of the sword would face its final and greatest test.

"You are sure that was Ambrose you saw?" Lance had asked the night Arthur had teleported into Thanatos.

"Who else could it have been?" Arthur had answered, yet he had fought with doubts of his own. The images he had seen in the dark city had been unlike those he had seen during any of his other jumps. He had been deceived often enough to question everything he saw, especially in that place. Still, his abilities and those of the others lent powerful support to the idea that Ambrose and the power he had wielded had somehow survived. Even though he still had moments when he doubted his judgment, his leadership skills, and his very sanity, Arthur had spent the past week leading the effort to gather Ambrose's supporters from the surrounding villages as Ambrose had asked. And what an effort it had been. Those among their number had been chased by Steel-Hearts, shot at by Seraf arrows, dressed down by an Elvish queen, and threatened with burning by the leader of a fire-cult. Amazingly, everyone had made it back alive, and—for good or ill—they would make their stand.

Arthur and Lance got hugs from the girls as they climbed down from the carriage. They introduced their new friends and talked excitedly about their adventures. They followed Arthur and Lance to the door of the chapel and fell silent when they saw Amos and Karissa sifting sadly through the wrecked furniture inside.

"I'm sorry about your church," Angie said.

Amos nodded. "At least they didn't destroy it completely." He turned to one of the children. "Lucas just made it back," he said. "Tell the others it is time."

Moments later nearly a hundred people had gathered at the steps of the chapel. Some were on foot, others were on horseback, and some—mostly Rael's gang—rode on mechanical conveyances.

"Thank you all for gathering here," Amos said.

"The time has come to make our stand for Ambrose Pendragon," Rael said. "As he took his stand for us. If we are to live, let it be as citizens of the new Camelot. If we are to die, let us die well. Lucas, come." Mr. Lucas took the stage beside him.

"I have heard much about this power you possess," Amos said. "I think these people could use a demonstration."

"I'm not so sure this is the time," Lucas said.

"My friend," Amos said. "I can think of none better."

"Very well," Mr. Lucas said. Then he began to sing. Lance smirked for a second or two, but then his expression changed to one of awestruck appreciation. As the teacher sang, images began to form in Arthur's mind, and he was sure the others could see them too. He could see roaring oceans, bright glades, fierce battles, lost cities, soaring mountain vistas.... Then he saw the rise of Ambrose Pendragon as he received his sword from the mysterious Lady of the Lake, as he moved among villagers working wonders and giving hope. In the last verse, and the last image, he held his sword high in triumph as dawn broke over the mountains. The images faded as the song ended. The crowd stood in silence for a moment before breaking into applause.

"Wow," Lance said as Mr. Lucas stepped down. "I...uh...didn't know you could sing."

"I haven't sung anything for quite a while," the teacher admitted. "I did it quite often when I was in college. Choir, opera, musical drama. I loved it, but after I graduated, I stopped singing. I had forgotten, until now, just how much it used to mean to me. Sometimes it almost seemed as if I were in the presence of God."

"Wow," Lance said again. "And all I can do is talk on magical cellphones."

"Your gift is more practical than mine," Mr. Lucas said, "but each of us plays a part. And, as I was telling Arthur, I think our gifts are expressions of who we are. The ability to connect with people and to connect them to each other is not something to be taken lightly. The gift of communication can really be quite powerful."

"Never thought of it like that."

"How did the people in the villages take your songs?" Arthur asked.

"The Elvish and the Seraf are as different as any two races you might encounter," the teacher said, "but one thing they have in common is a love of song. Songsmiths, it seems, are revered among them."

"That's cool."

Others in the crowd began to sing as they left the clearing. Singing and holding hands, they rode and marched through the village in an impromptu parade. Others joined them there, following them down the darkening forest trails that lay between the village and Samhain's gaudy lair. Arthur felt his pulse quicken as he saw the city of Thanatos looming ahead of them. The golden towers rippled in the night air. The place had never looked completely real. It would have been more at home in a mirage...or a nightmare. When they rounded the final turn and the clearing at the base of the city's entrance ramp came into full view, they could see a crowd gathered there. Many of them were Bre'on, but in the midst of them were more Elvish and Seraf people than Arthur had seen since his arrival in this strange world. Some of the people were poor, dressed in rags. Others wore robes embroidered with jewels. The flickering light of torches blended with the soft glow of colored glowstones.

Amos climbed upon the ramp that led upward to the city's waiting gates. They seemed more like jaws. Amos turned and faced the crowd of friends that had followed him. His face glowed in the blue halo of the lantern he held.

So Arthur, Lance, Angie, Stacy, Mr. Lucas, Marcos, Amos, Karissa, Prisca, Aquila, Malua, Rael, Pyras, Pax, Vita, Jess, Shreeokh, the former dwellers of Thanatos, and an odd assortment of Bre'ons, Merfolk, Seraf, and mixed races gazed into the weather -worn face of the sailor named Amos as he began to speak.

"I am not a speaker or even a man with much education. I just tell you what I have seen. Ambrose Pendragon was a friend of mine. I lived with him and traveled around with him for nearly four years. He was a good man. He has helped many of you. You have seen the power he had. But seven days ago tonight he journeyed into the dark heart of Thanatos and surrendered himself to save others. From there he was taken to the Isle of A'Vilian. His face has not been seen since, but one of our number has seen a spectre with his likeness. Before he was taken, our king said that we should meet here in this clearing tonight. He did not say why. He just said to gather all the friends of the Pendragon together here. And so we have.

"As we wait here, I bring you tidings of strange things. My brother, my friends, and I have told you many things when we visited you in your homes. We will now tell you of stranger things we have learned since then."

Amos called Marcos up. The young scholar opened a book of prophecies and began to read:

In the later days, the Valley of Wind will again be opened.
A warrior, twins of the mirror and twins of the spirit
And a maiden with the face of an angel shall pass through.
One twin, not of the flesh, will fall into shadow.
On the night of his fall into darkness, the power of the Pendragon
Will pass to the Children of the Wind.
Brothers and sisters will join hands against the Man of Shadows,
And the Pendragon shall return to his throne.

Marcos closed his book.

There was an uneasy pause. Arthur looked out at the faces of the people who stood in the clearing. He heard footfalls behind him, the sound of an army. Steel-Hearts poured from the forest and surrounded the friends of Camelot on every side.

"It was a trap!" someone cried out.

"We've been set up!"

A mechanical voice rang out: <WE COME IN PEACE. WE WILL NOT HARM YOU!>

"They've got us," Lance said.

"Not yet," Arthur said. "Not if what those prophecies said was true."

Bionic stormtroopers herded men, women, and children into the clearing in front of the city's entrance ramp.

If they die, it's our fault, Arthur kept thinking. His heart was pounding, and his mouth was suddenly dry.

<WE ARE A PEACEFUL ENVOY FOR OUR LORD, SAMHAIN,> one of the cyborgs proclaimed.

"Since when is Samhain peaceful?" Arthur mumbled to himself.

<OUR LORD DOES NOT UNDERSTAND THE NATURE OF THIS GATHERING,> the same Steel-Heart spoke again. <WHY DO YOU INCITE THESE PEOPLE TO TREASON WITH TALK OF PROPHECIES?>

"Because the prophecies are true," Marcos declared. "We have seen the proof."

<WHAT IS THIS PROOF YOU SPEAK OF?>

"We are the proof!" Arthur said as he stepped forward. "We come from the World of the Fathers! We come from a world you say doesn't even exist!"

There were a few murmurs from the crowd.

<WHAT PROOF DO YOU OFFER FOR WHAT YOU SAY?> the metal giant was unmoved. <MANY HAVE COME FORTH SAYING THAT THEY WERE OF THE WORLD OF THE FATHERS, YET NONE COME OFFERING PROOF.>

"I have watched your movements for this entire week," Arthur said. "You have searched for us, but we have evaded you at every turn."

<THAT PROVES NOTHING.>

"Your name is Darnak," Arthur told him. "I have heard you speak of your ambitions."

<LIES!> the cyborg cried.

"What about this?" Arthur pulled out his smartphone. He walked up the stairs and held it out to Darnak. "Technology from my world. You can talk to people who are far away."

<WHAT IS THE PURPOSE OF THESE SYMBOLS?>

"They're icons," Arthur said. "They open apps that...."

The cyborg closed his hand. Arthur gritted his teeth as he heard glass breaking. The Steel-Heart opened his hand. The ruined device fell to the dirt.

"That's not all," Arthur said. "You haven't heard Mr. Lucas' songs, seen Angies images, or seen Stacy glow." The three of them stepped forward, prepared to give demonstrations.

Darnak brushed it all aside. <USELESS.>

"What about our language?" Lance yelled up at the Steel-Heart. "Look at my lips. I'm speaking English, but you're hearing me in *Bre'on*."

"Yes," Arthur said. "We talk in one language and you hear another one. It's the power of the Sword."

The giant storm trooper seemed to shiver a little bit— or was it imagination?

<YOU SPEAK OF THE SWORD,>   the giant said. <WHERE IS THIS SWORD?>

"In us," Arthur said. "We have its power."

<BUT DO YOU HAVE THE SWORD?>

"Uh. Nope."

"Don't tell 'em anything," Lance snapped.

<YOU DO NOT HAVE THIS SWORD, YET YOU CLAIM YOU HAVE ITS POWER,> the Steel-Heart said. <CAN YOU USE THIS POWER TO DESTROY US?>

"Well," Arthur said. "I'm...."

"Right at this moment," a gruff voice said, "They do not feel that destroying you would be the right use of the power."

Everyone turned to Amos.

<DOES THIS MEAN YOU CANNOT DESTROY US?>

"It means we will not destroy you yet."

The gates of the city opened. A line of Steel-Hearts marched out onto the ramp and divided down the middle. Two goblins emerged behind them. They were small and pink with long arms and wide, empty eyes. They were carrying something on their backs. Blue lantern light fell upon a curtained box. It was a litter. Two other goblins carried the back part of the box. Amos moved aside as the four goblins marched down the ramp and set the litter on a landing at the base. The litter's curtains were almost transparent. Through them, Arthur could see the shape of a man seated on a throne. The dim silhouette could almost have passed as a shadow of the Lincoln Memorial statue.

<YOU STAND ACCUSED OF HIGH TREASON AGAINST YOUR LORD, SAMHAIN,> the Steel-Heart who had spoken before said. <ANY WHO WISH TO END THIS BLASPHEMY

AND RETURN TO YOUR KING MAY DO SO NOW AND FIND MERCY.>

"Return to me, swear your love to me, and denounce the name of Ambrose Pendragon and all will be forgotten," a raspy voice cut through the night. "I only want your love. I, Samhain I, speak to you."

"What's wrong with his voice?" Lance whispered.

"You're right," Arthur said. "It's too high."

"We're subjects of King Ambrose Pendragon!" Amos yelled out over the crowd. "We'll never come back to you!"

"Pen-dragon," someone began to chant. "Pen-dragon. Pen-dragon."

Other voices rose up and joined in: "Pen-dragon. Pen-dragon. Pen-dragon. Pen-dragon. Pen-dragon. Pen-dragon."

"Your leader is dead!" Samhain cried from inside the litter. "Will you swear allegiance to a dead man?"

"I say he's alive," Arthur yelled back.

Silence—complete silence—fell over the crowd.

"Ambrose had power over his sword," Arthur said. "Most of you know how nobody else could lift the sword or pull it out of anything."

Everyone was listening.

"Well, a week ago tonight, when Ambrose gave himself up to Samhain, he plunged his sword into a stone slab in the middle of the city, and no one else could remove it. Samhain had him taken to A'Vilian, but one night later, somebody walked into the city and stole the sword right under the noses of Samhain's guards."

Arthur thought he saw the shadow on the litter tremble a little bit.

Mumbles came from the crowd.

"What he says is ridiculous," Samhain scoffed. "Is that why you are all here? Is that what you have been told, that Ambrose Pendragon is *alive*? Yes, Pendragon left his sword. And I did have him taken to the Island. This much is true. But Ambrose Pendragon is dead, and I have his sword."

"You're saying the sword is still in the city?" Arthur

asked.

"Why, yes," Samhain said. "But you can never be sure of that because you have some superstition about entering my city."

"I visited your city by means you would not understand," Arthur said. "The sword was gone, and the block that held it was cracked."

"Even if you really had visited my city, you would not have seen the sword." The voice was calm. "I had it removed to my royal treasury."

"I say you're lying," Lance said. "Go get it and prove me wrong."

"I have been very patient," the rich baritone voice had a hint of a cold hiss at its edge.

"He doesn't have the sword," Arthur declared.

"I already told you," Samhain said. "The sword is in my royal treasury."

"Then why did your guard ask us if we had the sword?" Angie asked.

People started mumbling.

"I say the sword has been taken by the man you claim to have killed," Arthur said. "If I'm lying, prove it. Show me the sword."

Samhain held his peace until the crowd was silent.

"You will have the truth then," Samhain sighed. "The sword was in my royal treasury as I said. But—as this strangely dressed young man has said—it is there no longer. It was stolen from me days ago by the followers of Ambrose Pendragon."

"That's ridiculous."

"They wanted to start the rumor that Pendragon had come back and had taken the sword himself. You think your king is alive. What proof do you have? What proof do you have that Ambrose Pendragon is alive? A missing sword? A sword possibly taken by someone who wants to be a king. Someone like him."

The shadow on the throne pointed to Arthur Richards.

"Sure," Arthur said. "Why not? I admit it. I ran in and beat up six of his bionic guards and took it. I'm a bad man."

Amos and a few others laughed.

Something had been bothering Arthur since Samhain had first been hauled out. Why was the daemon hiding inside a curtained litter. What was his game?

"Before you tell us any more lies," Arthur said. "Why don't you tell us—or better yet—show us why you're hiding behind those curtains."

"The time for talk is ended," Samhain said. "I offered you peace, but you would not have it. I give you one final chance. Those who would take the blood-oath to me, forsaking all other oaths, all other loyalties, will obtain my mercy. Those who do not will die. If you would take the blood-oath, remove yourselves from among these traitors and step to my left."

The shadow in the box gestured with his left hand.

Silence answered him.

"Those who would take the blood-oath, move yourselves to my left."

There was a sound of shuffling, but no one moved away from the crowd.

"Sad times have a way of drawing people together," Rael, the son of Dran, answered. "Even warriors."

Someone ran past Arthur.

<FOOL!> one of the Steel-Hearts yelled. Lance, Arthur could see, was reaching for the curtains on Samhain's litter. Just as he grabbed a handful of cloth, cybernetic hands seized him and hurled him into the crowd. Metal rings snapped open as the curtains tore away from the litter.

"Look out!" Lance yelled as he plowed through the crowd, curtains tangled around him. As his brother got to his feet, Arthur turned to see the figure on the throne. Hateful yellow eyes glowed in the dark. Now illuminated by the blue glow of Elvish lanterns, the face of the creature on the throne was painfully familiar.

"*Chris*," Arthur gasped.

"Your friend is deader than your king," Samhain's voice croaked from between Chris's lips. The voice was not as deep as it had been in Thanatos, but the tone was the same. "On the morrow of Pendragon's death, my shell began to feel the weight of its age. Thus I have implanted my being into a younger shell."

Arthur was horrified, but his mind was strangely clear.

"Ambrose said some people thought there was a lifeline—sort of like an umbilical cord—that connects you to your world. It came through some magical doorway on the Island of A'Vilian. Now Ambrose has closed that doorway. He's sealed the abyss your people tossed him into. That's why your body fell apart, isn't it?" A new idea flashed into his mind. "That's why you've lost so much power that you can't even walk. You have to be carried everywhere, don't you? This is your last bluff. You think maybe you can reverse this if you get the sword back. That's it, isn't it? Isn't it?"

Arthur's heart was pounding. Sweat was running down his armpits.

"We will kill them slowly," Chris-Samhain said. "One at a time."

"No," Stacy said as she raised her arms to the sky. Light, soft and pure, radiated from her body. As before, Arthur felt himself surrounded by warmth and peace. Samhain and his troops recoiled in terror and rage. Arthur watched in stunned surprise as some of their bodies began to smoke.

"Kill her!" Chris-Samhain cried. The Steel-Hearts drew their weapons and tried to move in, but Stacy's light held them at bay. Arthur watched in amazement. The night she had discovered her ability, Stacy thought it was the most useless of abilities. Now she was using it to push back an army.

"Can you expand the bubble?" Arthur asked her.

"I'm trying," Stacy said. "This is as bright as I can make it." Arthur stepped up and took her hand. Maybe if they joined wills, somehow combined their abilities.... It was no use. The glow was getting weaker.

A Steel-Heart projectile whistled through the air. It struck Stacy in the chest and knocked her back onto the platform. She looked down in bewilderment as blood soaked the front of her shirt. She was dying...again.

Lance and Arthur ran to her. Mr. Lucas, Angie, and their friends from the new world surrounded them. Lance cradled Stacy's head as she gasped for breath.

"Kill them!" Chris-Samhain ordered. "Kill them all."

"Join hands," Arthur said as he took Stacy's hand in one of his and Angie's in the other. Lance took Stacy's other hand and joined hands with Mr. Lucas. As their hands were linked, Stacy's glow suddenly grew brighter. A burst of energy shot heavenward. The clouds rolled back as a vortex opened in the sky.

Chris-Samhain raised his left hand. Words formed on his lips but a low roar, a rumble like the bass register on a pipe organ, swallowed everything. Bright light bathed the clearing, but it was not the glow Stacy's ability created.

All eyes were on the sky as a mass of fireballs swarmed out of the vortex and spiraled through the sky like drunken comets. Suddenly they stopped and hung in the sky over the crowd.

Arthur glanced around at all the others—Amos, Angie—standing open-mouthed with the light reflected in their eyes, glowing on their faces.

The fireballs hovered directly overhead like so many blazing stars. Then they fell.

Screams were silenced by the roar. Bodies covered bodies as everyone in the crowd fell to the earth. Light swallowed everything.

19. /Back to Avalon

Arthur lay in a heap of bodies. His eyes were squeezed shut, but he could still see the glare. The seconds ticked past as he lay there expecting to be engulfed by searing heat and a bone-shattering weight. Every muscle in his body was tensed. His teeth ground against each other. In his mind, he began to count down.

Ten...nine...eight...seven...six...five...four...three...two...one.... zero?

Nothing happened.

Arthur raised his head and looked around. The glow was bright, but somehow it wasn't painful to look at. An army of armored figures on horseback stood in a sea of piled up human bodies.

"You've done well, my friends," a voice rang out over the roar.

A tall, lean man-shape with a sword sat on the lead horse, a winged creature that might have been mistaken for a marble statue if it had not been moving.

"Ambrose," Arthur said, but he couldn't hear his own voice over the roar. He saw his brother Lance raise up and saw the wonder on his face as he saw the armored figures.

"Children of Camelot arise," Ambrose commanded. "Our time has come at last."

Awestruck, the survivors came slowly to their feet. Arthur started to rise with them, but looked back at Stacy. Blood covered the whole front of her shirt, and her life was slipping away.

"Can you help her?" Lance asked.

"I can," Ambrose said. "But so can you. My power resides in you, too. Save her or release her. The choice is yours."

"What do we do?" Arthur asked.

"Save her," Lance said.

"What if she doesn't want to come back?" Angie asked. "Ambrose, what do we do?"

"You led wisely while I was away," Ambrose said. "What does your wisdom tell you now?"

"This is supposed to be the victory of light over darkness," Arthur said. "We can't let it start like this." He placed his hand on her upper chest. Lance, Angie, and Mr. Lucas placed their hands on top of his. Stacy's supernatural glow returned for an instant and the blood stain faded from the front of her shirt. Arthur and Lance helped her to her feet. The crowd around them applauded.

Ambrose nodded to them. "You have done well, Children of Earth. Knights of the new Camelot, I present Arthur Pendragon, the ruler of the old kingdom." Ambrose gestured toward a man with a gray beard and a jeweled crown who sat on his right. He nodded gravely and extended his right hand, palm facing outward, to the crowd before him.

"King Arthur," Arthur said in disbelief.

"And Merlinus Ambrosius, his faithful advisor."

Another bearded man, this one dressed in a strange and colorful robe, sat at Ambrose's right.

"And Merlin," Mr. Lucas said, his voice tinged with awe.

"And these are the knights of the old kingdom," Ambrose said as he indicated the others around him. "The resurrected Knights of the Round Table."

"SLAY THEM!" the Chris-Samhain thing cried.

The Steel-Hearts surged forward. Glowing swords drawn, the warriors of Old Camelot engaged them. Wings beating the air, their horses leaped into battle.

Arthur watched, in horrified interest, as one of the knights brought his sword down on an advancing Steel-Heart. The attacker vanished in a cloud of fire and red vapor. The blade had vaporized him on contact.

"Nothing touched by darkness can survive those blades," Marcos said.

"What about us?" Arthur asked.

"Your reflection is no longer in the blade," the scholar told him. "You will be safe. The power of the sword is in you."

The Steel-Hearts refused to retreat. One by one, they

stepped into the arching blades of Camelot's army and vanished. Arthur watched in horror as one of Camelot's warriors stabbed Chris through the heart. He shrieked as red smoke poured out of his mouth and nose. His eyes glowed red and then went dark. He stumbled back to the edge of his litter, fell to the ground, and lay still.

Camelot's knights withdrew. The Steel-Heart army had been destroyed.

"City of Thanatos!" Ambrose declared. "For too long, you have feasted on the souls of the ignorant, the unwary, and the proud. Release your captives!"

The ground began to shake. Low, rumbling tremors became violent pulsations—shivering like a giant, irregular heartbeat. A burst of water exploded through the city's gates, spilling a mass of thrashing figures onto the ground. At first, Arthur was not sure if they were people or dolphins. Then he realized they were Merfolk who had been captives of Thanatos.

One of them, a young woman, grabbed Arthur's ankle. Her pale green eyes were wide with fear. Arthur realized she was the one who had smiled at him from the tank as he was being driven through the crowd. Frantic to get her to water, he knelt down and scooped up her muddy form. She clung to him.

"They're dying," he said. "We have to get them to the lake."

"Not yet," Ambrose said. "The lake is poison to them."

"What can we do?"

"They can breathe air as well as water," Amos told him. "The girl continued to cling to Arthur. He noticed, to his chagrin, that she wasn't wearing anything but a necklace of shells. Still, there was an innocence about her.

"Evil city," Ambrose said. "I proclaim your doom."

The hard clay around the city broke into a spider's web of radiating cracks. Like creeping vines, they crept up the city's walls splitting, branching, and splitting again. Shards of golden glaze fell away. A giant piece of the wall fell in a shimmering avalanche. Screams and cries of rage erupted from the city. The ground was hemorrhaging water. The dust blackened into mud. Jets of steam hissed into the air. A crack split the city's foundation. The sundered sides fell inward upon each other, the cobra-headed minarets striking against each other and breaking off.

The vibrations ceased. For a moment the city was still. Jets of water and steam continued to pour up from below. The city exploded in one giant death-scream as it sank—coming apart as it went—and the fountains of the deep swallowed it whole. The surface of the lake boiled, rolled, and tumbled. They changed in color from a sinister black to a pale blue-green. The lake was healing itself. A pale subterranean light glowed from somewhere far beneath the foaming surface. At the edge of the lake, plants began to grow at a miraculous rate. Clawing vines engulfed the lake's jagged shores, encircled the rocks, and embraced the charred ground. Pale flowers opened like tiny hands.

Over the waters, an unearthly voice began to sing. A white figure hung in the fog over the lake, her pale garment rippling and shimmering like the wings of a dove.

"The Lady of the Lake has returned," Marcos said.

"The water is clean now," Ambrose told Arthur. "Take your friend to her new home."

Arthur took the young mermaid to the water's bubbling edge. Amos, Lance, Mr. Lucas, and the others helped the other Merfolk into the water. Arthur's friend smiled, kissed him, and rolled out of his arms into the waiting lake. She vanished beneath the waves only to emerge a moment later about thirty feet away. She waved to Arthur and smiled one last time before plunging into the depths. The last he saw of her was the pale dolphin's tail with its glistening membranes.

"Easy come, easy go," Lance said. "Hey! Look at that!"

Arthur followed his gaze out into the lake. The island of A'Vilian, no longer a charred ruin, was cloaked in mist but the shapes of trees blanketed its once-jagged contours.

"Avalon is restored," Mr. Lucas said.

"We can go home," Lance said.

Home, Arthur thought. He turned around and saw Chris's broken body lying twisted on the ground. The miraculous vines and flowers formed a wreath around him. Arthur walked slowly over to his friend's body. He remembered working on the school newspaper together, riding bikes down to the comic book shop, hiking in the woods. Chris would not be returning home with them. Arthur wondered how his disappearance would be explained. What would he tell Chris's mother? Would Mr. Lucas and the rest of them be charged with his murder?

"Do you believe I can save your friend?"

Who was Ambrose talking to?

"Arthur?"

"Yes?"

"Do you believe I can save your friend?"

Arthur turned to Ambrose.

"Save my—? You mean Chris?"

Ambrose nodded.

"What does it matter what I believe?" Arthur sighed.

"It matters."

"If anyone can," Arthur said. "...it's you."

Ambrose placed his hand on Chris's chest and closed his eyes.

***

Chris looked around him. He was standing on a platform overlooking an empty amphitheater. Samhain was standing beside his chopping block with his hooded executioner and female demons. Ambrose was holding up his sword and waiting.

"Will you come too, Chris Castle?"

Chris remembered hearing those words. He remembered diving headlong into the crowd, and losing himself in a hellish nightmare of corridors which never seemed to end. One twisting tunnel led to another. Staircases lined with locked doors dropped deep into the ground. He remembered being captured and almost feeling relieved. He remembered screaming as they cut away his clothes and strapped him to a table. He remembered the knives of pain ripping through him. Then that thing had somehow been pumped into his skull. Chris could watch and hear, but he could say or do nothing.

Then it all dissolved, and he was here.

The rest had only been a nightmare—or had it? No, Chris decided. The first time Arthur, Lance, and Stacy had been with him. There had been a crowd. This time only the key players remained. This was a private performance just for Chris.

"Will you come too, Chris Castle?"

Chris could see the eyes of his reflection, the guilty eyes of a fugitive—the eyes of a murderer.

"I was in the other car that night, you know," Chris said, "the car that ran Stacy off the road." He smiled sadly as tears fell from his eyes. "I was going about ninety miles an hour, and the curve wasn't banked. I was on the wrong side of the road trying to.... " He fought for control, shook his head. His voice cracked. "I saw the car rolling as it hit the ditch. I didn't even know it was her. All I could think of was getting away. I wasn't going to jail for killing some poor.... " He stopped. He covered his face.

Ambrose was nodding.

"She took the ditch to keep from hitting me," Chris's voice came from behind his hands.

"I didn't even stop to help!" he cried. "I didn't even care about them. All I could think of was getting away and not getting caught. I just drove off and left them lying there in that ditch. Just lying there ...." He just lay there and sobbed for several minutes.

"Join me," Ambrose said at last.

"Yes," Chris whispered. Then louder. "Yes. I'll ... I'll join you."

Ambrose touched him with the sword.

He looked into the sword and saw his own image ripple like a heat mirage and resolve itself into the face of Ambrose Pendragon.

"It is done," Ambrose told him.

"What will happen to me now?" Chris asked.

"Go in peace. The power of the sword will hold the Steel-Hearts immobile until you are safely away. I must die tonight, but the name and cause of the Pendragon line and of the Worldsmen must continue. You must be my son, my prince. Goodbye, my friend."

He raised his sword high above his head. It gleamed in the red light of the lamps. Then, with lightning speed, he brought the sword down, tip first, and impaled it into the stone platform.

SLLLLLLLLLLLLLLLLLLIIIIIIIIIIIIIIIIIISSSSSHHHHHH!

Metal hissed against stone. The blade was half-buried in polished stone. The earth had gripped it and no hand but Ambrose's could draw it back.

"I have laid down my weapon," Ambrose said. "Now I surrender myself to you..." he turned to Chris, "...for you."

"Take him," Samhain croaked, pointing a jabbing finger at Ambrose. "Put his hands on the block."

The succubi seized Ambrose by the arms, hissing and laughing as they dragged him to the dark-colored block that stood in the center of the platform. The executioner stood beside it, his dark and tattered hood drifting like fog. His skeleton's hands held the axe ready.

Ambrose's hands were laid on the block.

"You'll never raise a sword against me again, *Bre'on*," Samhain said. "Do it."

The executioner raised his axe and brought it down hard. Ambrose's scream ripped through the air and echoed out into the forest. Just then lightning seared the heavens and rain began to fall.

"Take him away," Samhain said. "Take him to A'Vilian."

It all melted away.

Chris and Ambrose stood on the banks of a newly-formed lake looking down at a crumpled body—Chris's body.

"That would have been me," Chris said. There were tears on his face. "It should have been me."

"That is the Chris Castle who came here from Earth," Ambrose said. "If you choose, you can bury him here."

"I don't understand," Chris said. "If he's dead, what will happen to me?"

"That is up to you," Ambrose said. "You can remain here with him, or you can return to your world."

"Now?" Chris said. "Just like that?"

"If you return home, you will die."

Chris gasped. He started to protest, then nodded.

"I guess that's what I deserve. But what was the point of saving me back there if I'm going to die anyway?"

"I'm giving you the chance to choose the manner of your death," Ambrose said.

Chris looked at the twisted body at his feet. "It's not much of a choice, is it?"

"No," Ambrose said. "It isn't."

"What about my friends?"

"Their time here is almost finished."

"Tell them I'm sorry for everything," Chris said.

"They will know," Ambrose said. "Are you ready?"

Chris took a deep breath and squared his shoulders. "As ready as I will ever be. Thank you for coming back for me." He closed his eyes. Ambrose placed his hand on Chris's heart. He felt his chest constrict. His body folded in upon itself as the world around him ceased to exist. He found himself falling into brightness and realized, to his amazement, that he really didn't mind. Then, suddenly, he was sitting behind the wheel of a speeding car. Rock music was blasting in his ears. He saw a pair of headlights speeding toward him.

Stacy!

It was the night of the accident. Ambrose had sent him back. He closed his eyes and turned the wheel.

***

"What happened to Chris?" Arthur asked. The body had vanished, but Ambrose had returned alone.

"He has been released," Ambrose said.

"Released," Arthur said. "From what?"

"His guilt," Stacy said. "That's it, isn't it?"

"Guilt?" Arthur was not sure he understood. "You mean, because he led us into the city?"

"Because he caused the accident," Stacy said.

"The accident?" Arthur gasped. "The accident that...."

"The accident that killed me."

Arthur gasped. That explains it, he thought. That explains it all.

"He couldn't live with himself," Lance said. "That's why he couldn't get along with anybody else."

"How long have you known?" Angie asked Stacy.

"Always," she said.

"Where is he?" Lance asked.

"Home," Ambrose said. "I sent him home."

"It was what he always wanted," Arthur said.

"And I was finally able to grant his wish for him," Ambrose said.

"Somehow," Arthur said, "I get the feeling there's something you're not telling me."

"Perhaps," Ambrose said, "but you'll have your answers soon enough."

"You have to tell him I forgive him," Stacy said. "I wanted to, but the time was never right. I guess maybe I wanted him to come to me first. I should have gone to him."

"Don't beat yourself up," Angie told her. "None of it was your fault."

"How did you do all of this?" Lance asked. "We thought you were dead."

"I was," Ambrose said. "But as you see, I got better."

"I'm serious," Lance said.

"It was the sword," Ambrose said. He held up his hands. White, well-healed scars encircled his wrists. "Before I surrendered myself to Samhain, I commanded my blade to return to my body and restore me on the night following my exile to the island. I didn't know if it would work. My body was seared to blackened bones by the flames of the isle, but my sword was able to reform me from the dust of death. Once I was on the island of A'Vilian with my sword, I was able to reopen some of the doors Samhain had sealed. Arthur, Merlin, and the others were free to return from the realm beyond the door."

"All's well that ends well," Lance said. "I guess."

"It has not ended quite yet," Ambrose said.

20./Departure

"Come," Ambrose said. "Avalon awaits."

The island lay, shrouded and mysterious, across the crystal lake. In a narrow finger of the lake, beside a run-down shack and a weathered dock, lay a long, rectangular raft. It was a ferry.

"Lucas," Ambrose said. "The ferry will bear you and your carriage across. Karissa and I will fly ahead. We have things to discuss."

"Fly?" Karissa said. Ambrose climbed onto the back of his winged horse. "You mean—fly?"

"Come."

Ambrose lifted Karissa into the saddle behind him. The horse took off across the grass, leaped into the air, and soared into the darkening sky. King Arthur, Merlin, and the rest of the knights of Old Camelot took to the sky behind them. The sky over Avalon was filled with gleaming apparitions on horseback. Arthur, Angie, and Lance climbed into Mr. Lucas' carriage as they had done so many times before. The teacher coaxed the faithful horses into motion. Arthur wondered if they envied their cousins or simply accepted the limitations of their earthbound existence without complaint.

The ferry Ambrose had spoken of waited at the lake's edge. In spite of their advanced age, neither the ferry nor the dock looked rotten. Amos guided Mr. Lucas along a narrow ramp of weathered wood. The horses' hooves knocked a hollow cadence against the planks beneath them as they stepped across to the waiting ferry. Marcos, Rael, and some of the others joined them on the raft. Once they were all safely aboard, Amos closed the gate and latched it.

Amos took up a long pole and pushed off with slow, steady pressure. The flat raft moved slowly away from the shore. Arthur looked back at the friends of Camelot still gathered there. He thought about the crumbling remains of

Thanatos, the city of death, lying somewhere far beneath them. Many of the city's occupants had no doubt gone down with their city, but there were no bodies floating on the surface of the lake. Arthur knew there would not be. He thought about the Merfolk at home in the depths of the lake, about the girl who had clung to him for comfort. Ten minutes passed, and the island of Avalon loomed close. Amos piloted the ferry up to a square slab of rock that stood at the water's edge and docked the raft there. He opened the gate, and Mr. Lucas drove his horses through the narrow opening and onto the waiting island. He stopped his carriage at the edge of the crowd. Arthur climbed out and took in the scene.

Blue-white Elvish lanterns were scattered over dunes of cool, green grass. Stately tree-shapes of black ink and glowing towers were framed against a star-speckled sky.

The shape of Ambrose Pendragon rose from a cluster of dark people-shapes. He held up a goblet as though making a toast.

"This is a time for rejoicing," he said. "The power to travel between worlds has once again been restored to the hands of the Worldsmen. Amos, step forward."

Amos looked nervously around as he came. Clearly he had no idea why he had been singled out. Suddenly a graceful figure dropped from the heavens on shining wings of white.

"Karissa?" Barak gasped.

"Neither Bre'on nor Seraf, our wise and kind Karissa has patiently endured life's difficulties. That patience has been rewarded. Now Karissa stands before you as both Bre'on and Seraf."

Unlike Shreeokh, who had wings instead of arms, Karissa had both. Clad in a sleeveless gown of white, she stretched her beautiful arms toward heaven and spread glorious white wings behind her.

"Even before this miracle," Amos said, his voice trembling, "I was unworthy to be wed to so beautiful a creature. Now I don't know what to say. My love, my gift of grace, no one deserves this more."

Amos and Karissa held each other as the crowd applauded.

"Our time of rejoicing is also a day of sadness," Ambrose said. "It is the sadness that comes from saying goodbye to friends. For Edmund Lucas, Arthur Richards, Lance Richards, and Angelina Stone, the World of the Fathers, a world called Earth, awaits." He looked at the faces of the young people and their teacher as they stood together. "My friends, it is time for you to go home. Say your parting words now."

We're going home, Arthur thought. He looked around at the others. The first thing Arthur felt was relief. Mom and Dad would know he was all right.

Then Arthur remembered the fun times at the Elvish village, the lazy afternoon on Malua's pond, the green day of riding through the mountains and villages.... He would never see New Logres again. And he wouldn't see Ambrose, Marcos, Amos, Karissa, Rael, Prisca, Aquila,...and Stacy? What about Stacy?

Arthur wiped his eyes and looked around at the faces of people from another world. The faces hung in blue-white light from Elvish lamps. They were the faces of aliens, and friends.

They were all crowded around Arthur, Lance, Angie, and Mr. Lucas.

"You have found a home with us," Amos said. He gripped Arthur's shoulders with rough hands. His voice cracked. "We will miss you."

"Remember us," Marcos said. The curly-haired, young scholar wept openly.

Embraces and tears and heartfelt words went all around.

"We won't forget you."

"I wish you could stay with us."

"We'll always be friends, whether we're together or apart."

The crowd opened up as Ambrose Pendragon stepped through. Manly tears flowed down his regal cheekbones.

"I wish you could stay and explore new worlds with

us," he said. "It simply could not be."

"Will we ever see you again?" Angie asked.

He smiled.

"Yes, child. You will."

The crowd started to move apart. Mr. Lucas climbed into the driver's seat of his carriage. Lance swung up beside him. Arthur and Angie climbed into the back.

"I have one last thing to show you before you go," Ambrose said. He gestured toward the crowd from Old Camelot. A man in chain mail and a young woman in a white, old-fashioned dress came forward.

"Lucas," the man said. "Is that you?"

"I know you," the teacher said. "Both of you." Hardly knowing what he was doing, he climbed down from the carriage and made his way to where they were standing. They embraced him, smiled, and spoke to him as though they knew him. Arthur, Lance, and Angie watched, intrigued. After what seemed like a long time, Mr. Lucas returned. There were tears on his face.

"Who were those people?" Lance asked.

"The young woman is called Evelyn," he said. "She was my first love. The man is a friend from my youth."

"They look so young," Angie said.

"And I look so old?" He laughed, but his eyes were sad. "Yes, I know."

"Why are they here?" Arthur asked.

Mr. Lucas lifted his hand and indicated the ring. "Do you remember when Ambrose asked me about this ring and where I had gotten it?"

"Yes."

"I told him I found it in a shop. That was true, but it was not the entire truth. I didn't know it then, but now the fog has lifted from my mind, and I remember everything. I have been here before. It was another time, another age. My memories failed me, but the ring led me back here to the place where it was forged."

"So we're here because of you?" Lance asked.

"Yes," the teacher said. "I think so. That is part of it, at least."

"It is as much as you need to know for now," Ambrose said. "Are you ready to go home?"

"I suppose we are," Mr. Lucas said. "Where should I drive?"

"Here," Ambrose said. He gestured toward a stone arch. It looked like an ordinary stone carving with bushes behind it clearly visible. Suddenly a blinding light flooded the portal. Mr. Lucas drove his horses toward the glow. The horses didn't jerk or hesitate. The light seemed to draw them.

Arthur looked back. He saw Stacy waving and smiling as she stood with Amos, Karissa, and Marcos. "Wait," he said. "We left Stacy. We've got to go back for Stacy."

Mr. Lucas made no move to pull back on the reins.

She's not coming, Arthur suddenly realized. Tears came to his eyes as the carriage began to float, and light swallowed up the images of the people behind them. The light dimmed and wispy fingers of gray fog shrouded everything. Mr. Lucas' buggy creaked blindly through the same gray nowhere-verse they had passed through on the first journey. All that remained visible was the dim glow of gas lamps shining somewhere in the fog.

Arthur felt his hair standing on end. Cold gripped his stomach, and the horses went wild. Mr. Lucas clung tightly to the reins, but the carriage didn't jerk or bounce. There was no sound of buggy wheels or hoofbeats because there was nothing underneath them. Arthur had the chilling thought that if he jumped out, he might fall forever.

In the distance, they heard a sound like wind and bells. They also heard singing, but the voices did not sound entirely human. The air was bitterly cold. Arthur felt Angie squeeze up against his side. Then he remembered Angie was sitting on the other side of him. Lights flashed through the fog like fireflies, only brighter. Then they popped.

The carriage bucked beneath them, and the sound of hoofbeats returned. Glad to be on solid ground again, the horses galloped furiously through the night. The fog thinned, and Arthur found that he could see the sky overhead. A crescent moon hung in a starry sky. The air was bitterly cold, and ice covered the trees. They were back.

21./Homecoming

"Whoa, Morgan," Mr. Lucas said as he drew back on the reins. "Whoa, Gawain."

Arthur looked down. He noticed he was wearing his coat, and found his smartphone, the one the Steel-Heart had crushed, still hanging from his belt. He pulled it free and looked at the time. It was only 8:15.

"It's the same night we left," Arthur said. "Look at our clothes."

Angie suddenly cried out and pulled up her sweater. "Look!" she said. "Look!" She was wearing a sports bra underneath.

"What's wrong?" Lance said. "Sudden urge to strip?"

"Her tattoos are gone." Arthur had suddenly noticed.

"So's everything else," Angie said. "I've gone from super-sized to skinny again." She dropped her sweater back into place.

"There's plenty of time to grow up," Mr. Lucas said, "and each age has its own unique kind of beauty."

"He's right," Arthur said. Then he gasped. "The note!" Arthur plunged his hand into his pocket and pulled out Stacy's note. His throat tightened as he unfolded it.

I'll be waiting, it said. *Don't forget.*

"What is that?" Lance said.

"It's from Stacy," Arthur managed to say as he passed it to his brother.

"Don't forget?" Lance said after he read it. "Forget her? Like that will ever happen."

"The night we found her," Arthur said, "I asked Ambrose if she was back to stay."

"What did he say?" Angie asked.

"He said it was yet to be determined," Arthur said, "that she was just a possibility."

"What does that mean?" Lance asked.

"I don't know," Arthur said. "There's a lot he said that I still don't understand. He said I would understand in time. I'm not so sure."

"I'm glad we saw her again," Angie said. "Even if she couldn't stay."

"Yeah," Lance said. "I am, too."

"We have another problem," Mr. Lucas said.

"Chris," Lance said.

"Indeed."

"What are we going to tell his parents?" Arthur asked.

"I have no idea," Mr. Lucas said.

"We could say he got upset and ran off into the woods," Lance said. "That's almost the truth."

"I won't lie to them," Angie said. "It's too cruel."

"If we tell the truth," Lance said, "they'll think we're lying."

"Maybe he'll be waiting for us when we get back," Angie said. "Ambrose said he had sent him home."

"Then why isn't he here?" Lance asked. "Everything else is back the way it was before, but not Chris."

As they rode out of the woods and into their neighborhood, they saw Christmas lights glowing from some of the homes. Arthur saw the gates of the cemetery ahead of them.

"She said she'd be waiting for us." Angie spoke through her tears. "Is this what she meant?"

"I can't look at it," Arthur said.

"Me, either," Lance said.

Arthur felt the vibration from his smartphone. He pulled it from his belt and read.

"This doesn't make any sense," he said.

"What is it?" Lance asked.

"It says, 'Chris is awake.'"

"Who is it from?"

"Mom."

"Ask her where he is," Lance said.

Arthur typed the message. The phone vibrated again. Arthur read.

"The hospital."

***

Mr. Lucas parked his carriage across the street from the hospital on a snowy vacant lot. As they stepped through the emergency room door, Arthur thought about the night of the accident and the terrible news they had received. Official visiting hours were over, but the nurse on duty smiled when she saw them.

"You're Chris's friends," she said. "I guess you've heard?"

"Mom says he's awake," Arthur said.

"Yes," she said. "Isn't it wonderful? Come on."

She led them to an elevator and held the door open as they all stepped in.

"How long has he been asleep?" Arthur asked.

"Nearly two months," she said. "We were sure he'd wake up when the swelling on his brain went down, but he never did."

"Two months?" Arthur and Lance looked at each other. "The accident?"

The doors opened, and the nurse led them down the hall to the ICU unit.

"You can't stay long," she explained, "but I think it would do him a world of good to see you."

Chris's mother was standing by the bed when they walked in. She was holding the hand of a mummy, a figure so swathed in bandages and plaster that he was almost unrecognizable.

"Honey," she said. "Your friends are here. And Mr. Lucas."

Chris's face, what little they could see of it, was pale and gaunt. A tube had been taped into his nose—a feeding tube, most likely. He looked terrible, but he was alive.

"Chris." Arthur swallowed hard. "What happened?"

Chris whispered something. Arthur leaned in closer to hear what he was saying.

"Second chance," he said, his voice weak. "Put things right."

"What did he say?" Lance asked.

"He said he got the chance to put things right."

Chris nodded and smiled. His bandaged hand gave Arthur a "thumbs up" sign.

"What's he talking about?" the nurse asked.

"I don't know," Chris's mother said. "He's been saying some pretty strange things."

"Oh?" Mr. Lucas said. "What sort of things?"

"Do any of you know a boy named Ambrose?"

Arthur heard the others gasp.

"What is it?" she asked. "What's wrong?"

"Nothing," Lance said.

"It's kind of a long story," Arthur said.

Chris spoke again. Arthur leaned in and asked him to repeat it.

"I'm free," he said. He closed his eyes and drifted off to sleep. Arthur was afraid he had died, but the wavy line on the heart monitor said otherwise.

"It may take him a while to get his strength back," the nurse said.

"We'll start physical therapy tomorrow."

"Will he be okay?" Arthur asked the nurse as she led them out.

"Eventually," she said. "It may be a few months before he can walk again."

"But he will be okay?"

"There's a good chance he'll make a full recovery," the nurse said. "There doesn't seem to be any permanent damage. He's pretty lucky to be so unlucky."

"That's reassuring, at least," Mr. Lucas said.

"He looks like King Tut," Lance sighed.

"No," Angie said. "The bandages are a cocoon. Chris is growing his wings."

"After some of what we've seen," Arthur said, "I almost believe you."

They rode the elevator back down to the emergency room level. Someone had set up a Christmas tree beside the door.

"A Christmas tree in an emergency room?" Lance said. "What's wrong with this picture?"

"It's a symbol of hope," Arthur said. "It's right where it needs to be."

The electric door slid open and a young blonde woman stepped in. She looked up, saw them all staring at her, and smiled.

"I told you I'd be waiting."

It was Stacy.

22./Epilogue

"What's wrong with all of you?" Stacy laughed a little nervously as they surrounded her. "You act like you haven't seen me in weeks."

"We didn't know if you could come back," Arthur said.

"Come back?" She shook her head. "What are you talking about?"

"What are *you* talking about?" Lance asked her. "When did you tell us you would be waiting?"

"I just sent you a text message," she said.

He checked his phone and found a new message: *Chris is awake. I'll see you at the hospital!*

"Oh, yeah. You did."

They stood and looked at each other until Stacy broke the silence. "Have you seen Chris?"

"Yeah," Lance said. "He's asleep again, but it's not a coma this time."

"Thank God," she said. She put her hand over her mouth. Tears formed in her eyes. "I don't think I could have lived with myself if...."

"Lived with yourself?"

"He did it for me. Drove into the ditch to keep from hitting me. It took them over an hour to cut him out of the car."

"He could have died," Arthur said.

"He did," Stacy said, "on the way to the hospital. Don't you remember? The paramedics brought him back. Can I see him? Will you go with me?"

"Sure."

"She doesn't remember," Angie whispered as they started down the hall.

"Of course she doesn't," Lance said. "For her, none of it ever happened."

Chris had his eyes closed when they walked back into the room.

"I heard he was awake," Stacy said, and his eyes opened wide at the sound of her voice. He spoke, but his voice was too faint to hear. His friends moved closer.

"Stacy," he said.

"I'm here," Stacy said. "What is it?" She took one of his hands, avoiding the IV.

"I'm sorry," he said.

"For what?"

"Way I treated you." His voice was raspy and weak. "Didn't believe...it was you."

"I don't understand," she said as she took his hand.

"It's okay." Chris smiled as his eyes closed.

"Do any of you know what he's talking about?" Stacy asked the others. They looked at each other but didn't answer.

"Not everything he says makes sense at this point," Chris's mother said. "He's come a long way though."

They waited around for a while, but Chris didn't say anything else. They talked quietly for a half hour or so. Finally they said goodbye to Chris's mother and left. As they stepped back out into the parking lot, Stacy saw Mr. Lucas' carriage sitting beneath the lights.

"Is that your carriage?" she asked.

"Yes," Mr. Lucas said. "Your friends and I have just returned from an adventure."

She frowned and shook her head.

"What is it?" Arthur asked.

"It's too strange," she said. Walked a circle around the carriage and patted the horses as she circled it.

"Mr. Lucas is about to take us all home," Arthur said. "Do you want a lift?"

"I brought my car," she said. She started to walk away, then turned back. "On second thought, I think I will ride with you. I can get my car later."

They loaded back into the carriage for one last ride. They rode for about two blocks before anyone spoke.

"What's going on, Stacy?" Arthur finally asked. "I mean really."

"It's too strange," she said, "but wonderful. On the night of the accident, something happened to me. I haven't told anybody about it until now. I was starting to wonder if I was crazy. It was so strange but so real."

"What happened?"

She paused for a moment and looked out at the Christmas lights. Then she continued: "You know how people talk about your life flashing in front of your eyes when you're about to die? That's what happened to me, but that's not all. I mean, I saw the tunnel and the light, but then it got really crazy. The next thing I knew, I was in another world. All of you were there, too, and Chris. You told me I was...dead."

They looked at each other.

"Did Ambrose send you back?" Angie asked her.

Stacy breathed a sigh of relief and smiled even though she was brushing away tears.

"Then it was real? You saw it, too?" She looked around at the carriage. "You just got back?"

"Yes," Arthur said. "It was real. I'm not completely sure what that means anymore, but we all experienced it together. What happened to you after Ambrose sent us back?"

"Not much," she said. "He sent me through the same doorway. I stepped into the light, and suddenly I was back in my car on the night of the accident...just in time to see Chris swerve to miss me."

"Ambrose must have given him another chance," Lance said, "a 'do-over.'"

"How many of us get a gift like that?" Arthur mused.

"I suppose all of us do," Mr. Lucas said. "Every time we learn from our experiences. This was extraordinary, though: a chance to relive the *same* experience and change one's path."

"And you said he died on the way to the hospital?" Arthur said.

"Yes," Stacy nodded. "The paramedics brought him back."

"Amazing," Arthur said. "I wonder what he'll be like after this. I wonder how it will change him."

"I think it's changing all of us," Angie said.

"Yes," Stacy agreed. "I think so too."

"One thing's for sure," Lance said. "Nothing like that will ever happen to us again."

"Don't be so certain," Mr. Lucas said. He smiled enigmatically and Arthur saw him touching his ring.

www.ingramcontent.com/pod-product-compliance
Lightning Source LLC
Chambersburg PA
CBHW031949170626
46807CB00006B/2415